MURDER AT
THE NATIONAL GALLERY

By Jim Eldridge

MUSEUM MYSTERIES SERIES
Murder at the Fitzwilliam
Murder at the British Museum
Murder at the Ashmolean
Murder at the Manchester Museum
Murder at the Natural History Museum
Murder at Madame Tussauds
Murder at the National Gallery

HOTEL MYSTERIES SERIES
Murder at the Ritz
Murder at the Savoy
Murder at Claridge's

a&b

MURDER AT
THE NATIONAL GALLERY

JIM ELDRIDGE

Allison & Busby Limited
11 Wardour Mews
London W1F 8AN
allisonandbusby.com

First published in Great Britain by Allison & Busby in 2022.

Copyright © 2022 by Jim Eldridge

A CIP catalogue record for this book is available from
the British Library.

First Edition

ISBN: 978-0-7490-2733-9

Typeset in 11.5/16.5 pt Adobe Garamond Pro by
Allison & Busby Ltd.

FSC
www.fsc.org
MIX
Paper from
responsible sources
FSC® C171272

Printed and bound by
CPI Group (UK) Ltd, Croydon, CR0 4YY

For Lynne, for always

CHAPTER ONE

London, February 1897

Daniel Wilson, formerly a detective sergeant with Scotland Yard and now a private enquiry agent, sat in his favourite wooden armchair in the kitchen of the small terraced house in Camden Town he shared with his partner in life and business, Abigail Fenton, the noted archaeologist and Egyptologist. They made an interesting couple, an apparent attraction of opposites: both were in their mid-thirties, Abigail, a Classics graduate of Girton College in Cambridge, tall, her red hair emphasising her high cheekbones adding to her elegance; and Daniel, the workhouse orphan, tall and muscular, his broken nose giving him the appearance of a bare-knuckle fighter. But sympatico is in the soul, not externals, and both Daniel and Abigail had found a deep empathy with one another when they'd first met three years previously, when Daniel was in Cambridge, hired to investigate a mysterious murder at the Fitzwilliam Museum.

They'd moved into Daniel's small house in what was generally considered the slum area of Camden Town because it was where Daniel had grown up, but since then they'd talked about moving to a better area, and – more importantly – getting married and formalising their relationship. In the poorer areas, like Camden Town, marriage was often considered an expense that couldn't be afforded; so couples moved in together and the woman adopted the man's surname; and, to all intents and purposes, they were a married couple. As the poor had no property there would be no arguments over sharing the proceeds of the marital house in the event of a split. If questions were ever raised by officials about their marital status, the usual reply was that the wedding certificate had somehow got lost. The fact was that their neighbours recognised them as married, their children and the children's mother bore their father's name, so they were married.

The same standards did not apply to those of the middle and upper classes. To Abigail's sister, Bella, who still lived in Cambridge, Abigail and Daniel were living in sin, and a disgrace to the family. Bella herself was married to a doctor, a very respectable situation.

Daniel and Abigail wanted to marry, not for society's sake but as a pledge of their love for one another, a relationship they both intended to be in for life. They'd come close to it a couple of times but always something seemed to interfere, usually a murder case at one of the nation's great museums that needed investigation. After their first case together at the Fitzwilliam, their reputation had grown and they'd been hired to investigate murders at the British Museum, the Ashmolean in Oxford, the Manchester Museum, the Natural History Museum and Madame Tussauds.

Now they were in a fallow period as far as detection was concerned, and Abigail could return to her first love: archaeological exploration. She'd agreed to lead an expedition, funded by Arthur Conan Doyle, to the sun temple of Niuserre at Abu Ghurob, part of the area in Egypt known as the Pyramids of Abusir. The plan was for the expedition to begin in June or July. At the moment, Doyle was making financial arrangements, while Abigail studied what was known about the pyramid they would be exploring. Both Daniel and Abigail had agreed that any thought of their wedding, or moving house, should be on hold until the expedition had been completed and Abigail returned to England.

Both of them viewed the expedition with mixed feelings: it would be the climax to an already brilliant career for Abigail; only one woman before, Lady Hester Stanhope, had led such an expedition and lent her name to it. But both of them were aware that Abigail would be in Egypt for a long time, and they would be separated. Daniel had determined to go and visit the dig while it was going on, but it wouldn't make up for the fact that for the past three years they'd spent barely a day apart.

Daniel looked fondly at Abigail as she sat at the kitchen table, studying maps and texts she'd been allowed to borrow from the British Museum, then returned to reading the morning's newspaper. He read the reports of the latest political arguments that were raging around the prime minister, Lord Salisbury, as once more efforts were made by the Home Rule faction to press the government to give independence to Ireland. It was an argument that had been going on for as long as Daniel could remember, with strong emotions on both sides of the debate. He turned the page and as his eye fell on a story on the second page, his mouth dropped open.

'My God!' he said, shocked.

'What?' asked Abigail.

'Walter Sickert's been arrested.'

'The artist?'

'Yes. They say he's being questioned over the murder of a prostitute whose body was found at the entrance to the National Gallery first thing yesterday morning. According to this, she'd been eviscerated.'

Abigail stared at him, bewildered.

'Walter Sickert?' she repeated.

'It's like déjà vu,' said Daniel. 'We had him in for questioning during the Ripper investigation, Fred Abberline and myself.'

Abigail came and took the newspaper from him and scanned the page.

'This is unbelievable,' she said.

'That there's been another murder in the same manner as the original Jack the Ripper killings, or that Sickert's been arrested on suspicion?' he asked.

'Both,' she replied. 'I see that Chief Superintendent Armstrong is in charge of the case.'

'*Chief* Superintendent? Another promotion? That man knows how to climb a greasy pole,' commented Daniel.

There was a knock at their front door, and Abigail handed the newspaper back to Daniel and hurried to open it. When she returned she was holding a small brown envelope.

'It's addressed to you,' she said.

Daniel opened the envelope and took out the single sheet of paper.

'Well, well,' he said. 'This is very timely. It's from Stanford

Beckett, the curator at the National Gallery. He wants our help.'

'No, he wants *your* help,' Abigail corrected him. 'It's addressed to you.'

'But Beckett's note asks for both of us,' said Daniel. He held out Beckett's letter to her.

'In that case why wasn't my name on the envelope?' she asked, obviously annoyed.

'I suspect it's to do with the fact that I've met Sickert before, during the Ripper investigations.' He stood up. 'Shall we go?'

CHAPTER TWO

Stanford Beckett, curator of the National Gallery, was the epitome of the Victorian gentleman: a man in his sixties with a high, starched white collar to his shirt, a neat but colourful tie, bushy side whiskers, and an elegant pinstripe suit in charcoal grey, the image slightly marred by the amount of cigar ash on the front of his jacket. He put his half-smoked cigar into the ashtray on his desk, where it smouldered, as he gave a heavy sigh and looked at Daniel and Abigail with mournful eyes.

'Tragic,' he said. 'Absolutely tragic.'

'Could you tell us what happened?' asked Daniel. 'All we know is what we read in the newspaper, that a prostitute was found murdered and mutilated at the entrance to the National Gallery yesterday morning, and that Walter Sickert has been taken in for questioning on suspicion of her murder and is currently being held at Scotland Yard.'

'Yes,' nodded Beckett, with a heavy sigh. 'Dreadful. Although it's unfair to label her simply as a prostitute. I believe she also engaged in . . . er . . . that profession, but primarily she was an artist's model.'

'Who modelled for Sickert, I assume,' said Daniel.

'Yes.'

'And do we know why Sickert was arrested? And so quickly?'

'No,' admitted Beckett helplessly. 'The police say it was the result of information received.'

'And he's been held in custody since yesterday afternoon?'

'Yes,' said Beckett. 'His wife, Ellen, informed me that the police came to the house with a warrant for his arrest and took him in, charged on suspicion of murder. Today I received a message from him asking me to get in touch with you. He seems to feel that you might be able to get him out of custody.'

Daniel frowned. 'A message? I find it hard to believe that Chief Superintendent Armstrong allowed him to write to you? The chief superintendent is notorious for applying the rules rigidly to people he takes into custody to ensure they have little outside contact while he's questioning them. Lawyers are allowed, of course, but even then, the chief superintendent has been known to make things difficult for them.'

'This message came through Ellen. She was allowed to visit her husband early this morning, although – as you suggest – not without difficulty.'

Daniel smiled. 'I can imagine. But, having met Mrs Sickert, she can be quite formidable.'

'Yes, although it was fortunate that when she called at Scotland Yard this morning, Chief Superintendent Armstrong had not yet arrived, so she was dealing with the turnkey, which is I believe the correct term. She managed to get a meeting with Walter, who asked her to ask me to contact you.'

'I can't see how I can be of much help in this case. I'm no longer with the police force and I have no authority with them.'

'Nevertheless, he asked if you'd at least see him.'

'I'm not even sure if we'd be allowed to,' said Daniel doubtfully.

'You might, if you're going on behalf of the National Gallery,' said Beckett. 'We are a highly reputable and well-respected organisation, and we believe Walter is one of Britain's truly great artists.'

'I'm not sure if that will have any sway over Chief Superintendent Armstrong,' said Daniel. 'He's not known for his appreciation of art and artists.'

'Won't you at least try?' asked Beckett appealingly. He gave a slight shudder as he added: 'When Ellen came to see me this morning, she was very angry and insisted that I do something.'

'Yes, I have seen Mrs Sickert when she's angry,' said Daniel, doing his best not to smile. 'Very well, we'll try, but we'll need something to say that we're acting on behalf of the National Gallery.'

'That will be no problem,' said Beckett, relieved. 'I'll give you a note over my signature saying you've been authorised to act on our behalf.' He took a sheet of letterheaded notepaper from a small pile on his desk, dipped his pen into his inkwell, and began to write a brief letter. When finished, he pressed it on his blotting pad and passed it to Daniel.

'I suggest we leave it until we're sure the ink is dry,' said Daniel. 'We don't want to take a smudged letter in with us, it'll lessen the impact. While we're waiting for it to dry, perhaps you can show us where the unfortunate woman was found.'

'Of course,' said Beckett getting to his feet and leading the way.

'Do you know her name?' asked Abigail. 'There was no mention of it in the newspaper report.'

'Her name was Anne-Marie Dresser.'

'And she modelled for Walter Sickert.'

'Among others. Her face is quite recognisable when you look at some of the portraits by different hands.'

'Have you some on display?'

'We have one by Walter and one by Edgar Degas.'

'Degas painted her?' asked Abigail. 'Here, in England?'

'Yes. Degas was a frequent visitor to these shores before his eyesight began to fail. He's also great friends with Walter. Walter says that it was Degas who taught him how to represent reality on canvas. They shared many interests.'

'Including the same model,' commented Abigail drily.

'Er . . . yes. I believe that may have been the case,' said Beckett, forcing an awkward smile.

They passed through the main doors and into the portico-covered entrance of the National Gallery, overlooking Trafalgar Square with its four stone lions protecting the imposing edifice of Nelson's Column.

'She was found here,' said Beckett, pointing to the low wall at the side of the entrance area.

Daniel crouched down and examined the flagstone area.

'The newspaper said she had been eviscerated. Ripped open and her internal organs taken. I assume your staff have done a good job of cleaning up all traces of the blood.'

'That was one of the unusual aspects,' said Beckett.

'There was, in fact, very little blood.'

'Suggesting that the crime was committed somewhere else and her body was dumped here,' said Daniel.

'Yes,' nodded Beckett.

'Who found the body?'

'The cleaners, when they arrived for work. They saw her lying there and thought she must be some tramp, or someone drunk. Her face and body were turned into the wall. It was only when they shook her by the shoulder to wake her up that the body rolled and the horror of what had been done to her was revealed.'

'Have the police spoken to the cleaners?' asked Abigail.

'I believe so,' said Beckett. 'Will you wish to speak to them?'

'At the moment this is a police investigation and our role, as I understand it, is just to try and get Walter Sickert out of custody. Unless you're asking us to investigate the murder?'

'Not at the moment,' said Beckett. 'That would be a decision for the Board of Trustees, and only if it was felt appropriate. At the moment we're putting our faith in the police to carry out their investigation. What we'd like, as Walter has requested, is for you to try and obtain his release. That is our priority. If you're unable to, then we shall inform Ellen and leave it to her to decide the next course of action. Whatever happens, you will of course be paid.'

'Thank you,' said Daniel. 'We'll collect the letter from your office and head for Scotland Yard.'

'Before we do, can we see the two portraits of Anne-Marie you mentioned, by Sickert and Degas?' asked Abigail.

'Of course, Follow me.'

As they walked back into the building and followed the

16

curator through the galleries, Beckett said: 'Of course, much of this will be changing when the National Gallery of British Art opens at Millbank later this year.'

'The Tate Gallery,' said Abigail.

'Yes, I believe that is what people are calling it, and perhaps that will eventually be its official title.' He saw the puzzled expression on Daniel's face and explained: 'It was founded and paid for by Sir Henry Tate, the sugar magnate. It will house works by British artists born after 1790, so Sickert's paintings will be transferred to there.' He stopped in front of a large picture of a nude woman standing in a bowl of water in a bedroom and wiping her naked body with a flannel. 'Here we are, Walter's portrait of Anne-Marie.'

'It's full of life,' commented Abigail. 'And he's captured the apparent poverty of her surroundings.'

'I think he may have exaggerated the poor conditions,' admitted Beckett. 'As far as I know, she lived in a room that was furnished quite reasonably. I suspect he may have chosen a less salubrious location for this picture. Walter does like to play what he calls "the proletariat card" in his work. Ordinary working people at leisure, and not engaging in what could be called "genteel pastimes".'

'In other words, he likes to shock,' commented Abigail.

'I think there may be an element of that,' Beckett agreed.

He then led them through to a gallery where French painters were on display. The woman in the picture he stopped in front of was recognisable as the same woman in Sickert's picture. Both artists had captured the hungry, almost vulpine look in the woman's eyes, made more so by her pale face, high cheekbones, and long, lank, greasy dark hair hanging down. In

Degas' picture of her she was standing in front of a full-length mirror admiring herself. The artist had captured both her back view and the reflection of her naked front in the mirror. As with the Sickert painting, Degas had caught the life force of her. Here she was living, animalistic, vibrant. And now she was dead, butchered.

'She's very confident in her nakedness,' observed Abigail.

'She was a very confident young woman,' said Beckett.

As they left the gallery, Abigail asked Daniel: 'What did you think of the paintings?'

'They're different to what I've been used to,' he admitted. 'They're almost semi-finished sketches. But I liked them. I thought they brought her to life more than some of these paintings that are painted to perfection.'

'It's called post-Impressionist,' said Abigail.

'Post-Impressionism?'

'It follows on from the original Impressionists: Manet, Monet, Renoir, all French. Our own Turner was said to be an inspiration for them.'

'Turner?'

'Joseph Mallord William Turner. *The Fighting Temeraire*. Very impressionist.'

'This is all foreign to me,' admitted Daniel. 'I can see that if this becomes a case for us, you're going to have to be my guide.' He turned to her and said: 'You already knew all that about the new Gallery of British Art, didn't you?'

'Yes,' said Abigail. 'It was in one of my magazines. But I didn't like to spoil Mr Beckett's telling us about it.'

CHAPTER THREE

Chief Superintendent Armstrong wasn't at Scotland Yard when they arrived, to Daniel's relief as he'd always had a difficult relationship with him. It had been hard enough when Daniel had been a detective sergeant, but it had got worse since Daniel retired from the force, especially because of his successes as a private enquiry agent, something that Armstrong seemed to take as a slur on the police, and himself in particular. This situation wasn't helped by those journalists with little liking for Armstrong who'd invented the title of 'The Museum Detectives' for Daniel and Abigail, highlighting their successes in those cases and making a point of contrasting them with Scotland Yard's failures.

Their old friend, Inspector John Feather, was in, and it was to him that Daniel showed the letter from Stanford Beckett. Feather grinned as he handed it back to Daniel.

'Good, this'll cover my back if the chief superintendent

finds out you've been here.'

'Don't tell me we've been barred from Scotland Yard again,' said Abigail indignantly as they followed Feather up the wide ornamental staircase to his office on the first floor.

'Not officially. It's just in this case, with your past experience in the original Ripper killings, Daniel, he'd prefer it if you weren't involved.' He gestured at the letter from Stanford Beckett as Daniel put it back in his pocket. 'He'll be upset when he hears about this.'

'What do you know, John?'

'Anne-Marie Dresser, part-time artists' model, part-time prostitute. Her body was found yesterday morning outside the entrance to the National Gallery. Her abdomen had been ripped open and her internal organs removed.'

'And you arrested Sickert. Why?'

'Two things,' said Feather as he walked into his office and gestured for them to sit. 'One, the murder was a copy-cat of the Jack the Ripper killings from nine years ago. And you especially, Daniel, will remember that Sickert was a strong suspect at the time, you and Abberline being in the thick of it. I was only a detective constable then, but even I did my bit, as did every copper on the force, because it was such a big case.'

'It's still not enough to arrest Sickert,' said Daniel.

'No, but this was the clincher,' said Feather. He reached into his desk and took out a sheet of paper, which he passed to them. 'It was left at the front desk late yesterday afternoon.'

On the paper were the words 'The tart wot was killed at the National Gallery. It was the painter Sickert wot dun it.'

'Interesting,' mused Daniel. 'They can't spell "what" and "done", but they can spell "National Gallery".'

'Yes,' nodded Feather, taking the letter back and putting it back in his desk. 'Someone educated pretending to be semi-literate? Anyway, we went in search of Sickert and found him at home, packing to leave for Venice. Doing a runner, in the chief super's opinion.'

'So you brought him in.'

'We did. He claims he hadn't seen Anne-Marie for three days.'

'But he admits knowing her. She was his model.'

'A bit more than that,' chuckled Feather. 'In fact, he told us he brought her back with him after one of his trips to France. From Dieppe, which is where he met her. He set her up in a room in Cumberland Market.'

'Did his wife know about this arrangement?' asked Abigail.

'I don't know,' said Feather. 'We didn't get a chance to ask her. She was pretty angry when she found out why we were there and spent most of the time hurling abuse at us. It didn't seem the right time to ask her.'

'She's quite a character,' smiled Daniel. 'I remember meeting her during the Ripper enquiry. She and Sickert had quite a tempestuous relationship.'

'They still do, by all accounts,' said Feather. 'At least, that's the impression we get from the servants. So, what's your angle in all this? Don't tell me the National Gallery have brought you in to solve the murder. I'd have thought it's a bit soon for that.'

'No,' said Daniel. 'They want us to try and get Sickert released.'

'Not a chance,' said Feather. 'The chief super's firm on this. He's sure that Sickert did it. He wants to nail him. He's aiming to get a confession from him before the lawyers get on to the case.'

'How's he keeping them at bay?' asked Abigail. 'It's a legal requirement that a person accused has access to a solicitor.'

'Armstrong's an old hand at this game,' said Feather. 'He keeps pulling obscure bits of legislation out of the hat. It won't last – give it a day or so and Sickert will get to meet his legal people. But the chief super's hoping by then he'll have enough to proceed.'

'Can we at least see Sickert?' asked Daniel. He tapped his breast pocket where the letter was stored. 'So we have something to tell the National Gallery.'

Feather hesitated, then nodded. 'You're lucky Armstrong's not around or the answer would be no. But, as he's not here, I can't see why not. And if he asks, I'll tell him about that letter of authority.'

'Can we see him on our own?'

'You certainly can,' said Feather cheerfully. 'That way I can say it was nothing to do with me, I wasn't even there, I was just following instructions issued by the boss of the National Gallery.'

A short while later, Daniel and Abigail found themselves sitting at a bare wooden table in an austere interview room in the basement of Scotland Yard. Across from them on the other side of the table were two further chairs. The door opened and a uniformed constable ushered in a short, stocky man in his late thirties. He was dressed in civilian clothes that looked as if he'd slept in them, which they guessed was the case. His trousers were crumpled, as was his shirt, which was unbuttoned.

'I've been told to leave Mr Sickert with you,' the constable told them, a strong note of disapproval in his voice. 'If he plays up, just shout. I'll be right outside the door.'

With that, the constable left.

Sickert gave a broad smile. 'Detective Sergeant Wilson!' he said as he walked to the table and took one of the chairs.

'Sergeant no longer,' said Daniel. 'I'm now in private practice. This is my partner, Miss Abigail Fenton.'

'The brilliant Miss Fenton,' beamed Sickert. 'I've read about you. The famous archaeologist, and now one of the Museum Detectives, as I believe you call yourselves.'

'We don't call ourselves that, that's a title dreamt up by the newspapers.'

'Ah yes, the newspapers,' sighed Sickert. 'They don't like me, you know. They call my work vulgar because it depicts real life. Real women, not those idealised depictions so loved of the Renaissance. When did you ever see a Renaissance nude with sagging breasts? I look at you, Miss Fenton, and I see—'

'If you are going to comment on my breasts, Mr Sickert, perhaps you'll allow me to comment on your equipment,' retorted Abigail.

The smile was wiped off Sickert's face and he glared angrily at Abigail, then at Daniel.

'I do not appreciate gossip about me being spread,' he snapped at Daniel.

'I can assure you I have never discussed your anatomy with anyone, and that includes my partner,' Daniel snapped back.

For a moment, Sickert seemed discomforted and confused. Then he turned back to Abigail, forcing a smile.

'I was going to say that it would be an honour to paint your portrait, Miss Fenton.'

'I do not appear naked for anyone except my husband and

my physician,' said Abigail firmly.

'I do not only paint nudes,' said Sickert. 'You appeal to me. Your statuesque poise, your red hair.'

'Can we get back to the matter in hand?' said Abigail curtly. 'You asked for Mr Wilson to try to get you released. That is why we are here.'

Sickert nodded. 'I did not kill Anne-Marie,' he said. 'She modelled for me, and that was all.' He leered as he added: 'We may have dallied, but we were consenting adults who found pleasure in one another's company.'

'We've been told she was a prostitute,' said Daniel.

'She was. Women without the financial security of a husband often need to earn money that way.'

'Not all women with husbands are financially secure,' Abigail countered. 'In many cases, the husband is a drain on their limited resources.'

'True,' admitted Sickert.

'You paid her?' asked Daniel.

'For modelling for me,' said Sickert. 'And now and then for sex. She was fond of me and sometimes money entered into it. But I did not kill her. I could never harm Anne-Marie. Or any woman.' He turned to Daniel. 'You must know that from our previous encounter, Mr Wilson. You and Abberline spent long enough probing into me.'

The sound of the door crashing open and slamming against the wall made them all jerk round. The bulky figure of Chief Superintendent Armstrong stood framed in the doorway, his face purple with fury. Behind him they could see John Feather in the corridor.

'What the hell's going on?' Armstrong raged.

Daniel took the letter from the National Gallery and held it out towards the chief superintendent.

'We've been authorised by the National Gallery to ask for the release of Mr Sickert—' he began, but was immediately cut off by the furious Armstrong.

'Yes, I've been informed about this spurious letter . . .'

'Hardly spurious,' said Daniel. 'It's signed by the curator, Stanford Beckett.'

'I couldn't care if it's been signed by God himself! It has no jurisdiction here. And nor have you two.' He stepped into the room and pointed at the open doorway. 'Get out!'

Daniel rose to his feet. 'Legally, Mr Sickert has the right of representation . . .'

'Neither you nor Miss Fenton are lawyers,' grunted Armstrong. 'You have no official grounds for being here, or for talking to Mr Sickert. Either you leave or I'll have you both arrested for trespass and obstruction of the police.'

Daniel gave Abigail a look of weary resignation, and she got to her feet.

'You are making a serious mistake, Chief Superintendent,' she said. 'I'm sure that Mr Beckett will wish to take this matter up with your superiors.' With that, she turned to Sickert and gave a polite but icy nod to him. 'Goodbye, Mr Sickert. I'm sure we'll meet again.'

'Not if I have anything to do with it!' growled Armstrong.

Abigail and Daniel left the room. As they passed Feather, the inspector grabbed a quick glance into the interview room to make sure that the chief superintendent had his back to them, then gave Daniel and Abigail a conspiratorial wink, before stepping into the interview room himself.

CHAPTER FOUR

'What did you think of Sickert?' asked Daniel as they headed back to the National Gallery.

'He's an odious man. A very different kettle of fish from his sister.'

'His sister?' queried Daniel.

'Helena,' said Abigail. 'Highly intelligent, honest, forthright, very caring about other people, unlike her brother. We were at Girton at the same time, although our courses were different. Mine was Classics, hers was psychology. She was appointed lecturer in psychology at Westfield. You may know her better as Helena Swanwick, the suffragette and campaigner for women's rights. She married Frederick Swanwick, a lecturer at Manchester University.'

'No, I'm afraid I don't know her at all,' admitted Daniel. 'But then, I don't move in those circles. So you don't approve of Walter Sickert?'

'No I don't. He preys on women, especially lower-class women. He's vain and a blatant self-publicist. He's a despicable person and I don't believe we should be helping him.'

'I agree with you about his character,' said Daniel. 'That was my impression of him when we interviewed him about the original Ripper murders. But this isn't about whether we like him as a person, it's about whether he's guilty of these murders, or is he being framed by someone, as he alleges. This is about justice being done.'

'What about natural justice?' challenged Abigail. 'These women he's preyed on?'

'Who all got paid, I believe,' said Daniel.

'I don't know,' said Abigail doubtfully. 'Are you sure he's not using you as some kind of smokescreen? For all we know he may well have done it, but because he knows from his previous experience of you that you're an honest person who believes in justice, he wants you as protection, and also to aid his claims of innocence.' She frowned and gave Daniel a puzzled look. 'What was all that about when he had a go at you for discussing his equipment? He seemed really angry.'

'When we brought Sickert in for questioning during the Ripper investigations, the guv'nor had the idea of giving him a medical examination, and we discovered that his penis was disfigured. It was a congenital defect. Not that it seemed to stop his sexual adventures.'

'And he thought that was what I was referring to?'

'Yes,' nodded Daniel. 'He's very sensitive about it.'

'I hope he was reassured that you hadn't spoken about it to me. I was just getting back at him for presuming he could talk to a woman about her breasts.'

'We don't know he was going to say anything about your breasts,' said Daniel. 'You didn't give him a chance to finish what he was saying.'

'Why raise the subject if he wasn't going to continue it?' asked Abigail.

'Yes, good point,' admitted Daniel. 'And Sickert's perfectly capable of raising subjects like that, just to shock. He likes shocking people, which is why he's quite proud of the fact that some people see his work as vulgar.'

Stanford Beckett was waiting for them when they arrived back at the National Gallery. Regretfully, they told him their mission had not been a success.

'We saw Mr Sickert, who seemed to be in good spirits, but we were ordered off the premises by Chief Superintendent Armstrong. I'm afraid he seems extremely reluctant to release Sickert.'

Beckett gave a weary sigh. 'I'm sorry you had an abortive journey,' he said apologetically. 'But I'll arrange payment for your time on your usual terms. I hope that will be acceptable?'

'Very acceptable,' said Daniel.

They left the gallery and began their walk up Charing Cross Road towards Camden Town.

'Well, that's that,' said Abigail resignedly. 'I didn't like Sickert, but it's a great pity that he remains in custody of that oaf Armstrong, who I'm sure will try and break him down and confess.'

'Oh, I'm not sure if that'll be the end of it,' said Daniel. 'From our point of view, yes. But Ellen Sickert isn't the sort of woman to give up her husband that easily.'

* * *

28

Chief Superintendent Armstrong paced around his office as Inspector Feather scribbled down his superior's instructions.

'Anne-Marie Dresser's movements,' he said. 'We need to find out who she saw the night she was killed. Who she was planning to see. Talk to her friends. Neighbours. Find out if any of them saw Sickert near that room of hers during the evening.'

'He says he was at home the whole time, and that his wife will bear that out,' pointed out Feather.

'Balderdash!' snorted the chief superintendent. 'A wife's alibi isn't worth anything.'

'He says his servants will back it up. And there's this character . . .' He flicked back through his notebook. 'Edwin O'Tool.'

'A complete figment,' derided Armstrong. 'Sickert's the one. All we've got to do is break his alibi, and we do that by proving he and this woman Dresser saw one another that night.'

There was a loud and imperious knock at the door. Before Armstrong could say 'Come in!', the door had been pushed open and the tall and bulky figure of Sir Bramley Petton was framed in the doorway. Petton was a very well-known barrister, possibly one of the most familiar faces at the Old Bailey. He was in his sixties, with a mass of unruly greying hair, and a large stomach that battled to burst out of his very expensive tailor-made suit. He carried a bulky envelope under one arm. Petton eyed Armstrong and Feather with a glinting and accusing glare, developed over many years interrogating witnesses in the highest courts in the land.

'Chief Superintendent Armstrong,' he boomed, his voice filling the office.

'Indeed, Sir Bramley,' said Armstrong. 'What can I do for

you?'

By way of answer, Petton dropped the bulky envelope on Armstrong's desk.

'You can release my client, Mr Walter Sickert.'

Armstrong stared at the barrister, bewildered. Petton pointed at the large envelope he'd just deposited.

'These are signed affidavits from Mrs Ellen Sickert and four of the servants of the Sickert household which swear to the fact that Mr Walter Sickert was at home during the evening and the night of the 14th February, when this heinous crime was committed. Also, there was one Edwin O'Tool, a carpenter, who Mr Sickert had invited to celebrate with him. They drank copiously and Mr O'Tool was obliged to stay the night on the floor of the Sickert's drawing room next to the settee. Mr Sickert occupied the settee. If Mr Sickert had got up during the night, he would have trodden on Mr O'Tool and woken him. Ergo, Chief Superintendent, my client did not and could not have been murdering and disembowelling anyone that night. Therefore, I insist you release him from custody. Failure to do so will result in my presenting these affidavits to the police commissioner and the home secretary for them to authorise his release.'

Armstrong fixed the barrister with a grim look.

'There was absolutely no reason for this overreaction—' he began.

'Overreaction!' exploded Petton.

'. . . because I had already decided to release Mr Sickert. Is that not so, Inspector?' he said, turning to Feather.

Feather looked at him in awkward surprise, then at Bramley Petton, before saying, 'Yes, sir.'

'But by all means leave these affidavits here,' continued Armstrong. 'They may contain evidence that will help us in our investigation.'

Petton gave him a withering look and gathered up the envelope. 'These are the property of our firm,' he said. 'If you decide to take Mr Sickert into custody again, then, and only then will they be relinquished to you. I look forward to my client being released and brought to me.'

Armstrong swallowed, then turned to Feather.

'Inspector, have Mr Sickert released and taken to the reception area.' He turned to Petton. 'You may collect him there, Sir Bramley.'

CHAPTER FIVE

'Why was Sickert a suspect in the first Ripper investigation?' asked Abigail.

The pair had arrived home and it was Daniel's turn to prepare food for them. At first Abigail had been suspicious of his offer because Daniel's favourite meal seemed to be pie and mash from the local pie and mash shop, but today he'd used the range to roast potatoes and a chicken, which they were eating now, along with a glass of beer each.

'For the same reason he's a suspect now,' replied Daniel. 'You said yourself, as well as his society portraits, he also paints women from the lower classes, often prostitutes.'

'More than paints them,' she said scornfully.

'Yes, we did find that he also enjoyed their favours.'

'But, as you pointed out to me earlier, that doesn't make him a murderer,' she admitted.

'No. But rumours came to us that he and a friend of his used to take nocturnal trips to Whitechapel, and that some of these trips had occurred when the murders were committed.'

'Who was the friend?' asked Abigail.

'Prince Albert Victor Christian Edward.'

'The Queen's grandson?' said Abigail, shocked.

Daniel nodded.

'But jaunts like that mean nothing!' said Abigail, recovering her composure. 'You're surely not saying that the Queen's grandson, and heir to the throne . . .'

'Second in line,' Daniel corrected her. 'His father, the Prince of Wales, is the immediate heir.'

'There's no need to be pedantic,' said Abigail irritably. 'You know what I'm saying.'

'That we shouldn't suspect him because of who he is?'

'No, I'm not saying that.' Then she gave a rueful sigh. 'Yes, I suppose I am. But he died, didn't he?'

'Five years ago, in 1892 at the age of 28. Pneumonia.'

'Very convenient,' said Abigail tartly. 'But that was four years after the murders, so I assume you couldn't find any evidence against him. Or against Sickert.'

'Actually, the decision not to proceed wasn't that straightforward, even though we learnt that on 30th September 1888, the day that Elizabeth Stride and Catherine Eddowes, two of the Ripper's victims, were killed, Prince Albert was 500 miles away at Balmoral, so he couldn't have been involved. But there were questions about the dates of the other murders. Mary Ann Nichols was killed on 31st August. Annie Chapman was killed on 8th September. Mary Jane Kelly was killed on 9th November.'

'But no one was ever charged with the crimes, so I assume you had no proof against Prince Albert Victor or Sickert.'

'We never had the chance to dig deeper into them, although my guv'nor wanted to. At that time Armstrong was a chief inspector, and he stepped in and told us that the powers that be didn't want any further investigations into Prince Albert Victor, Walter Sickert or Sir William Gull.'

'Sir William Gull?' queried Abigail.

'He was the third member of the alleged conspiracy. Rumours said that all three were involved in these nocturnal trips to Whitechapel, and were involved in the killings. We had eye-witness reports that Sir William's carriage, which was quite distinctive with a coat of arms on it, was seen in Whitechapel on the night of at least two of the murders.'

'Why wasn't he investigated?'

'We talked to him, but then we were warned off. Sir William Gull just happened to be the personal physician to the Queen. Gull died in 1890.'

'Abberline retired from the police, didn't he?'

'He did, in 1892, a year before I did. The same year that Prince Albert Victor died.'

'Did Sir William Gull and Prince Albert Victor also get a medical examination, like Sickert?'

Daniel smiled. 'No chance. We were only allowed to talk to Sir William briefly before the shutters came down. And we were barred from meeting the prince.'

'Why did Armstrong interfere?'

'To protect the good name of the royal family.' He gave a scowl as he added: 'It was surely no coincidence that, shortly after, Armstrong was promoted to superintendent.'

'A reward for quashing the investigation?'

'That's what Fred Abberline thought. It was also around the same time, in 1889, there was another scandal involving Prince Albert Victor: the Cleveland Street Scandal.'

'You've mentioned that before. Wasn't it a homosexual brothel?'

'It was. Fred Abberline and I were called into investigate. We discovered that telegraph boys were being used as homosexual prostitutes at a house in Cleveland Street, but when we moved to make arrests, we only managed to get hold of one man who was involved, the house was empty. But we found a list of clients, many of them very well connected.'

'Prince Victor again?'

'Someone from his household, and some others he was known to associate with.'

'What happened in the end?'

'Most of the clients whose names were on the list fled abroad.'

'So no one was charged.'

'No one of any social importance. A few lesser individuals were arrested, including some of the telegraph boys, who received light sentences.'

Abigail frowned. 'What I don't understand,' she said, puzzled, 'is if Armstrong quashed the investigation into Sickert, the Prince and Gull nine years ago, why is he arresting him now over this one? Surely he runs the risk of raising why Sickert was let off the hook the first time, which will call his position into question.'

Daniel chuckled. 'What do you think of Sickert?' he asked.

'I've already told you,' said Abigail, her face tight with her disapproval. 'He's an odious man. Vain and despicable.'

'Exactly,' nodded Daniel. 'And it's been his vanity that's been his downfall here. After our original investigation was ended, Sickert took delight in boasting to his friends that he was untouchable. That the police kept their hands off him because he "knew things". The implication was that he had something on Armstrong. Being Sickert, he was clever not to repeat that too often, but word got back to Armstrong, and the superintendent was angry. No – more than angry, he was incandescent. But what could he do? Sickert hadn't actually said anything specific, just hinted that he couldn't be touched. And, so long as he didn't do anything illegal, he couldn't be. He may be disreputable, a lecher, a frequenter of prostitutes, but none of that's illegal. And all the time Armstrong simmers over the injustice of what he knows Sickert has said behind his back. So now, this is revenge. This is something he can pull Sickert in for. And it's not just about Sickert, it's a message to people like Bram Stoker, for example. You know the animosity there is between Armstrong and Stoker.'

'Stoker? How does he come into it?'

'He and Sickert are old friends. Years ago, Sickert was an actor at the Lyceum in Irving's theatre company.'

'My God! I've always thought it was a small world, but it just got smaller. Sickert, Stoker, Irving and Armstrong?'

'I know,' said Daniel. 'There are lots of long memories involved here.'

There was a knock at their front door.

'I'll go,' said Daniel, getting to his feet.

Abigail heard voices from the front door, then Daniel reappeared with a brown envelope similar to the one that had been delivered to them that morning. This one had been opened.

'It was a messenger from Stanford Beckett,' Daniel said.

He held out the single-page letter to her.

'Dear Mr Wilson and Miss Fenton,' she read. 'Walter has been released from custody and asks if you can meet him here at my office tomorrow morning at 10 a.m.'

'I told the messenger to tell Beckett that we'd be there,' said Daniel. 'I hope that's all right with you.'

'How did he come to be released?' asked Abigail, stunned. 'Armstrong was so determined to keep him.'

'But I expect Ellen Sickert was even more determined to get him out,' said Daniel. 'As I said, she is a formidable woman.'

CHAPTER SIX

John Feather could see that Chief Superintendent Armstrong was still seething with anger when he arrived at Scotland Yard the following morning.

'Have you found anything?' demanded Armstrong angrily. 'Anything that puts Sickert with the victim that night?'

'No, sir,' said Feather. 'I went to the room she had at Cumberland Market and spoke to her neighbours, but none of them recall seeing her that night. They believe she was out. And none of them saw any men around her room, certainly none answering Sickert's description. And most of the neighbours knew Sickert, because he was a frequent visitor.'

'So maybe he'd arranged to see her somewhere else, away from her room?' suggested Armstrong.

'There's always the possibility that whoever wrote that note accusing Sickert did it because they had some kind of resentment against him, not because they actually knew anything,' said Feather.

'No!' growled Armstrong. 'It's Sickert. I feel it in my bones.' He banged his fist hard on his desk. 'How does he do it? How does he get to use people like Sir Bramley Petton? He's not cheap, you know. And for Petton to come here himself, not just send a solicitor . . .' He shook his head, lost for words. 'I doubt if there were even any affidavits in those papers. A lawyer's trick. I've seen him in court pulling that kind of stunt.' He looked at Feather as he asked: 'Did you put a tail on Sickert like I said?'

'Yes, sir, I did that first before I went to Cumberland Market. There was a note from him waiting for me at the reception desk just now.' He took a piece of paper from his pocket. 'Subject arrived at National Gallery at 9.45 a.m.'

'Back to the scene of the crime,' growled Armstrong.

'D Wilson and A Fenton arrived ten minutes after,' continued Feather.

'What?!' bellowed Armstrong, leaping to his feet. He reached out and snatched the piece of paper from Feather's hand. 'What's going on?' he demanded.

Daniel and Abigail sat in Stanford Beckett's office and studied Walter Sickert, who lounged in a leather armchair beside Beckett's desk. They'd gone through the usual formalities, handshakes and polite smiles, when they first walked in, before settling themselves down.

'Congratulations on your release,' said Daniel. 'There's been no mention of it in the press, but I assume Chief Superintendent Armstrong changed his mind about your guilt.'

'Alas, no,' said Sickert. 'Fortunately for me, Sir Bramley

Petton, the eminent barrister, turned up at Armstrong's office with a pile of affidavits from my wife and my servants, all swearing that I was at home the whole night of February 14th. There was also one from an acquaintance of mine, a Mr Edwin O'Tool. He and I indulged in a little too much alcohol on the evening and as a result I spent the night on the settee in the drawing room while Mr O'Tool slept on the floor next to the settee. He gave a statement that said I could not have got up and left in the night without treading on him and waking him. As a result, Armstrong was reluctantly forced to let me go.'

'He doesn't believe the statements?'

'No, he doesn't. And I have to admit, if I were in his shoes, I would have doubt about them. One's wife and servants would be expected to say I was at the house all night, and Mr O'Tool has issues with drink that could make him a suspect witness.' He smiled. 'But, faced with the eminence of Sir Bramley, the chief superintendent had little choice but to release me. However, I'd like to hire you to prove my innocence.'

'The police will already be investigating.'

'I doubt it. I believe that Chief Superintendent Armstrong is convinced I'm guilty, so he'll be spending his time waiting for me to make a slip that will give me away. He's already got his bloodhounds trailing me. There was a constable outside my house this morning and he accompanied me all the way here. I expect he'll be waiting outside when I leave.

'In the meantime, in the eyes of everyone, I'm guilty and getting away with it. And I'm sure that Armstrong will be keen to remind people – in some oblique way – that I got away with it before, in 1888. My reputation, and therefore my living, is at stake as long as this hangs over me. I have many portraits commissioned, and already people are backing off from going ahead. Will you take on this commission on my behalf and find the real guilty person?'

Daniel shot a look at Abigail, who hesitated, then nodded. 'We will,' she said.

'How will you begin?' asked Sickert.

'First, we'd like to talk to your wife and servants, and also see these affidavits,' said Daniel.

'You do not trust my wife and me?'

'It's not a question of trust, it's a matter of looking at everything that's germane to the case. If we are to prove your innocence, the first thing we need to do is assure ourselves that you are, indeed, innocent.'

'Very well,' Sickert nodded. 'I've already let Nellie know that I hope to engage you, so she'll be expecting you. I'll also tell Sir Bramley to let you see the affidavits. When will you call?'

'Later today?' suggested Daniel.

'That will be fine. I shall depart for Venice tomorrow, as I originally intended.'

'Does Chief Superintendent Armstrong know you intend to leave?'

'He may do,' shrugged Sickert. 'He knows I was on my way to Venice when they took me into custody.'

'He may not let you go.'

Sickert smiled. 'After the intervention of Sir Bramley Petton, I doubt if he'd be so foolish as to prevent me going. My hope is that you'll be able to find the guilty party while I'm away, so that I can return and get on with my work.'

'It will help us if you can share with us any idea who might have wanted to frame you.'

'I have no idea,' said Sickert.

'Enemies?'

'Not enough to warrant killing Anne-Marie, I would have thought.'

'Then let's consider it from another angle. People who know both you and Anne-Marie.'

'Many,' said Sickert.

'She was an artist's model. She modelled for you. Do you know who else she modelled for?'

'I didn't ask.'

'She modelled for Simon Anstis,' put in Beckett.

Sickert let out a laugh of derision. 'That so-called excuse for a painter?'

'I know he was very fond of her,' added Beckett.

'He lusted after her, and she kept him dangling on a string for her amusement,' sneered Sickert.

'It would be useful to talk to him,' said Daniel. 'Do you have his address?'

'No,' said Sickert. 'I have no interest in him. He is a would-be painter who desperately wants to be Van Gogh. The only way he could be in any way like him is if he cut off his ear.'

'I think you're being a bit harsh, Walter,' said Beckett with polite reproof. 'He's young and still finding his way as an artist.'

'He's not an artist and he never will be,' snapped Sickert. 'That's why I call him a painter. Truth be told, he's more of a dauber.'

Beckett turned to Daniel. 'I can let you have Simon's address.'

'That wasn't a very useful meeting,' commented Daniel as they walked away from the National Gallery.

'Who's Nellie?' she asked.

'That's the name his wife, Ellen, is known as by her family. It came up when we met her before, in 1888. Her sister, Jane, was with her and she called her Nellie.'

'So do we call her Nellie when we meet her?'

'No. We'll stick to the formalities. Mrs Sickert.'

'Sickert doesn't give much away,' observed Abigail. 'He does this casual lounging and puts on an air of indifference. But he cares. He especially cares about not letting people know what's going on. He keeps secrets.'

'He doesn't trust people,' observed Daniel. 'And that includes us. He's worried if he opens up and admits things, they might go against him. He's not going to Venice simply to paint, he's going to hide.' He looked at Abigail and said in hopeful appeal: 'I'm also going to need you to translate this world of art and artists for me. For example, what was that reference of Sickert's about Van Gogh?'

'You don't know the work of Vincent Van Gogh?'

'No. To be honest, this whole art world is a closed world to me. I guess from his name that he's Dutch.'

'He was Dutch. He died nine years ago after shooting himself. But before that he had a breakdown, during which he cut off one of his ears and apparently gave it to a prostitute as a present.'

'My God!' exclaimed Daniel. 'I always think of painters as sedate people, happy to paint pictures of horses or plants, or portraits. But after meeting Sickert again, and now this Van Gogh character, I'm beginning to think the art world is dangerous.'

'What do you think our next move should be?' asked

Abigail. 'Talk to this Simon Anstis? He is the only name that we've been given.'

'I think first we need to look into these affidavits that claim to prove Sickert's innocence,' said Daniel thoughtfully.

'Claim?' echoed Abigail. 'You think he might be guilty?'

'I don't know,' admitted Daniel. 'But, to be frank, the evidence of a wife and servants isn't the strongest.'

'There's also this man, O'Tool.'

'Yes, it will be interesting to talk to him.'

'So, we go to Sir Bramley Petton's office?'

'No, we go to see Ellen Sickert first. We need to get her on our side if we're going to get Sickert to be honest and open with us.'

CHAPTER SEVEN

Walter and Ellen Sickert's residence was a large, white-fronted Regency house in Clarence Gardens, near to Regent's Park.

'They've moved up in the world since I last saw them,' said Daniel as he tugged at the bell pull. 'When we were doing the Ripper investigation they were in South Hampstead. Walter had his studio on the top floor.'

A young girl of about fourteen, a maid in a striped apron and wearing a small white cap, opened the door to them. They introduced themselves and said they had come to see Mr and Mrs Sickert. Before the girl could head into the house to check, they heard a woman's voice call: 'Who is it, Doris?', and then a stately looking woman in her late forties appeared.

'Mrs Sickert,' said Daniel, with a slight bow of his head. 'I'm Daniel Wilson and this is my partner, Abigail Fenton.'

'Yes, I remember you. Walter said you might be calling.'

Ellen Sickert was a tall woman, dressed plainly in a long skirt and loose blouse, her dark hair pulled into a bun at the back of her head. She gestured for them to enter, and they followed her to a drawing room. There was a settee in the middle of the room, and Daniel wondered if this was the one on which Sickert claimed to have slept while his companion, the mysterious Edwin O'Tool, slept on the floor. If so, Sickert's alibi had been blown. The settee was distant enough from the nearest wall for Sickert to have climbed over its back without disturbing anyone sleeping on the floor.

Ellen Sickert motioned for them to sit and she herself took the settee.

'Walter said he was hoping to hire you to find the killer,' she told them.

'Yes. That's what he's asked us to do,' said Daniel.

'So you're on the other side of the fence now. I remember last time when you were trying to prove Walter guilty. You and Abberline.'

'We were just conducting enquiries, Mrs Sickert. As we are now.'

'You thought he did it. Killed those women.'

'If we'd believed that he'd have been charged. He wasn't.'

She scowled, not entirely satisfied. Then she turned to Abigail. 'And you, Miss Fenton? Do you believe my husband's innocent of this latest killing?'

'That's what he's asked us to prove by catching the person who committed it.'

'That's not an answer.'

Abigail weighed up her response before replying. 'On any investigation it's important to keep an open mind, but the

46

evidence so far, particularly the note that was left at Scotland Yard naming him, suggests someone killed Anne-Marie Dresser in order to frame him for the murder.'

'Yes, that's what Walter says.' She looked at them, slightly mollified. 'Very well, what can I do to help?'

'We understand that you and your household staff, along with a gentleman called Mr O'Tool, have already given affidavits to Sir Bramley Petton confirming that Mr Sickert was here all night on 14th February, the night she was killed.'

'That's right,' said Ellen.

'Mr Sickert has told us we can examine them, so we'll need a letter of authority to Sir Bramley from yourself or Mr Sickert . . .'

'I'll give you one today,' she said. 'I'm the one who arranged for Sir Bramley to intercede on Walter's behalf. Sir Bramley is an old friend of my father's.'

'We'd also like to hear from you and your staff about that night.'

'Why?' she demanded. 'You'll have the affidavits.'

'Because we might want to ask questions about some of the statements.'

'You don't trust us?'

'I always like to clarify things if I'm unsure of something,' said Daniel.

'You want to trick us,' she said. 'See if our statements today are the same as the affidavits we gave to Sir Bramley.'

'I just want to see things for myself,' said Daniel. 'For example, we understand that Mr Sickert spent the night sleeping on the settee, while a Mr O'Tool slept on the floor.'

'That is so,' said Ellen.

'Out of curiosity, is this the room where they spent the night?'

'It is,' she said.

'And is this that same settee?'

Ellen Sickert's lips tightened into a line. 'You are suggesting that he could have climbed over the back?'

'It has occurred to me,' said Daniel. 'Unless the settee's been moved since that evening.'

'Walter was drunk,' she said curtly. 'He did not go anywhere that night.'

'But he could have,' said Daniel. 'As you yourself have just said, he could have climbed over the back and got out without treading on Mr O'Tool.'

'I did not say that,' she corrected him. 'I said that *you* are suggesting he could have done that. He did not.'

'We'd like to talk to this Mr O'Tool. Do you have an address for him?'

'No. He was just some casual acquaintance of Walter's he met in a pub and brought home. He's always doing that, bringing home lame ducks and misfits. They're usually material for his work. I believe Sir Bramley may have an address for him.'

Ellen's head turned towards the door as they heard the sound of the street door opening and closing and footsteps in the hallway.

'That could be Walter,' she said.

It was. Walter Sickert appeared in the doorway and beamed at them.

'Ah, visitors! My private investigators!'

'Mr Wilson has a question to ask you,' said Ellen, her voice heavy with disapproval. 'Is this the settee on which you spent the night when Mr O'Tool was your guest?'

'The very same,' said Sickert cheerfully.

'Mr Wilson has observed that even with Mr O'Tool sleeping next to it, you could have climbed over the back.'

For a moment, Sickert was dumbfounded. Then he said: 'I must have moved it since that night. I'm sure it was against the wall.'

'Which wall?' asked Daniel.

Sickert pointed to the rear wall. Daniel walked over to the wall and paced his way carefully along it, looking at the carpet.

'That settee has not been against that wall in the last couple of days,' he said.

'Well then, it was against one of the other walls,' said Sickert defensively.

Daniel looked at him inquisitively, then said politely and calmly: 'Mr Sickert, if we are to represent you, we need you to be truthful with us.'

'Yes, all right, dammit,' blustered Sickert. 'The settee was where it is now. But I did sleep on it, and Mr O'Tool was beside it, and I assure you I did not clamber over the back. I never got up from it until the maid came to bring me and Mr O'Tool a cup of tea each in the morning.'

'Thank you,' said Daniel. 'With your permission, we'd like to talk to your servants.'

'Can't it wait until tomorrow?' asked Sickert, pained. 'As I told you, I'm off to Venice tomorrow and I need the servants to help me pack.'

Daniel and Abigail exchanged questioning looks, then Daniel nodded. 'Very well,' he said. 'Do you have an address for Mr O'Tool?'

Sickert shook his head. 'I met him at the Mother Redcap pub. I have no idea where he lives. Sir Bramley might have it.'

Daniel turned to Ellen. 'In that case, if you'll give me that letter of authority to Sir Bramley Petton, Mrs Sickert, we'll call on him to look at the affidavits, and we'll return tomorrow to talk to you and the servants. Will that be acceptable?'

She nodded, then rose. 'I'll go and write that letter of authority.'

As Daniel and Abigail made their way to Sir Bramley Petton's chambers in High Holborn, Abigail commented: 'So it seems it was Ellen Sickert who arranged for Sir Bramley Petton.'

'And paid for it, I expect,' said Daniel. 'That was one of the things we turned up before, Sickert isn't that well off. It's Ellen who's got the money.'

'Where from?'

'A trust fund set up in her father's memory. He was Richard Cobden.'

'The radical politician? The repeal of the Corn Laws and free trade?'

'The same. But he was also a businessman and that's where he made his money. She's supported Sickert financially ever since they were married so he could paint.'

'Despite the fact he seems to be serially unfaithful to her?'

'Plenty of marriages seem to work on different rules,' observed Daniel.

Sir Bramley Petton's chambers were on the first floor of the tall redbrick building, and when his clerk told them he had visitors, and who they were, Petton invited them into his office, which was an untidy sprawl of papers tied with red tape and books piled on every surface. Petton read the letter of introduction that Ellen Sickert had given them, then nodded as he handed it back. He gestured towards the two chairs opposite his, and they sat.

'I know of you by reputation, of course,' he said. 'Ellen says you wish to look at the affidavits.'

'We do,' confirmed Daniel.

Petton took a thick brown envelope from a nearby pile and pushed it across the desk to them. Daniel undid the string that secured the envelope and took out the bundle of papers. Only six sheets of paper at the top of the sheaf were written affidavits, the rest were sheets of paper, some handwritten, some printed, which seemed to have no relation to the Sickerts or the case. Daniel and Abigail looked inquisitively at Petton, who shrugged.

'Subsidiary documentation,' he said airily.

'Or bulk to intimidate a chief superintendent?' asked Daniel.

'We all play games,' shrugged Petton.

Daniel and Abigail read through the six affidavits, one each by Walter and Ellen Sickert, one by the mysterious Edwin O'Tool, one each from the housekeeper, Mrs Stanton, and Johnson, Sickert's manservant, and finally one from the maid, Doris. All had been written by the same hand, presumably Petton's. The statements from Walter and Ellen Sickert and the housekeeper and Johnson had been signed by them, and those from Mr O'Tool and the maid were marked with a cross.

'Thank you,' said Daniel, replacing the sheets of paper in the envelope and passing it back to Petton. 'However, that business with the settee doesn't hold up under examination. It's in the middle of the drawing room. Walter Sickert could

51

have climbed over the back and got out without disturbing Mr O'Tool.'

'I thought you were on our side,' said Petton, annoyed.

'We are,' said Daniel. 'But the first move of any detective worth their salt is to examine the evidence, both from the prosecution and the defence. We'd like to talk to Mr O'Tool. Do you have an address for him?'

'No. He appeared at my office and said he needed to make a statement. I asked him for his address, but he said he was currently without a permanent address.'

'Who brought him to your office?' asked Abigail.

'It was Johnson, the Sickerts' manservant,' replied Sir Bramley.

'Did he say where he'd found him?'

'No. I assume he'd found him in a pub somewhere.' He leant forward, his piercing eyes fixed on Daniel. 'You were involved in investigating the Ripper murders, Mr Wilson. Do you believe that Walter Sickert could have carried them out?'

'I have no opinion on that,' said Daniel. 'Not one I'm prepared to share.'

'But you have accepted the engagement to clear his name.'

'Everyone is entitled to justice,' said Daniel blandly. He stood up. 'Thank you, Sir Bramley.'

'What do you think?' asked Abigail as they made their way out to the pavement.

'About Sickert, or about Sir Bramley Petton?'

'All of it.'

'The affidavits are worthless, and Petton knows that. The whole thing was a charade played out by a bombastic would-be actor.'

'Which was successful,' added Abigail.

'Yes, that's what he does,' said Daniel.

'But we're no nearer to knowing if Sickert is guilty.'

'No, although my own assessment of him is that he's a watcher rather than a doer.'

'So we look elsewhere for our killer?'

'We do.'

'And Mr O'Tool?'

'We'll talk to Johnson and ask him where he found Mr O'Tool, and how he knew where to find him. But I think that whole settee business is a red herring. I think our next move is to look into Anne-Marie Dresser's life.'

'You think she was killed by someone she was involved with?'

'It's possible, but I believe we need to find out where Sickert's and Anne-Marie's lives intersect. The note naming Sickert is the crux of it. Either it was written because someone knew that Sickert had killed her; or it was written to frame him. In which case, it's likely that the killer wrote that note. The obvious deduction, if that's the case, is that the killer is someone who knows Sickert and hates him enough to kill someone.'

'Why doesn't he just kill Sickert?'

'Because he wants to discredit him publicly, and for him to hang as a murderer. If that's the case, then it's someone who knew Anne-Marie was a part of Sickert's life.'

CHAPTER EIGHT

Anne-Marie Dresser had lived in a shared house in Cumberland Market, which was just a street away from the Sickerts' house in Clarence Gardens.

'He was playing a dangerous game,' mused Abigail. 'Keeping his mistress so close to the family home.'

'Hiding her in plain sight,' suggested Daniel. 'She was his artist's model as well, remember.'

Anne-Marie's room was on the first floor. Their knocking at her door, just in case anyone was at home, led to the door of the adjacent room opening.

'She's not there,' said a tall, very thin, pale-faced woman in her thirties. Her long blonde hair was betrayed as dyed by the black roots that stood out.

'No, we know,' said Daniel. 'My name's Daniel Wilson and this is my partner, Abigail Fenton. We've been hired by Mr

Sickert and the National Gallery to find out what happened to her.'

'She was killed,' said the woman. 'The night before last. The police told me.'

'Yes, we know,' said Daniel. 'We've been asked to find out who did it, and we're starting by talking to people who knew her. Did you see much of her?'

The woman nodded. 'She would come in and talk. Like her, I'm not married so it was nice to have someone to talk to.'

'Do you mind if we ask your name?'

'Not at all. Vera Mattisson. I've already given it to the police. A nice man, an Inspector Feather.'

Daniel nodded.

'Yes, we know Inspector Feather. As you say, a very nice man.'

'You are working with him?'

'We will be, but at the moment we're following our own line of enquiry. We're trying to find out about Anne-Marie's life.'

'She's French. From Dieppe. But she spoke good English.'

'We know she modelled for Walter Sickert, the painter,' said Abigail.

Vera laughed. 'That's one word for it.' And she laughed some more.

'Were there other artists she modelled for?'

'One or two. Mostly she was busy, doing what she did.' Vera smiled. 'Artists don't pay much. The other thing she did, pays better.'

My guess is that Vera's in the same game, thought Abigail, and she shot a meaningful look at Daniel, who nodded.

'Did you know Mr Sickert?' asked Daniel.

She smiled. 'Of course.'

'Did you model for him?'

'No. Just the other thing.'

'Did Anne-Marie bring her . . . ah . . . clients to her room, or did she go to their places?'

'That depended,' said Vera. 'Sometimes they came here, sometimes she went there. She preferred bringing them here. She said it was safer. She knew where she was.' She paused, then added: 'She kept a knife under her pillow, within easy reach, in case of trouble. There are some bad people out there.'

'And one of them killed her,' said Daniel. 'Did she have any trouble with anybody in particular?'

Vera shook her head. 'Anne-Marie was cute. She could read people, like she had a secret sense about them. And most of the men who came to her were like little boys. Weak men, sneaking away from their wives.'

'Would you count Walter Sickert to be like that?'

'No. Walter is weak, but in a different way. He's also very gentle. Kind. Nice.'

'What about the other artists she modelled for?'

'There was one she sat for a couple of times called Adrian Ford, but she didn't like him, so she stopped going to his studio.'

'Why was that?'

'He stank and he farted all the time. He never washed. Anne-Marie said it was disgusting. The smell!'

'But no other reason. Was he ever violent to her?'

'No, he just stank.'

'The other artist? You said she sat for a couple of others beside Walter Sickert.'

At this, Vera gave a sly smile and chuckled again. 'Yes. Her little pet. She took delight in tormenting him. He was madly in love with her, but she wouldn't let him so much as touch her and it drove him mad.'

'His name?'

'Simon Anstis,' said Vera.

'Simon Anstis again,' said Abigail as they left the house.

Daniel took a piece of paper from his pocket. 'Mr Beckett gave me Anstis' address. He has a room, which doubles as his studio, not too far from here, in Great Portland Street. I suggest that's our next port of call.'

Simon Anstis was a short man, unshaven and with long hair that curled down to the smock he wore, which was daubed with oil paints in various colours. He had been reluctant to let Daniel and Abigail in, insisting that he was working on a private work that the person who'd commissioned it wanted to remain unseen until he was ready to reveal it. Abigail's suggestion that he put a cloth over the painting to conceal it while they were in his studio was grudgingly conceded. Anstis disappeared inside his studio, reappearing a few moments later to open the door to them.

Daniel had questioned a few painters in his time when he'd been on the Metropolitan Police, and all their studios had been heavy with the smell of turpentine. Simon Anstis' was the exception; the smell of oil paint and turpentine was muted by comparison, which allowed them to become aware of an unusual perfume that emanated from the coat rack just inside the door.

It was a small room in an attic at the top of the house in Great Portland Street and the one piece of furniture in it was a sofa, which they guessed also doubled as his bed from the way the cushions had been piled up at one end. There was a skylight in the ceiling, which let in light, and gas mantles around the walls. The picture that Anstis insisted was secret stood on an easel, covered with a brown cloth.

The young artist looked at them with suspicion.

'You say you're detectives,' he said warily. 'What are you detecting? And why do you think I can help you?'

'We've been hired by the National Gallery to investigate the murder of Anne-Marie Dresser,' said Daniel. 'We understand that she modelled for you.'

Anstis stood staring at them, his lips moving but no sound came out. Then he began to shake. Daniel and Abigail exchanged looks of concern. Was Anstis about to have an attack of some sort?

'Mr Anstis—' began Daniel.

Suddenly Anstis collapsed onto the sofa and began to sob.

'Anne-Marie!' he moaned. 'I loved her! I would have done anything for her!' He wept some more, great heaving sobs, then stammered: 'She taunted me! She'd be here, naked, and flaunt herself. She'd sit on the stool and deliberately open her legs and thrust herself forward and lick her lips, but she'd never let me so much as touch her. It drove me mad!'

'Why didn't you stop painting her?' asked Abigail.

'Because I loved her! I needed to look at her. But all she'd do was talk about that damned Sickert and what they did together. She did it to inflame me!' And he began to sob again.

'We know this is a difficult time for you,' said Daniel, 'but we do have to ask questions of everyone who knew her if we're going to find out who killed her.'

'It wasn't me,' Anstis sobbed.

'We're trying to trace her movements on the night she died. Was she here?'

'No. I wish she had been. If she had, she'd still be alive.'

'Where were you on the night of the 14th February? The night that Anne-Marie died.'

'Here,' he said. 'Working.'

'Was anyone with you?'

'No one. I was alone.' He leapt up, walked to the easel and snatched the brown cloth away, revealing the concealed picture. It was of a young woman, nude, sitting on the same sofa. 'I was working on that. It's Anne-Marie.'

They looked at the picture. Unlike Sickert's picture of Anne-Marie, or that by Degas, both of which had been impressionistic in style, Anstis had gone for a realistic portrayal. But somehow, it hadn't worked. Both Sickert and Degas had captured an animal spirit in their images of her, had given her life. Anstis' portrait of her was flat and mundane by comparison.

'Can you think of anyone who might have wanted to harm her?' asked Daniel.

Anstis shook his head.

'No,' he replied, his voice full of anguish. 'Everyone who met her loved her.'

'What did you think of him?' asked Daniel as they walked away from the house.

'As a suspect or a painter?' asked Abigail.

'Both, but primarily as a suspect?'

'He's certainly on edge and, I feel, unstable because of the intensity of his feelings for Anne-Marie. He also hates Sickert. It's possible he could have done it in a blinding rage, but I'm not sure. As far as his painting is concerned, I have to agree with Sickert. He's a dauber, not an artist – someone who can copy an image but it always looks flat. No vitality.'

'Yes, I thought the same,' said Daniel. 'And I'm a person who has no understanding of art.'

'You don't need to understand art to know if something feels good to you,' said Abigail. 'Art can mean different things to different people. But in my eyes, Sickert and Degas captured Anne-Marie, like catching lightning in a bottle. She lives in their canvases. Simon Anstis' picture was of a nude woman, but it could have been of a bunch of flowers, or a bowl of fruit. There was no life to it.' She looked at Daniel and asked, puzzled, 'By the way, what was that perfume smell?'

'Lemon and bergamot,' said Daniel. When Abigail looked at him in surprise, he explained: 'There was a member of the Detective Squad who used it. Dabbed it on his clothes. Everyone could smell him coming a mile off. Fortunately, he left Scotland Yard.'

Madge Potts and her small army of cleaners gathered at their usual assembly point at Nelson's Column. Madge preferred this place to all of them meeting up on the steps of the National Gallery at 6 o'clock in the morning. For one thing, there was more room in Trafalgar Square. For another, the fountains were available for the early arrivals to sit down on their marble edges while they waited for the latecomers to turn up. There was also entertainment to be had in watching the pigeons strutting around. The only exception was if it was raining, in which case the cleaners assembled under cover of the portico of the Gallery's entrance.

There were ten cleaners, already wearing their aprons beneath their coats. Madge made a quick count to make sure everyone was there, then she led them across the road to the National Gallery like a general leading her troops into battle. Or, to be more accurate, like a sergeant major leading the troops; generals were notorious for staying back from the action, sometimes a mile or so.

It was Mary Higgins who first spotted the bundle of what looked like rags tucked against the low entrance porch's wall.

'Look at that,' she said. 'Someone's dumped a pile of old clothes.'

'No,' said Sally Evans. 'It's a woman. Asleep or drunk.'

Madge stepped up to the bundle, which was now definitely a woman with her back to them and faced into the wall, and shook her by the shoulder.'

'You can't stay here,' she said. 'You'd better be off.'

The woman didn't move or respond in any way. Madge gave a sigh and pulled on the woman's shoulder, rolling her towards them. As she did so and the woman came to rest on her back, Mary screamed.

'My God!' she said, stumbling back, covering her mouth as she felt the vomit rise. 'It's another one!'

CHAPTER NINE

Daniel and Abigail arrived at the National Gallery to find a mass of people being kept away from the entrance by a line of uniformed police officers. Daniel recognised a few newspaper reporters among them, and one of them hurried over as soon as he spotted them.

'Mr Wilson!' he said. 'Have they called you in?' He turned to Abigail and smiled. 'Miss Fenton, it's a pleasure to actually meet you face to face.'

'Jerome Robbins from the *Daily Telegraph*,' introduced Daniel. 'He can be trusted. Unlike some of his colleagues.'

'So, have you been called in? If so, who by? The police, or the National Gallery?' He grinned. 'It'll be a turn around if Chief Superintendent Armstrong's called for you.'

'At the moment we're here in a private capacity,' said Daniel. 'But who for?'

'All will be revealed in good time,' said Daniel, and, taking Abigail's elbow, he steered her through the crowd to the line of policemen. Once there, he took the letter they'd received just half an hour before and showed it to a uniformed sergeant he recognised.

'Mr Stanford Beckett has sent for us,' he said.

The sergeant grinned. 'Come here to ruffle the super's feathers?' he chuckled. He handed the letter back to Daniel and ushered him and Abigail through the line.

John Feather was standing in the stone porch entrance to the gallery beside a body covered in a blanket.

'Let me guess,' said Feather. 'Mr Beckett sent for you.'

'He did,' said Abigail. 'He said there'd been another murder, the same as the first.' She looked towards the body beneath the blanket. 'Another woman?'

'Her name's Kate Branson,' said Feather. 'The local constable who was first on the scene recognised her. She's a prostitute with a beat near Charing Cross Station, just across the road.'

Daniel looked at the crowd. 'Where's the chief superintendent? Inside with Mr Beckett?'

'No, he decided against coming himself. He knew it would be a circus, with loads of reporters, and I don't think he fancied being besieged with questions he couldn't answer. He'll be holding a press conference later.' He looked questioningly at Daniel and Abigail. 'Have the National Gallery actually hired you?'

'Yes,' said Daniel. 'In order to prove Sickert is innocent.'

'And is he?'

Daniel gave a rueful sigh. 'At this stage, who knows? Is there a connection between him and this victim, like there was with Anne-Marie?'

63

'I don't know,' said Feather. 'That's what I'm hoping Stanford Beckett might be able to tell us.' He gestured at the blanket. 'Want to take a look?' To Abigail, he added: 'You might not want to, Abigail. She's been butchered. But Daniel, he's seen it all before.'

'I can take it,' said Abigail. 'If I can cope with what we saw in Manchester, I can cope with this.'

'I wouldn't be so sure,' said Feather.

He led them to the blanket-covered figure, calling, 'Make sure everyone else stays back!' to the constables keeping the reporters away as he saw the journalists were about to try and surge forward to catch a glimpse of the body.

Feather pulled the blanket back far enough for them to see the butchery. Kate Branson had been sliced open from just below her ribs down to her groin, then the flesh cut again so it could be peeled back in two flaps, exposing her internal organs. Her womb, her kidneys, her bladder and her intestines were missing, her empty interior scarred with blood clots.

'Hardly any blood on the ground around her,' commented Daniel.

'Same as the last one,' nodded Feather. 'So, she was killed and butchered elsewhere and then brought here and dumped.' He looked at Daniel. 'Remind you of the Ripper victims?'

'Very much so,' said Daniel. 'The same kind of cutting. But then, the hideous injuries the Ripper inflicted were well publicised in the press at the time. I remember there were even illustrations in the cheaper sensational papers.'

'Who found her?' asked Abigail.

'The cleaners. They arrive for work at six o'clock.'

'Where are they now?'

'Inside,' replied Feather. 'Their leader, Madge Potts, insisted they had to get to work. I'm just waiting for the van to arrive to take the body to the Yard, then I'm going in to talk to Stanford Beckett.' He hesitated, then said: 'As they've called you in, and as the chief superintendent isn't here, why don't we go and see Mr Beckett together? It would save time for all of us, rather than me hearing from you later what he told you, and me doing the same for you.'

'That makes sense,' said Abigail.

Feather gave a shrill whistle, and the burly figure of Jeremiah Cribbens, Inspector Feather's detective sergeant, detached himself from a group of bystanders and came towards them, his notebook and pencil in his hand.

'Miss Fenton, Mr Wilson,' smiled Cribbens at the pair. 'I thought you might be turning up sooner or later.'

'Good to see you again, Sergeant,' said Abigail. 'I trust you are well.'

'I am indeed.'

'And Mrs Cribbens?'

'She is indeed. Thank you for asking.' He patted his notebook. 'Just trying to get some witness statements. Not that they're worth much. No one saw the body being dumped.'

'I'm just going in to see Mr Beckett, Sergeant,' Feather told him. 'I'd like you to stay here and wait for the van to arrive to take the body away. Make sure no one gets too close. Arrest anyone who tries.'

'Yes, sir,' said Cribbens, and he took up a position in front of the body, ready to protect it against all potential intruders.

Feather headed for the door of the gallery, Daniel and Abigail close behind him.

Inside the gallery they saw some of the cleaners intent enough on their work to ignore these new arrivals.

'Have you spoken to them?' asked Abigail.

Feather nodded. 'There's not much they could tell us. They thought she was a drunk or a tramp until they rolled her over.'

'And yet they still go to work after seeing that?'

'The poor can't afford to take time off,' said Daniel. 'No work, no pay.'

They reached the door marked 'Stanford Beckett, Curator' and Feather knocked at it.

'Enter!' came Beckett's call.

They walked in, and Beckett stood up, a look of relief on his face as he saw Daniel and Abigail. 'You got my message?'

'We did indeed. Inspector Feather has just been showing us the body.'

Beckett gestured for them to sit.

'This is a tragedy! What sort of monster could do such a thing? And why deposit the bodies here?'

'We've been told by the local constable that this latest victim is a prostitute called Kate Branson.'

'Yes,' said Beckett with a sigh.

'You sound as if you knew her,' said Feather.

'Not in that capacity, I can assure you!' retorted Beckett primly.

'Do we assume she also modelled for artists?' asked Abigail.

Beckett gave a sad nod. 'Yes,' he said. 'I recognised her.'

'Was Walter Sickert one of those she modelled for?' asked Feather.

This time Beckett hesitated before giving a reluctant nod. 'Yes,' he said.

'Who else?'

'I don't know,' said Beckett. 'The only one I recognised her from is a painting by Walter Sickert. It's of a woman getting out of bed.'

'Is it here? At the National Gallery.'

'No, it was sold to a private collector.' He looked at them, anguished. 'It's all connected with Walter in some perverted way, isn't it? The fact that both women modelled for him, and their bodies were both left here, at the National Gallery.'

'It would certainly seem so,' said Abigail. She looked towards Feather. 'Although the police may have their own theories.'

'At the moment we're reserving judgement,' said Feather carefully.

'I can't believe that Walter is capable of such an atrocity,' Beckett said to them imploringly. 'Someone must be trying to incriminate him.'

'But why?' asked Daniel.

Beckett shook his head helplessly. 'I have no idea,' he sighed.

'What about his enemies? Or people who don't like him?'

Beckett sighed. 'I'm afraid that's quite a long list. Mostly it's jealousy.'

'Other artists?'

'And . . . ah . . . related to his other activities. I think some of the women he was involved with wanted more.'

'How does his wife tolerate his infidelities?' asked Abigail. 'Surely she doesn't just accept them. When we met her she seemed a very strong woman.'

'She is,' said Beckett. 'You know about her political activism?'

'No,' said Abigail. She looked at Daniel. 'You met her before. Did you know about it?'

'No,' said Daniel. 'Our concentration was on Walter himself. And he was just one aspect of our investigation, we had lots of other avenues to go look at.'

'Ellen – or Nellie as her family call her – was a fervent supporter of Home Rule for Ireland,' Beckett told them. 'In 1887, she and her sister Jane travelled to Ireland to support William O'Brien, the Irish MP, who was on trial for advising Irish tenants not to leave their houses after the government ordered them to be evicted for non-payment of rents. She spent the next two years campaigning for an end to British rule in Ireland.'

'She seems a very determined lady,' said Abigail.

'And then, of course, there's her involvement in the women's suffrage movement. She is a committed suffragist, campaigning for women's rights.'

'Which makes it even more odd that she puts up with her husband's serial infidelities.'

'The truth is, it's only recently that she discovered the extent of his . . . ah . . . activities,' said Beckett.

'I find that hard to believe,' said Abigail. 'She's an intelligent woman.'

'She's also very much in love with Walter. In fact, she still is, despite the fact that, as I understand it, she's intending to start divorce proceedings against him. I believe the truth is she didn't want to think that he could be so unfaithful. She did catch him out a couple of years ago when she found a compromising letter from one of his mistresses, but Walter swore it had happened just once and it would never happen again.'

'And she forgave him?'

'She did. In spite of her sister, Jane, warning her that he

would never change. Walter told me recently that Ellen had caught him out again, and that she'd told him she intended to divorce him. He pleaded with her not to, but he said she seems firm in her determination, although, as far as I know, it has not actually been put into the hands of solicitors. She still has a kind of belief in him.'

'The blindness of love,' sighed Abigail.

Feather waited until the three of them had left the gallery before giving his opinion.

'I think Mr Beckett is right,' he said. 'Someone's trying to incriminate Sickert. So Sickert's the key.'

He looked towards the spot where the body of Kate Branson had lain and saw it was now empty. Sergeant Cribbens appeared from the road, and they saw the police van parked behind him.

'The van's here, sir,' he said. 'They've loaded the body and are about to take it to the Yard. I've asked them to wait in case you're ready to go, and we can get a lift.'

'Good thinking, Sergeant,' said Feather. He turned to Daniel and Abigail and said: 'I'll report to the chief superintendent. What's your next move?'

'I thought we'd go and see Sickert and tell him about this latest victim, see what he can tell us about her,' said Daniel.

Feather nodded. 'Fine. We'll catch up later.'

Feather and Cribbens made their way down the steps to the waiting police van.

'Sickert's off to Venice today,' Abigail reminded Daniel.

'In that case we'll get hold of him before he leaves.'

'What do you think about what Stanford Beckett told us?' asked Abigail.

'Which part? The fact that Ellen Sickert is planning to divorce her husband?'

'I was thinking more about rivalries and jealousies in the art world. It's a real hotbed of deep and angry emotions.'

'Enough to murder someone?'

'I'm sure that Whistler felt he could happily have murdered Ruskin after he was declared bankrupt.'

'Explain,' said Daniel.

'Surely you know about the famous libel case: Whistler versus Ruskin,' said Abigail.

'No,' said Daniel.

'John Ruskin is a famous art critic. In 1878 he wrote a piece of criticism of a work by Whistler in which he said he was asking two hundred guineas to fling a pot of paint in the public's face. Whistler sued and won, but the judge – who didn't much care for Whistler's work – awarded him just one farthing in damages. As a result, with legal costs, Whistler was bankrupt within six months.'

'Yes, that's enough to want to vent your anger on someone,' said Daniel. 'This is James McNeill Whistler you're talking about, I assume.'

'Yes,' said Abigail, surprised. 'I thought you said you didn't know anything about art and artists.'

'Sickert was Whistler's assistant when he was first starting out as an artist,' explained Daniel. 'I learnt about Whistler while looking into Sickert's life during the original investigation.'

'Sickert again!' said Abigail. 'This world keeps getting smaller.'

Daniel smiled. 'Mind, I do remember a scandal about it. Didn't Whistler get his own back by seducing Ruskin's wife?'

'No, that was long before the court case. She had an affair with, and married John St Millais, the pre-Raphaelite painter. That was in 1855, after she'd divorced Ruskin on the grounds that their marriage had never been consummated. The talk was that Ruskin had only ever seen nude women in the form of classical sculptures, and when he realised on their wedding night that she had pubic hair he was put off, and never got over it.'

Inspector Feather returned to Scotland Yard to find the chief superintendent waiting for him impatiently in his office.

'You took a long time,' Armstrong complained.

'There was a lot to do, sir. We had to keep the reporters from invading the scene, then we had to arrange for the body to be removed, and also talk to the curator, Stanford Beckett.'

'Where's Sergeant Cribbens? Don't tell me you left him there with that rabble of reporters. God knows what he'll say to them.'

'Sergeant Cribbens is eminently capable of dealing with the sort of questions they throw at him, sir.' He grinned. 'He usually ignores them. Right now, he's in the mortuary checking the victim in.'

'Who is she?'

'A prostitute called Kate Branson. The local beat constable identified her.'

'Injuries the same as the other one?'

'Yes, sir. Hacked open and her internal organs removed. And, as with the first one, it looks as if she was killed and butchered elsewhere and then dumped.'

'Why the National Gallery?' asked Armstrong. 'Is there a

71

connection with the art world, like the previous one?'

'Yes, sir, and it's the same. She also modelled for artists.'

'Let me guess: Sickert?'

'Yes, sir, according to Mr Beckett.'

'Any others?'

'Not that he knows, just Sickert.'

'Sickert again!' scowled Armstrong. 'This is no coincidence, Inspector.'

'What do you want to do, sir?'

'Right at this moment, nothing.'

'There's another thing, sir. The National Gallery have hired Daniel Wilson and Abigail Fenton to look into the murders.'

'Have they, by Jove!'

'Yes, sir. Wilson and Fenton arrived this morning when I was there. Mr Beckett had sent them a note telling them about this latest murder and asking them to call.' He looked apologetic. 'I know how you feel about them, sir, but I could hardly send them away, as they'd been invited by Mr Beckett.'

The chief superintendent nodded. 'It's not your fault, Inspector.' He gave a thoughtful frown. 'In fact, it might be useful. Unofficially, of course.'

'Sir?'

'They can't stand me, and the feeling's mutual. But they like you. Keep in with them, find out what they find out. We're going to need all the help we can get if we're going to solve this.'

There was a knock at his door, which opened to reveal a constable who handed him a piece of paper. 'This was left at reception, sir. No one saw the person who left it.'

Armstrong took the note and as he read it he scowled. He passed it to Feather.

'Sickert doing a runner abroad today,' read Feather aloud.

'Oh no he isn't,' growled Armstrong. 'Bring him in!' Then he stopped and scowled. 'No, if we do it'll be just the same as last time. Sir Bramley bloody Petton turning up with more affidavits.'

'It's a bit suspicious, sir,' said Feather. 'This note turning up so soon after the body's been found. And the writing's the same as before.'

'Yes, it is,' nodded Armstrong. 'You think he's being framed?'

'It does seem likely.'

'Yes,' mused Armstrong thoughtfully. 'In which case whoever's trying to frame him is our killer. And Sickert's got to know him.' He looked at Feather with a sudden determination. 'We can't afford to let him leave the country, if that's what he's planning. He's got the information we need, whether he's aware of it or not. Right, Inspector, go and find Sickert and tell him he's not allowed to leave the country because he's a material witness. Make sure you stress that phrase: *material witness*. Not a suspect. Make sure he knows that. I don't want any further visits from that vain peacock, Sir Bramley. Go and see him and tell him. I'll arrange a warrant to back it up.'

CHAPTER TEN

Daniel and Abigail found Sickert carefully packing a trunk with artist's materials: brushes, pencils, small bottles of different coloured paints.

'Paper and such I can find in Venice. In fact, some of the best paper for art is produced in Italy. But my brushes are special to me.'

'You're not taking canvases?' asked Abigail.

Sickert shook his head. 'I prefer doing preliminary sketches and such on paper, and then reworking them in oils on canvas in my studio. It's not just that oils take a long time to dry, I want to consider my studies and take the best aspects from them in order to produce a work.'

'When are you actually leaving for Venice?' asked Daniel.

'In about two hours I'm catching the boat train for Dieppe where I shall stop overnight to catch up with old friends, and then on to Venice tomorrow.' He stopped packing and looked at them quizzically. 'But I haven't asked the purpose of your visit. Have you found out anything about Anne-Marie's murder? Are you any nearer to finding the culprit and removing this cloud from me?'

'No. We've come to tell you about a second murder.'

'A second?' repeated Sickert, puzzled.

'A woman called Kate Branson. Killed and eviscerated in the same way as Anne-Marie, her body dumped sometime last night on the steps of the National Gallery.'

Sickert stared at them, horrified.

'Kate Branson?'

They nodded. Sickert gulped and stammered: 'But-but she modelled for me.'

'We know,' said Daniel. 'Stanford Beckett informed us when we were called to the gallery early this morning.'

'And you are here to . . . what?' demanded Sickert. 'Accuse me?'

'On the contrary,' said Daniel. 'In our view it suggests that the murders were done by someone who wants to incriminate you. The fact the two victims had both modelled for you.'

Sickert sat down heavily in a chair, his face that of a man bewildered.

'First Anne-Marie, then Kate,' he said numbly.

'Where were you last night?' asked Abigail.

'Here,' said Sickert.

'And Mrs Sickert can verify that?'

Sickert shook his head. 'Nellie went to see her sister, Jane, and decided to stay overnight. I'm expecting her back before I leave.'

They heard the sound of the doorbell, and Sickert leapt to his feet.

'That'll be her!' he said, alarmed. He looked at them in appeal as he begged: 'Please, don't tell her this latest news. About Kate. We're having a . . . bit of a difficult time lately.'

'She may well have heard about it already,' said Daniel. 'Although it won't have made the newspapers until the late morning editions appear.'

The door opened and the housekeeper appeared. 'Inspector Feather from the police,' she announced.

Sickert looked at Inspector Feather as he entered the room, with an expression of outrage mixed with panic.

'You can't arrest me again!' he burst out. 'I didn't do it!'

Feather looked enquiringly at Daniel and Abigail.

'We've just told him about Kate Branson,' said Abigail.

'I didn't do it!' repeated Sickert urgently.

'I'm not here to arrest you, sir,' said Feather politely. 'I've been detailed to come and inform you about the murder of Kate Branson, which I now see you already know about, and to ask you to keep yourself available as a potential material witness.'

'What do you mean?' demanded Sickert. 'Keep myself available.'

'He means you aren't to leave the country,' said Daniel.

Sickert looked at Daniel, stunned, then back at Feather.

'But I'm off to Venice today!' he burst out angrily. 'I'm booked on the boat train.'

'I'm sorry, sir, but we've received information that requires me to ask you to remain in this country while our investigations continue.'

'You're arresting me again!'

'Not at all. As I said, information has been received . . .'

'What sort of information?'

'A note arrived at Scotland Yard saying that you were fleeing the country today. In the light of what has happened—'

'I was not fleeing!' Sickert burst out, furious. 'You know I was going to Venice. I told you that when you arrested me.'

'How did you know that Mr Sickert was leaving for Venice today?' asked Abigail.

'I didn't know it was Venice,' said Feather. 'Or where he was going, in fact. We had an anonymous note that said he was leaving the country today.'

'Similar to the anonymous note that said he killed Anne-Marie Dresser?' asked Daniel.

Feather nodded. 'The same writing.'

'This is a vendetta,' said Daniel. 'A deliberate attempt to incriminate him.'

'That does seem likely,' agreed Feather. 'So we need to find out the identity of the person behind these anonymous notes, and who might want to implicate Mr Sickert. And for that, sir, we need you to stay near at hand. I must warn you that you will not be allowed to board any boat heading out of this country.' He nodded politely to Sickert, and to Daniel and Abigail, and then withdrew. Shortly after, they heard the front door close.

'Well?' Sickert demanded of them. 'What are you going to do?'

'What we've been hired to do,' said Daniel. 'Find out who killed these two women.'

'I'm talking about my being kept prisoner in this country.'

'Hardly a prisoner,' said Daniel.

'I'm being prevented from going where I want to go,' insisted Sickert. 'Can't you do anything about that?'

'No,' said Daniel. 'My advice is that you take it up with Sir Bramley Petton, he seems to be the expert in that line.'

'This is appalling!' said Sickert.

'It's not very good for the two women, either,' said Abigail primly.

Sickert looked as if he was about to give a retort, then he subsided and nodded. 'You're right,' he said apologetically. He looked at Daniel. 'As an ex-policeman, Mr Wilson, what does it mean, that both women were painted by me? I suppose that increases suspicion of my guilt.'

'And also the anonymous letters sent to the police, especially this last one telling them you were about to flee the country.'

'I was going to Venice to paint, not flee!' protested Sickert.

'But the letter must have been sent by someone who knows you and knows your plans. Who else, besides your wife and servants, knew you were intending to go to Venice today?'

'Anyone who knows me, I suppose,' said Sickert ruefully. 'People know I go to Venice.' He groaned. 'Oh God, what will Nellie say when she finds out?'

Chief Superintendent Armstrong sat alongside Inspector Feather at the table in front of the audience who'd assembled for this sudden press conference at Scotland Yard. Despite the short notice, the room was packed, not just with newspaper reporters who'd taken the seats at the front, but local government officials who were under pressure to afford more protection for their citizens, and – at the back of the room – a variety of people who were claiming to be interested parties or relatives of the two deceased women, but were mostly there to gossip and pick up the horrendous details of the killings.

Armstrong rose to his feet and rapped on the table to call the meeting to order, then began his address.

'My name is Chief Superintendent Armstrong. Alongside me is Inspector Feather who is leading the enquiry into the recent outrages that have occurred on the steps of the National Gallery in Trafalgar Square. I refer, of course, to the bodies of the two women found there, both of whom had been murdered and a form of butchery inflicted on their bodies.

'On Monday 15th February the body of Anne-Marie Dresser was found in the early hours, and today the body of Kate Branson was discovered at the same place. Again, she was found in the early hours of the morning by the cleaners when they arrived for work at the gallery.

'At this moment in time it is too soon to give any details of our enquiries, especially as this latest murder only occurred a few hours ago. But our enquiries are progressing. I will now take questions from the gentlemen of the press.'

Immediately a mass of hands went up from the first three rows. Armstrong avoided those he knew were both anti-police and given to lengthy political diatribes in the spurious form of a question, and selected Charles McGiver from *The Times*.

'Chief Superintendent, on Tuesday it was reported that you had arrested the artist, Walter Sickert. Can you tell us why, and why you released him?'

'Mr Sickert was not arrested, he was invited for questioning as the result of information we received. Our investigations showed that he could not have been responsible for the death of Anne-Marie Dresser.'

Next was a question from *The Tribune*: 'Is Jack the Ripper back?'

'There are similarities between these two deaths and the Ripper murders from nine years ago, but there is nothing to suggest that the same person or persons who committed those murders in 1888 is involved in these latest two deaths.'

'But these two women were both prostitutes, as were the Ripper's victims,' called out a man from the back of the hall.

'We are still looking into the lifestyles of the two recent victims,' said Armstrong calmly.

Jerome Robbins from *The Telegraph* raised his hand, and Armstrong reluctantly pointed at him. Reluctantly, because Robbins was intelligent and also had been a critic of Armstrong in the past, but the chief superintendent knew that he wouldn't be able to avoid answering his question during this session.

'We understand the Museum Detectives, as they are popularly known, Daniel Wilson and Abigail Fenton, have been hired by Walter Sickert to find the killer and establish his innocence. Do you have any comment to make on that?'

Plenty, thought Armstrong sourly. Aloud, he said: 'No. What private individuals choose to do is up to them, providing they do not interfere with the police investigation.'

At the back of the hall, two men exchanged concerned looks, then the taller of the two nodded towards the door and the two men left. Outside on the pavement, the shorter man said: 'Did you hear that? Wilson and Fenton working for Sickert.'

'Not for much longer,' said the other grimly. And he set off, his companion hurrying after him.

CHAPTER ELEVEN

As Daniel and Abigail walked away from the Sickerts' house, Abigail said thoughtfully: 'This second murder.'

'Kate Branson,' nodded Daniel.

'Why so soon after the first one?'

'You have a theory?'

She nodded. 'It strikes me that someone did it knowing that Sickert, as a result, would be prevented from leaving the country.'

'Yes, that's a good thought,' agreed Daniel. 'I think it's worth going to see John Feather and making that point to him.' He stopped and turned to make in the direction of Scotland Yard, but Abigail stopped him.

'Do you mind if you went to see him on you own?' she asked. 'Only I've been preparing duck confit for the past two days, rubbing in the spices, and I need to finish it off. I've planned it for lunch, and after all that work I'd hate it to spoil.'

'Duck confit?' asked Daniel.

'It's a delicacy,' said Abigail. 'I told you about it. You take the legs of a duck and rub salt and thyme into them—'

'Yes, absolutely,' said Daniel hastily.

'If you don't take on board new ways of cooking . . .' began Abigail, annoyed.

'I do,' said Daniel. 'And I will. But right now I need to talk to John Feather. But I promise you, I will be looking forward to this duck confit with great anticipation.'

'I hate it when you just say things to placate me,' complained Abigail.

'I'm not, I promise you,' Daniel assured her.

She looked at him intently, then said: 'A lot of work has gone into it.'

'And I'm sorry if I was offhand about it,' apologised Daniel. She smiled.

'Go,' she said. 'And you can moan to John Feather about me and my special recipes.'

'I would never do that,' he protested.

She leant forward and kissed him. 'Go,' she said again. 'I'll see you at home.'

As Daniel walked away, he told himself off: *She was right. I was just placating her. I'll make it up to her.*

He was just weighing up the best way to make it up to her, what to give her as an apology present, when he felt a blow on the back of his neck which sent him staggering forward. Before he could recover his balance, strong arms had gripped his shoulders and forced him down, while at the same time a scarf was thrown over his head and pulled back, blinding and gagging him.

He felt knees fall on his back, pinioning him to the pavement, and his struggles managed to dislodge one corner of the scarf blindfold. Not enough to see properly, but he caught a glimpse of heavy boots appearing by his head and thought for a moment he was going to be stamped on. Instead, as he was held down, a voice above him hissed: 'Why are you on Sickert's side, Wilson? You knew it was him last time. You and Abberline. He may have got away with it before, but no longer.' The toes of the boots moved out of sight and were replaced a moment later by a trousered knee and a fist. The skin on the wrist above the fist had the end of a tattoo of what looked like part of a capital L in blue ink. Then another voice, close to his head, snarled threateningly: 'Stop protecting Sickert or your woman will be the next one carved up. And we mean it.'

Daniel felt cord being tied around his wrists, and then his ankles. Meanwhile the scarf was made tighter around his face.

He listened as he heard the footsteps leave, then he set to work to try to extricate himself, but whoever had tied him had done a good job and all his tugging and pulling just seemed to make the knots that held him tighter.

'Hello, what's going on?' demanded a voice, and Daniel smelt the odour of stale alcohol.

'I've just been attacked and left tied up,' Daniel managed to speak through the cloth, hoping that whoever had arrived wouldn't take advantage of his position and rob him.

'Hang on,' said the voice.

The scarf around his head was the first to be removed, and Daniel saw that the man who'd come to his rescue was wearing a long, grubby coat. As the man turned his attention to the bonds that held Daniel's ankles, Daniel saw the words Dickens

BREWERY in large letters on the back of his coat.

'I was just on my way to work when I saw you,' said the man. He frowned. 'Whoever did these knots knew what they were doing.' He reached into his pocket and pulled out a folding knife, which he opened and used it to cut through the cords around Daniel's ankles, then around his wrists.

'Thank you,' said Daniel, getting to his feet. He held out his hand. 'I'll take the bits of string and scarf, thank you.'

The man looked puzzled, but handed them over.

'They might help me work out who did it to me,' Daniel explained.

'Ah, a copper,' said the man.

'Ex-copper,' said Daniel. He dug into his pocket and pulled out a two-shilling piece, which he held out to the man. 'Thank you.'

The man looked at the coin, then shook his head. 'No need,' he said. 'Just one bloke helping another, even if you used to be a copper. A kindness done for no reward is supposed to bring good luck, so maybe I'll get lucky.' With that, he walked off, whistling.

Sir Bramley Petton looked up in annoyance as the door of his office burst open and Walter Sickert rushed in, closely followed by Petton's harassed-looking clerk, Leonard Watts.

'I'm sorry, Sir Bramley, I told him you were busy . . .' apologised Watts.

'Yes, all right,' grunted Petton. He looked at Sickert with a grim expression and demanded: 'I suppose there's a reason for you crashing in unannounced?'

'There's been another killing!' said Sickert.

'Yes, I know,' said Petton.

'The police think I did it.'

'Have they told you as much?'

'No, but they've barred me from leaving the country! It's outrageous! I was on my way to Venice again, but they say I'll be stopped from leaving Britain.'

'Yes, I had a letter from Chief Superintendent Armstrong informing me, as your legal representative, that they require your presence in this country as a material witness.'

'It's the same! They're keeping me locked up.'

'They're not,' said Sir Bramley. 'You are free to go wherever you wish, providing you do not leave these shores. Armstrong has been quite clever. He informs me that the police suspect these murders were done by someone with the aim of incriminating you. His evidence is the anonymous notes he's received naming you, the latest of which was received by Scotland Yard this morning.'

'Yes, Inspector Feather told me the same.'

'His hypothesis is that the killer must be someone who you have had some acquaintance with who is determined to have you blamed for these murders. To that end it is vital you remain in the country in order for the police to have immediate access to you, should they consider someone as yet unknown as a possible suspect, for your intelligence on that person.'

'But that's outrageous! Surely there's something you can do?'

'Yes, I can get on with this very important piece of work that you have interrupted,' snapped Petton. 'My advice to you, Walter, is stay at home and wait until all this blows over.'

Abigail, her hands covered in flour and duck fat, looked up in surprise, and then concern, as Daniel walked into the kitchen.

'There's dirt on your trousers and jacket,' she said. 'What happened? Did you have an accident?'

'I'm afraid it was quite deliberate,' said Daniel. 'I was attacked.'

'Who by?'

'Two, possibly three men. I didn't get a proper chance to look at them, they pulled a scarf over my head and bundled me to the ground.'

He told her about being tied up, and about the threats.

'They want us to stop digging for evidence that would prove Sickert is innocent?' she said, astonished.

'And if we don't, they'll harm you. In fact, the threat was that what happened to those two women would happen to you.'

'This is appalling!' she burst out angrily, going to the sink and rinsing her hands of the flour and fat. 'We have to do something!'

'Yes, you have to leave London. I suggest you go and stay with your sister, Bella, in Cambridge.'

'What? Absolutely not!'

'You're in danger here. I can't protect you, and nor can the police.'

'You don't know that.'

'Yes I do. I was in the police. Unless you have officers guarding you 24 hours a day your life is at risk. I'm not even sure if you'll be safe in Cambridge.'

She shook her head.

'No,' she said firmly. 'I refuse to live like that. We need to let Chief Superintendent Armstrong and John Feather know about this.'

'All they'll do is give you the same advice. With the best will in the world, they can't protect you.'

'There must be an alternative.'

Daniel sat down in his favourite chair, his face creased in thought. Then he said: 'There may be a way.'

'What?'

'It depends on Armstrong.' He stood up. 'I'll tell you on the way to Scotland Yard.'

Chief Superintendent Armstrong was in when they got to Scotland Yard, and Daniel and Abigail were invited into his office, along with John Feather, once the inspector had reported on the reason for their arrival.

'They threatened to kill Miss Fenton?' said Armstrong, shocked.

'They did,' said Daniel. 'And the same way the two recent victims had been killed.'

'You have to leave London,' Armstrong told Abigail. 'You're not safe here. If someone wants to kill you, we can't protect you 24 hours a day.'

'I know,' said Abigail. 'That's what Daniel said. And I'll say to you the same thing I told him.'

'She won't go,' groaned Daniel.

'Why ever not?' demanded Armstrong.

'I refuse to be a victim,' said Abigail. 'I will not be bullied like this. I intend to see that justice is done in this case.'

'Then what do you want us to do?' asked Armstrong helplessly. 'We're doing all we can to catch this murderer.'

'As are we,' said Abigail.

'I think there's another option to handle this threat,' said Daniel. 'The attack on me shows that these people want Sickert in the frame for the murders. So Sickert didn't kill these women, these people did.'

'You can't be sure of that,' said Armstrong.

'No, but I'm now sure that Sickert didn't kill them. The first thing we need to do is ensure Abigail's safety. And that means getting Sickert out of London. Once he's gone, they won't kill any more women here. Their whole strategy is to implicate Sickert. Get Sickert out of the country, and with a show of publicity, and the killings will stop. And so will the threat to Abigail.'

'So he gets what he wants,' scowled Armstrong, disgruntled. 'Venice!'

'I was going to suggest Dieppe. It's near enough we can bring him back if needed. And he's known there.'

'The killers might follow him there.'

'I doubt it, somehow. From their voices when they had me trapped, these men are working-class Londoners. They'd feel out of their depth on the Continent. And we fudge it by saying he's gone to Venice, which would mean they'd have to go there to make sure he's there. I can't see them doing that. These are working men, I doubt if they speak either Italian or French.'

'You're still taking a chance with Abigail's life,' said Armstrong. 'They might not kill her and butcher her the same way as the other two, but they could still carry out their threat to harm her.'

'I know,' said Abigail. 'And I'm prepared to take that chance. I've been threatened before, remember.'

Armstrong sat, thinking, weighing up what he'd just heard, then finally he nodded. 'Very well,' he said. 'I'll leave it to you to tell Sickert. He's your client.'

'Thank you,' said Daniel. 'There's another thing. When I was face down on the pavement, my nose was close to the boots of one of them. They smelt of blood and sawdust.'

'Blood and sawdust?' frowned Armstrong.

'A butcher,' said Daniel.

'There was a butcher suspect in the first Ripper murders,' mused Armstrong.

'There was,' said Daniel. 'But that was nine years ago. That particular butcher was in his sixties, so he'd be about seventy now. The voice of the man who made the threats about Abigail was younger. About eighteen or twenty, something like that.'

'You think a butcher did these killings?'

'I don't know,' admitted Daniel. 'But it's a possibility.'

'But why? And why try and get Sickert blamed for it?'

'Let's suppose that this butcher was related to one of the women who were killed by the Ripper, maybe a son, and he heard the stories that were circulating around Whitechapel at the time naming Sickert, Prince Albert Victor and Sir William Gull.'

'Which were poppycock,' said Armstrong uncomfortably. 'No evidence was ever presented against them.'

'Because our investigation into them was stopped,' said Daniel quietly.

'I'm not getting into this,' said Armstrong. 'That was nine years ago. It's water under the bridge.'

'But say it isn't to this young man. Say he believes those stories naming those three men as the Ripper. Gull's dead. Prince Albert Victor's dead. That leaves Sickert.'

'You're saying he blames Sickert and wants revenge?'

'I'm saying it's a possibility,' said Daniel.

Armstrong fell silent, then said: 'All right, we'll look into it.' He turned to John Feather. 'I'll leave that to you, Inspector.' He then turned back to Daniel and Abigail. 'In the meantime, you two make sure Sickert leaves the country today. And before nightfall. And make sure that everyone knows he's gone. We don't want any more dead women turning up on the steps of the National Gallery.'

CHAPTER TWELVE

Sickert stared at Daniel and Abigail in bewilderment.

'You're telling me to leave the country?' he said, stunned.

'Yes.'

'Is this with Chief Superintendent Armstrong's agreement?'

'Yes.'

Sickert scowled. 'I'm not sure if I will. I refuse to have my life kicked from pillar to post at the whim of that oaf.'

'It's not that oaf, as you call him, who wants this. We do. And we need you to leave urgently, and with enough of a show so that people know you've gone.'

'Why?' Sickert asked, puzzled.

They told him about the attack on Daniel, and the threat to Abigail. 'If anything proves your innocence, this does. But if we're to stop them killing and butchering Abigail, or any other woman, you need to go abroad.' As he saw that Sickert was still weighing things up, he added: 'You must also be aware that your own life is in danger. You're their target. They may decide to just kill you instead.'

'Yes, I'm aware of that,' said Sicket tersely. 'It wasn't that that was giving me pause. As soon as you said Miss Fenton's life was in danger, you'd sold it to me. I was just weighing up where to go.'

'I suggest you tell people you're going to Venice, but actually you get off the boat at Dieppe and stay there. You have a place there, I believe.'

'Yes, I do,' said Sickert. 'But why tell people I'm going to Venice?'

'If these people decide to go after you, they'll head off to Venice on a wild goose chase. My own feeling is that they won't leave the country, but it's not worth taking a chance.'

'Very well,' said Sickert. 'I'll make my arrangements and spread the word that I'm off today to Venice. I know one or two reporters who will be eager to hear about this. I'll do my best to get it in this evening's editions. That might hopefully save some poor woman from suffering the same dreadful fate as poor Anne-Marie and Kate.' He looked enquiringly at Daniel and Abigail. 'Who do you think it is who's after me? And why?'

'We don't know. We believe it might be a butcher.'

'A butcher?'

'Someone in their late teens, early twenties.'

'For God's sake, why? What harm have I ever done to a butcher?'

'Is Mrs Sickert back at home?' asked Daniel, curious.

Sickert looked uncomfortable. 'No. I believe she's decided to stay a further day at her sister's. Do you wish to talk to her?'

'It would be interesting to hear anything she might have to say.'

'Very well. I'll give you her sister Jane's address.'

As they left the house, Daniel observed: 'It's interesting that Mrs Sickert hadn't come back to say goodbye to him.'

'If you ask me, that's deliberate,' said Abigail. 'Remember what Stanford Beckett said about her deciding to divorce him. And I don't blame her, after the abominable way he's treated her with this string of infidelities.' Then she asked: 'You really think this is connected with the original Ripper murders?'

'I do. It's the anger the man had against Sickert. And he actually said to me, "You knew it was him last time. You and Abberline. He may have got away with it before, but no longer".'

'So what do we do to find him?'

'We start with my notebooks from the time,' said Daniel. 'I listed each victim, their marital state, and their children if they had any. I haven't looked at them since I left the force. It's time for us to dig them out.'

Walter Sickert stood on platform two at Victoria Station beside the waiting boat train that would take him to the south coast, where he would catch the boat to Dieppe. His luggage was already aboard and steam and smoke drifted along the platform from the engine as it was fired up. Two reporters stood with him, notebooks open and pencils poised, a junior reporter from *The Times* who was unknown to Sickert, and the familiar figure of Jerome Robbins from *The Telegraph*. Both newspapers had responded to messages Sickert had despatched to their news editors, in his opinion the news of his departure for the

Continent in both should do the trick.

'Are you leaving the country with the permission of Scotland Yard?' asked Robbins.

'Absolutely,' smiled Sickert. 'Chief Superintendent Armstrong has realised that I am completely innocent of anything to do with the dreadful deaths of these two women, and he has given me permission to go anywhere I choose. When I told him I intended to go to Venice, he gave me his full support.'

'Why Venice?' asked the junior reporter from *The Times*, who looked about fifteen, thought Sickert. *Let's hope he can spell.*

'The light, dear boy!' said Sickert. 'The light in Venice is unlike anywhere else in the world. I would encourage everyone to experience its wonder.'

'How long will you be away for?' asked Robbins.

'At least a month,' said Sickert. 'Possibly longer. It depends how the muse takes me.'

Two men stood watching this from the shelter of an arch in the red brick wall.

'What do we do?' asked one. 'Follow him and kill him on the train?'

'I don't want him just dead, I want him disgraced!' scowled the other. He gave a grim smile. 'I think someone else has to die at his hands.'

Daniel and Abigail sat at their kitchen table, going through Daniel's notebooks from the original Ripper enquiry from nine years before. They sat side by side studying the pages that Daniel selected, because sometimes Daniel's scribble from that time was unintelligible to Abigail.

'We also need to talk to people who knew Kate Branson,' said Abigail. 'Find out if there had been any of her clients she was particularly afraid of. The killer may have been keeping watch on her, sizing up the best time to attack her.'

'I agree,' said Daniel. 'But right now, I think our killer may well be somewhere in these old notebooks, so before we go digging into Kate Branson's life, I'd like to go through them, see if anything leaps out that might be something worth following.'

'Fine,' said Abigail.

'The first victim was Mary Ann Nichols, aged forty-three,' said Daniel, when he'd found the page with her details, 'She had five children: Edward, born in 1866, so he'd be thirty-one now. Her second son, Percy, was born in 1868, so he'd be twenty-nine.'

'He's a possibility, if his voice sounds younger than he is,' said Abigail.

'Alice, born in 1870, and Eliza, born in 1877. Then there's Henry, born in 1879.'

'So he'd be eighteen now,' said Abigail.

'Definitely worth checking him out,' agreed Daniel.

He moved on to the next entry.

'Annie Chapman, forty-seven years old. Three children: Emily, born in 1870, Annie, born in 1873; and John, born in 1880.'

'Now seventeen years old. Another possibility?'

Daniel shook his head. 'He was born severely crippled. He was put into an institution for the severely disabled. My attacker definitely wasn't him.'

He flicked through to the next entry. 'Elizabeth Stride. Forty-five when she was killed. No children.' He flicked through the pages again. 'Catherine Eddowes; three children. No information on any of them.'

'Why?'

'She was in a common-law marriage to a former soldier called Thomas Conway. After he found out she was selling herself as a prostitute, he left her, taking the children with him. He changed his surname to Quinn so she couldn't trace him. The rumour was that he'd moved back to Birmingham, taking the children with him.'

'So, no hope there,' said Abigail. 'What about the fifth victim?'

'Mary Jane Kelly. No children.'

'So that leaves us with Mary Ann Nichol's sons, Percy and Henry,' said Abigail, before adding: 'Of course, it doesn't mean it has to be a child of one of the women. It could be a nephew, or someone who was close to one of them.'

'It could,' agreed Daniel. 'I think we'll find out more about the families, and what happened to the children, if we go to Whitechapel. That's where the murders occurred, and that's where the families lived. There was a station sergeant there who was very helpful, very approachable when Fred and I were there, Sergeant Whetstone. I'm hoping he's still there. He knew everyone on his beat, and I think he's the person we need right now. But first, let's do as you suggest and talk to people who knew Kate Branson. And we'll start with the local constable who recognised her.'

CHAPTER THIRTEEN

They returned to Scotland Yard and found that John Feather was engaged in a meeting with Chief Superintendent Armstrong, but Sergeant Cribbens was able to give them the information they were after.

'Police Constable Pete Wurzel,' he said. 'Decent bloke. You'll find him at the Strand police station. If he's not there, they'll be able to tell you in which part of his beat you'll find him.'

As Daniel and Abigail headed for the Strand, Abigail asked 'Is prostitution legal in certain parts of London?'

'Not to my knowledge,' said Daniel. 'Not unless the law's changed since I left the force.'

'I ask because this Constable Wurzel knew where Kate Branson operated, at Charing Cross Station, but there was no talk of him arresting her.'

'Ah, that's a grey area,' said Daniel.

'What, Charing Cross Station?'

'No, the whole business of the police and prostitutes, at least at beat level. Prostitutes can be valuable sources of information to the local constable, able to bargain with stories they pick up, like who may have carried out a robbery recently, or even committed a murder.'

'And is it possible that this mutually benevolent relationship extends to other mutual benefits?' asked Abigail, her tone heavy with sarcastic innuendo.

'It has been known,' admitted Daniel. 'A lack of prosecution in exchange for . . . er . . . intimacy.' Then he added hastily. 'But I assure you I never indulged when I was a copper on the beat. Offers in kind are just as much a bribe as cash or other favours.'

'But some do.'

'Some do,' said Daniel. 'And not just beat coppers. Some senior officers were known for it.'

'Chief Superintendent Armstrong?' asked Abigail amused.

'No,' said Daniel firmly. 'He may be many things, but he's not corrupt, I'll give him that.'

'But he got a promotion for stopping you and Abberline investigating Sir William Gull and Prince Albert Victor.'

'If he hadn't, the police commissioner would have stopped us. Or the home secretary, or someone equally important.'

'It's still corruption.'

'It's the way it is,' said Daniel wryly.

'I'm sure the police constable having sex free of charge with a prostitute would say the same thing, if challenged,' commented Abigail.

* * *

PC Wurzel was having his tea break at the Strand police station when Daniel and Abigail arrived, and was thrilled to sit in the canteen with them and engage in conversation with the famous Museum Detectives.

'Yes, I knew Kate Branson,' he told them. 'You, Mr Wilson, as a former policeman yourself, know it's a good thing to keep a friendly eye on people involved in underworld activities, particularly those on what could be called the fringes, because they're the ones who often know what's going on.'

'Information,' nodded Daniel.

'Exactly!'

'What we're looking for are people who would have known her.'

'The other prostitutes?' asked Wurzel.

'If they're the best ones.'

'They are,' said Wurzel. 'They look out for one another.'

'They didn't do that very successfully this time,' commented Abigail.

'No,' agreed Wurzel with a sigh of regret.

'Where can we meet these women?' asked Abigail. 'We need to talk to them, find out if Kate Branson ever mentioned difficult clients to them. Violent ones.'

'They start working early evening,' said Wurzel. 'I'm on duty from seven tonight. If you meet me at Charing Cross Station around that time, I'll introduce you to the ones who knew her most.'

'Seven o'clock,' nodded Daniel.

'I'll be by the ticket office.'

As they left the police station, Abigail asked: 'Well, does he or doesn't he?'

'Engage in sex with prostitutes?' asked Daniel. 'I think it highly likely. Although, if challenged, he'd deny it. But it's the sort of inside information that could well be useful to us.'

'I think his name should be Weasel, not Wurzel,' said Abigail in deep disapproval. 'He's a sex pest, preying on those women.'

'Who are in turn preying on this obviously corrupt beat constable to avoid being arrested,' countered Daniel.

'I think it's sordid,' said Abigail.

'It is,' agreed Daniel. 'But now to meet someone on the force I think you will approve of: my old friend, Sergeant Whetstone at Whitechapel.'

Their journey by bus to Whitechapel took what seemed like hours. Traffic on all the roads going east was packed, hansom cabs, buses and wagons nose to tail in a stop-start procession. The going was made slower because two horses collapsed in the road, one pulling a brewery dray, and the other hauling the very omnibus Daniel and Abigail were on when they were in the narrow streets of the City of London by Liverpool Street Station.

'We'll walk,' decided Daniel. 'It's not far from here.'

Sergeant Stanley Whetstone was still based at Whitechapel police station, and was on duty at the reception desk when Daniel and Abigail walked in.

'Sergeant Wilson!' he said, his face lighting up with pleasure. 'Or, rather, Mr Wilson now.'

'Indeed, Stanley,' grinned Daniel. 'And this is Miss Abigail Fenton.'

'A pleasure, miss,' beamed Whetstone, shaking her hand. 'We already know about you here, of course, from the papers.'

He chuckled. 'The Museum Detectives.'

'You don't need to believe everything you read in the papers,' smiled Abigail.

'Very true, miss. My old man used to say the only thing you can rely on in the papers is fish and chips, and even then it has to be taken with a pinch of salt.' He laughed. 'What can I do for you? You're a bit off your patch, and these murders by the New Ripper are up west.'

'Is that what they're calling him?' asked Daniel. '"The New Ripper?"'

'The people around here are calling him that, so my guess is the papers will jump on the bandwagon sooner or later.'

'In a way it's connected,' said Daniel. 'Do you remember the original investigation when Fred Abberline and I were here?'

'I'll never forget it!' said Whetstone. 'It was the biggest thing that had ever happened here. The biggest thing in the whole country, and there's been nothing like it since. Even these latest ones, the two up west at the National Gallery, don't compare, although it's like whoever did 'em is copying him.'

'The thing is, we're starting to wonder if these new murders aren't connected to the previous ones,' said Daniel. 'We were wondering if one of the original victims' kids might be involved in some way.'

Whetstone looked at Daniel, stunned. 'You're not serious?'

'It's just a line of enquiry that might well lead nowhere. But if you remember, the first time we looked into everything, no matter how mad it seemed.'

'Leather Apron,' nodded Whetstone. 'Jill the Ripper. Montague Druitt.'

'The ones we're interested in are the sons of Mary Ann

Nichols, Percy and Henry.'

'Why?'

'Just a hunch at the moment. Are Percy and Henry still around?'

'Percy joined the navy. As far as I know he's on some ship far away, serving Queen and country. Henry moved away. I heard he'd got apprenticed to a tailor in Bethnal Green.'

'Do you know which tailor?'

'No, but I can find out. Do you think he's involved in this latest business?'

'It's clutching at straws, to be honest. Someone mentioned that maybe someone was doing it out of revenge over what had happened to the earlier victims.'

'A bit odd,' frowned Whetstone. 'Why would killing those women be revenge in any way?' Then his face lit up. 'Wait a minute! A few days ago, the papers said that Walter Sickert had been arrested for the first woman who was done at the National Gallery, but then he was released. I remember you and Fred Abberline were quite keen on Sickert at the time. The word on the street was that him and his two posh mates – very, *very* posh mates – were the ones, but they got off. And Sickert's two posh mates died. So is that what this is about? Someone who's got it in for Sickert over what people reckoned he did and is bumping these women off and trying to put Sickert in the frame.'

'It's a theory,' admitted Daniel. 'A bit far-fetched, I agree, but we have to look into everything.'

'If you give me your address, I'll try and find out which tailor Henry's working for and drop you a note. Are you still in Camden Town?'

'I am,' said Daniel. He took a pencil and wrote their address on a piece of paper and passed it to the sergeant. 'The other thing is, do you know if any of the Ripper's victims' children became butchers?'

'Butchers?' said Whetstone. He shook his head. 'Not as far as I know. But, again, I'll ask around and if I hear anything it'll be in the same note.' He studied them. 'You think a butcher did it?'

'It's possible,' said Daniel. 'If none of the women's kids went into the butchery trade, how about relatives? Someone who was about ten or so during the original enquiry, so they'd be about twenty now.'

'That's very specific,' observed Whetstone. 'Have you got hold of some good information?'

'Yes and no,' said Daniel. 'I'm not sure how good it is, which is why I'm checking it out.'

Whetstone looked thoughtful, then he asked: 'Are you still in touch with your old guv'nor, Fred Abberline?'

'We exchange Christmas cards,' said Daniel. 'To be honest, when he retired from the force, I got the impression he didn't want anything more to do with the Met, and then when I left the Met and went private I was busy building up my new practice. We sort of lost touch.'

'Is he still in Clapham?'

'He was last Christmas, according to his card.'

'It might be worth going to see him, or at least drop him a line,' suggested Whetstone. 'Remember, he was an inspector for quite a few years here at Whitechapel before he transferred to Scotland Yard. That's one of the reasons they put him in charge of the Ripper enquiry.'

'I knew he'd served in Whitechapel before we came here from the way he knew his way about, but I didn't know how long for. I only joined his team six months before the Ripper murders started. He never talked much about his time here before the Ripper investigation.'

'He transferred here from Highgate as a local inspector in 1878. I was just a young copper then, but we were all very impressed by him. He was here for nine years. He moved to Scotland Yard in 1887. We were pleased for him, the promotion to Inspector First-Class and everything, but sad to see him go. We were dead chuffed when we knew he was coming back to lead the Ripper enquiry, coming home, so to speak.'

'Yes, he did seem to know everyone, and every place around here.'

'He knew most of the butchers.' He grinned. 'He was always partial to a pound of sausages, was Fred.'

'Yes, I remember,' nodded Daniel.

'I know he was upset you didn't land him,' said Whetstone. 'The original Ripper, that is. I got the impression he was fairly sure who it was, but someone was pulling strings somewhere.'

'Yes, that's the impression I got,' said Daniel carefully.

As they walked away from the police station, Abigail observed: 'Tailors use very large and very sharp shears.'

'Yes, I was thinking the same,' agreed Daniel. 'We'll have a word with Henry Nichols once we get his address from Sergeant Whetstone. In the meantime, there's this mysterious butcher to find.'

'Which is going to be like looking for a needle in a haystack,' said Abigail. 'There must be thousands of butchers in London.'

'I think we're looking for one based in Whitechapel,' said Daniel. 'Most working-class people stay where they were born and brought up.'

'Like you, still in Camden Town,' said Abigail with a smile.

'Guilty,' Daniel smiled back. 'I suppose it's where we feel safe. Surroundings we know. I suggest we have a word with our local butcher, Bob Bones. He knows most of the butchers because they all congregate at Smithfield to buy their meat. We can ask him to introduce us to butchers around twenty years old who come from Whitechapel.'

'Yes, but before we do, I suggest we make contact with Ellen Sickert and let her know about Walter leaving for the Continent,' said Abigail. 'She's as much our client as he is. More so, if she's the one paying the bills.'

'Yes, good point,' said Daniel. He took the piece of paper that Sickert had given him from his pocket with the address of Ellen Sickert's sister, Jane. '10 Hereford Square, Kensington,' he said. He looked inquisitively at Abigail and asked: 'Do you fancy taking the underground railway? It will get us all the way to Kensington and be quicker than getting a succession of buses, especially at this hour when the roads are packed.'

'Yes,' said Abigail. 'It's something I've been meaning to do since I moved to London, but somehow never managed.' Suddenly her face lit up as she spotted a large sign over a series of open doorways, which bore the legend 'Whitechapel and Mile End Station'. 'We're in luck, we're right by the station.' She smiled. 'But then, you knew that already, which is why you suggested it.'

'Not exactly,' said Daniel. 'Whitechapel and Mile End is on the District Railway Line, and all the changing at different stations we'd have to do can be a pain in the neck. It'll be easier to walk to Aldgate and get a train there. Aldgate is on the Inner Circle Line, so we'll just have to board one train and get off at South Kensington.'

A short while later they were walking down the stairs of Aldgate Station to the platforms.

'It's strange,' mused Abigail, 'as an archaeologist I spent so much of my time in tunnels inside the pyramids, but this is the first time I've tried it in London. If, as you say, it's quicker, I'm surprised you haven't suggested it before.'

'I must admit, I prefer to be above ground,' said Daniel. 'And mostly you and I have been able to get wherever we wanted to by walking, or on a bus or a cab. But today, as we're going from one side of London to the other, it seemed a good idea.'

'I keep thinking of the underground railway as new, but it's not, is it?'

'It's been around since 1863, when the world's first ever underground railway opened. The Metropolitan Line between Paddington, or Bishops' Road as it was called then, and Farringdon Street. It's expanded since, and the District Railway Line opened in 1868. The line we're taking, the Inner Circle Line, was finally operational in 1884, just thirteen years ago. The City and South London Railway opened in 1890, so it is relatively new, when compared to the above ground railways.'

Abigail looked up at the arched ceiling high above them.

'The ceiling's much higher than I expected it to be,' she commented.

'That's so the smoke from the engine can rise up to the air vents and avoid suffocating the people on the platforms.' There was a mechanical clanking sound from deep in the tunnel and the metal rails began to vibrate. 'Here's our train.'

The engine appeared, belching smoke, and pulled to a halt at the platform with a screech of brakes and a hiss of steam.

There were three windowless wooden carriages. A guard stationed in each carriage opened the doors of his carriage to let the passengers off, and then Daniel and Abigail joined the waiting passengers in boarding. The carriages were narrow, with wooden slatted seats, and with gas lamps for lighting.

The guard pulled the door of their carriage shut and the train began to move, jolting and shaking on its way.

'No windows,' said Abigail as they took their seats.

'That's because otherwise the smoke from the engine would blow back and creep in through them. The City and South London Railway run electric trains to get away from the problem of smoke filling the tunnels. They say that one day the whole of the underground system will be electrified in some way, either by making an electric train, or electrifying the rails. Also, the rail company said that underground travellers don't need windows as we're in tunnels, so there's nothing to see.'

'Except when you come to a station,' said Abigail. 'How do you know where you've come to?'

Daniel gestured to where the guard sat beside the door of the carriage.

'His job is to open and close the doors and shout the name of the station the train's just arrived at.'

'Say he gets it wrong?'

'He won't,' said Daniel confidently. 'They do this all the time, it becomes second nature to them.'

As if to prove his words they could feel the train slowing down, then pulling to a halt. The guard shouted 'Tower Hill!', and when the train pulled to a juddering halt he opened the carriage door.

In what seemed a surprisingly short time, they arrived at South Kensington Station.

'I must admit, it's quicker than by bus,' said Abigail as they came out into the open air. 'No traffic jams. No horses dropping dead in the road. I can see this as the way to travel across cities in the future.'

Hereford Square was an upmarket location made up of tall, four-storey houses built of white stone.

'Very desirable residences,' commented Abigail.

'I did say that Ellen and her sister inherited a trust fund from their father,' Daniel reminded her.

They went to Number 10 where a housekeeper opened the door to them, and after they'd given her their names, they were shown into a plain but expensively furnished drawing room, where they found Ellen Sickert sitting on a settee, with two other women in their thirties. One of the women rose to her feet and came towards them, a welcoming smile on her face.

'Abigail!' she beamed. She held out her hand. 'How lovely to see you again after all this time.'

'It is indeed,' Abigail smiled in return as she shook Helena's hand. She gestured towards Daniel. 'Daniel, this is Helena Swanwick. We were at Girton together. Remember, I mentioned her to you?'

'Walter Sickert's sister,' nodded Daniel. 'It's a pleasure to meet you, Mrs Swanwick.'

'You must be Daniel Wilson. The other half of the famous Museum Detectives,' said Helena, amused, as they shook hands.

The other woman got up from the settee. 'I'm Nellie's sister, Jane,' she introduced herself, but there was a wariness about her that echoed the decidedly cool reaction from the still seated

Ellen Sickert as she looked at them, which was in stark contrast to the warm reception they'd received from Helena Swanwick.

Helena, suddenly contrite, gave Ellen Sickert a look of apology. 'I'm so sorry, Nellie. These are your guests and I'm hogging them quite unfairly.'

Ellen Sickert regarded them warily.

'I am assuming you have come with news of Walter?' she said.

'We have indeed,' said Abigail. 'He's left the country, ostensibly for Venice, but in actuality he will be staying in Dieppe. He caught the boat train from Victoria earlier.'

'I see,' said Ellen Sickert, but her manner remained distant and aloof. 'Was there a reason why Chief Superintendent Armstrong gave him permission to leave? I understood he had been told he had to remain in the country after the latest outrage.'

'Something happened that persuaded the chief superintendent that it would be best for everyone if Mr Sickert was allowed to leave the country.'

'What?' asked Jane.

'We were threatened,' said Abigail.

'Threatened?' asked Helena, puzzled.

'By two men who said we were interfering with their scheme to implicate Mr Sickert in the murders, and they wanted us to stop our investigation. The chief superintendent agreed that this shone a new light on the culprits and exonerated Mr Sickert.'

'I would have thought that Walter would have called Nellie here to tell her this first, rather than rush off to the Continent,' said Jane. 'He could have left going until tomorrow.'

'I'm sure that's what he would have preferred to do, but we asked him to leave the country as a matter of urgency, and make sure his departure was noted in the press,' said Daniel diplomatically.

'Why?' asked Ellen.

Daniel explained about the attack on him and the threats to Abigail. 'It struck us that as long as Mr Sickert was still in the country there was a danger of the real culprits killing either Abigail, as they threatened, or some other unfortunate woman with the intention of your husband being blamed for it.'

Ellen Sickert sat down heavily on the sofa.

'Thank you,' she said, and for the first time her face softened as she looked at them. 'For believing in him, and for persuading him to leave, for his own safety and that of others.'

'It's what he asked us to do,' said Daniel.

'Yes, but . . . I wasn't sure of you at first,' said Ellen. She got to her feet and walked towards them, and then – to their surprise – gave Abigail a hug of gratitude. 'Thank you.'

'We'll leave you now with your family,' said Daniel. 'But, if we hear of anything new occurring, we'll report to you.'

Ellen released Abigail and dabbed at her eyes with a handkerchief. 'I haven't even offered you tea,' she said.

'That's not important,' smiled Abigail. 'We have another visit to make to check on something else that has arisen.'

'You are continuing with the case, despite being threatened?' asked Jane.

'Abigail is not easily deflected,' said Daniel.

Helena gave a light laugh. 'No, indeed. I remember her at Girton flooring a member of the University rugby team with a right hook when he refused to stop his overzealous attentions to her.'

'He was drunk,' said Abigail. 'Too drunk to listen to words and reason.'

As Daniel and Abigail made for the door, they were stopped by a call from Helena Swanwick: 'One moment!'

They turned back to Helena as she said to Ellen: 'I'll be off as well, Nellie. This is an opportunity to catch up with Abigail. It's been many years since we've seen one another, we lost touch after Girton. I hope you don't mind.'

'Not at all,' said Ellen. She turned to Abigail and Daniel and said with deep sincerity: 'Once again, thank you both for everything.'

Outside in the street, Helena asked: 'Where is your next port of call?'

'Smithfield meat market,' said Daniel.

'In that case, I won't join you,' said Helena. 'Though I wanted to talk to you about Walter.' She gave a sigh. 'The reason I came to see Nellie was because Walter asked me to. He begged me to entreat Nellie not to divorce him.'

'You're aware of that?' asked Abigail.

'Everyone who knows them is aware,' said Helena with a sigh. 'The sad thing is that Walter is not the bad person people think he is. Most of it's bravado. He's actually a kind person.'

'Kind?'

'He'd never hurt anyone. Not intentionally.'

'But unintentionally. Can you think of anyone who would feel so much anger at him they'd go to these terrible lengths to implicate him as a murderer?'

Helena hesitated, then said: 'There was a situation about a year ago. Edmund Heppenstall, a well-known surgeon, commissioned Walter to paint a portrait of his wife, Catherine, and – unfortunately – things went further than they should have.'

'He seduced her?'

'The rumour was that it was she who seduced Walter.'

'I wouldn't have thought she found that too difficult,' commented Abigail.

'True,' Helena admitted sadly.

'What happened? Did Mr Heppenstall divorce her?'

'No. She left.'

'Left?'

'She just left one day and never returned. Whether it was because he'd got angry and was violent to her in some way, although I think that unlikely. Mr Heppenstall was one of the gentlest of men, his patients considered him almost a saint. I can't imagine him striking anyone, certainly not his wife.'

'Where did she go?'

'No one knows. She just vanished.'

'And there's been no trace of her?'

'None.'

'Did she have family somewhere?'

'I've no idea,' said Helena.

'How long had she and Mr Heppenstall been married?'

'About two years.'

'Did you ever meet her?'

'Yes. I visited Walter at his studio, and he was doing some studies of her.' She frowned, thoughtfully, then said: 'I think Walter said she was originally from Clapham. She was a singer. I understand Mr Heppenstall had met her when he went to a cabaret where she was appearing, and she gave up her idea of a career and settled down with him.'

'How old was she?'

'Young. In her twenties. Younger than Mr Heppenstall, who's in his fifties.'

'Did Mr Heppenstall make any attempt to trace her?'

'Not to my knowledge. All I know is there was a scandal and Walter did what he always does, he ran away. I believe he went to Dieppe. I imagine you already know he has a place there.'

'Indeed,' nodded Abigail.

Helena reached into her handbag and produced a pasteboard calling card, which she handed to Abigail. 'Please take this. It's my address. I know you're working for Nellie and reporting to her, but if anything comes up that you think I can help with, do get in touch with me. I'm absolutely sure Walter didn't do these murders.'

'We don't believe he did, either,' said Abigail. 'Our job now is to prove it by catching the real murderer.'

CHAPTER FOURTEEN

Under pressure from Abigail, who was eager to repeat the experience of travelling on the underground, they caught the Inner Circle Line train from South Kensington and got off at Euston Square. The noise of the clanking train made talking difficult, unless shouted, so they waited until they had left Euston Square and were making their way through Somers Town towards their home before they talked about what Helena Swanwick had told them.

'So Edmund Heppenstall seethes with anger over Walter Sickert's affair with his wife. He wants revenge,' said Daniel.

'It's a bit drastic to kill two women and try to implicate Walter just to get revenge on him for an affair. I mean, to actually kill someone deliberately, and butcher them the way these women were,' said Abigail.

'Unless he's killed before.'

'His wife?'

'It's possible. There's been no sign of her. And he's spent the past year letting the guilt for killing her build up, and all the time blaming Sickert for it.'

'And finally it boils over in him?'

'I've known it happen,' said Daniel. 'And he is a surgeon, perfectly capable of carving up those women.'

'At the moment it's just a theory, with nothing to back it up,' Abigail pointed out.

'We need to find out what happened to Catherine Heppenstall,' said Daniel.

'Aren't we in danger of getting away from the course of action we've set for ourselves?' asked Abigail. 'The butcher. This business of Heppenstall could just be a red herring.'

'Perhaps,' agreed Daniel. 'But it may not be. And I've been thinking about what Sergeant Whetstone suggested about talking to Fred Abberline. If Fred spent nine years as a local inspector in Whitechapel, he might well know the extended families of the murdered women. And he might also know something about Catherine Heppenstall, since she came from Clapham.' He looked enquiringly at her. 'I think it might be a good time to renew an old acquaintance.'

When they arrived home, Daniel wrote a letter to Frederick Abberline asking if he and Abigail could visit them. Meanwhile, Abigail sorted out her books and maps on the sun temple of Niuserre at Abu Ghurob. She expected that at any time now Conan Doyle would be in touch to arrange their trip to the Pyramids of Abusir, and she wanted to be ready when that happened.

Daniel put his letter in an envelope and said to Abigail: 'I'm going to the post office to send this off; then I'm going to call on Bob Bones and ask if he can help us with finding our mysterious butcher. Every trade and profession is a small circle where everyone knows everyone else, and butchery is no exception. Do you want to come?'

Abigail shook her head. 'I really need to catch up on my research for the visit to Egypt with Doyle. It's a big responsibility to lead an expedition, and I don't want to let him down.'

'All right,' said Daniel. 'But don't answer the door to anyone. Keep it bolted. I'll call through the letter box when I come back.'

'You still feel I'm at risk, even though Sickert's left the country?'

'I don't know. I just don't want to take any chances.'

Once he'd posted the letter to Abberline, Daniel made for Bob Bones's butcher shop in Camden High Street.

'Afternoon, Mr Wilson,' Bones greeted him cheerily. 'What can I do for you today? I've got some lovely mince. Perfect for a shepherd's pie.'

'Not today, thanks, Bob. I'm after a favour. Would you take me and Abigail to Smithfield the next time you go?'

'Why?' asked Bones, puzzled.

'I'm looking for a butcher, aged about nineteen or twenty, born and raised in Whitechapel but he could be working in North London.'

'Let me guess, this is the New Ripper, as they're calling him?'

'To be honest, Bob, I'm clutching at straws. I may even be barking up the wrong tree, but it's all I've got to go on so far.'

'You had a butcher in your sights before, I remember, with the original Ripper.'

'Not for long. It was someone who had a grudge against him who gave us his name. Wrongly, as it turned out.'

'But this time?'

'All I know is I've had a tip-off that we might be looking for a butcher, originally from Whitechapel, who'd be in his late teens or early twenties. So I wondered if you could take us to Smithfield and maybe introduce us to anyone like that you know.'

Bones nodded.

'You're welcome to come with me, if you can put up with the smell.'

'We'll cope.'

'You might but will Abigail? She's a bit upper class, she might not be used to it.'

Daniel grinned.

'Don't let her accent fool you, Bob. She's been in places like that before, maybe worse. Especially now Smithfield's been smartened up. By all accounts, the markets in Egypt aren't the sweetest-smelling.'

Bones nodded.

'All right, but it'll be an early start.'

'When you say *early*?'

'Two o'clock tomorrow morning. Butchers go to Smithfield in the early hours to make sure they get the best meat.'

'We'll be here at two,' said Daniel. 'And thanks, Bob.'

As Abigail sat at the kitchen table going through her notes on the Pyramids of Abusir, her thoughts went back to the conversation she'd had with John Tussaud of Madame Tussauds when they'd talked about the proposed expedition to the sun temple of

Niuserre. Conan Doyle had told her he wanted to explore not just the physicality of the sun temple and the complex at Abu Ghurob, but the belief the ancient Egyptians held that the pyramids had restorative powers. It was John Tussaud who'd given her the explanation for Doyle's obsession with looking into the pyramids and specifically the sun temple of Niuserre.

'I'm not sure how much you know of Mr Doyle's wife's health,' Tussaud had said.

'Nothing at all,' Abigail had replied. 'It's not a subject that has arisen between us.'

'Her name is Louise, although he calls her Touie, his affectionate nickname for her. About three years ago she was diagnosed with tuberculosis and she suffers terribly with her lungs. Early last year Mr Doyle moved them to Davos in Switzerland in the hope the air there would offer some relief, and it did, for a while. The reason I'm telling you this is because I've gained the impression that Mr Doyle's interest in the pyramids of Egypt is more to do with the restorative powers they are supposed to have. I may be wrong, but I feel that's his real motive in undertaking this expedition, to try and find out if there is truth in the idea of the life-enhancing properties of the pyramid, and if so that there might be a way of utilising it to improve his wife's health.'

Was she undertaking this expedition on false pretences, Abigail wondered? She did not believe the pyramids had the power to bring the dead back to life, or to extend the life of a living being; but Doyle obviously hoped they might. She could not believe her good fortune in being invited to take part in the expedition, and especially to be appointed as its leader, but she worried that she and Doyle – who was the person financing it – had very separate aims.

She heard the door open and Daniel appeared.

'All arranged,' he told her. 'Bob will take us to Smithfield at two o'clock tomorrow morning.'

'Two o'clock!' she said, aghast.

'According to Bob, butchers go to Smithfield in the early hours to make sure they get the best meat.'

'Yes, but two o'clock!'

'You don't have to come,' said Daniel. 'I was the one who was attacked, I'm the one who saw him. Well, his boots and his left wrist with the tattoo on it.'

'Of course I'm coming,' said Abigail crossly. 'We're partners.'

There was a knock at their front door and Daniel went to open it, while Abigail put her notes about Egypt into a briefcase.

'It's John Feather,' said Daniel, returning to the kitchen.

'Good afternoon, John,' said Abigail. 'I'm guessing something's happened to bring you calling.'

'It has,' said Feather. 'There's been another murder.'

CHAPTER FIFTEEN

Feather sat with Abigail at the kitchen table while Daniel made tea.

'Another murder?' said Abigail, puzzled. 'But not at the National Gallery, I presume, or we'd have surely had a message from them.'

'No, this one was in Sickert's studio in Robert Street. We went there following an anonymous tip-off. Do you know it? It's off Albany Street.'

'I know where Robert Street is, but I didn't know Sickert had his studio there,' said Daniel. 'When we interviewed him and his wife in 1888 they were living in a house in South Hampstead and he had a studio on the top floor.' He turned to Abigail and told her: 'Robert Street is between Clarence Gardens, where Sickert and Ellen live, and Cumberland Market where he kept Anne-Marie.'

'I assume Sickert decided to separate his studio from his home in view of his extra-curricular activities,' commented Abigail wryly. 'So, was it another of his artist's models?'

'No, this time it was a man,' said Feather. 'He's been identified as Edwin O'Tool. His throat was cut.'

'The man who gave Sickert his alibi for the first murder,' said Daniel, putting the cups of tea on the table for them.

'The doctor reckons he was killed sometime late this morning. As a result, the guv'nor's now thinking that maybe Sickert is in the frame, after all.'

'That's ridiculous,' said Abigail.

'The timing fits,' said Feather. 'He could have killed him before he caught the boat train.'

'The timing may fit, but where's the motive?'

'The guv'nor thinks he killed O'Tool to stop him blabbing the truth about the night he was supposed to have spent beside the sofa.'

'No, Abigail's right. That's ridiculous,' said Daniel. 'This is someone trying to frame Sickert again.'

'Your butcher?' asked Feather.

'Possibly,' said Daniel. 'We're going to Smithfield tonight with our local butcher to try and talk to some of those who might be likely.'

'Tonight?' echoed Feather.

'Two o'clock in the morning,' Abigail confirmed.

'Rather you than me,' said Feather. 'The guv'nor sent me to ask if you've got an address for Sickert in Dieppe.'

'He wants to take him into custody again?' asked Daniel.

'No, he wants to find out if Sickert knew that O'Tool was staying at his studio, and who else knew.'

'Nearly everyone who knows Sickert, I expect,' said Abigail. 'He and Ellen seem to live a life that's an open book.' She frowned thoughtfully. 'Which is why it still strikes me as strange that Ellen Sickert apparently was unaware of just how serial an adulterer he's been.'

'People often only see what they want to see,' said Feather sagely. 'Despite them having this tempestuous relationship, by all accounts she's always been very much in love with him.'

'Yes, that's true,' said Daniel. 'That was what we picked up when we talked to them during the first Ripper investigation, and it's been reinforced by everything we've learnt about them during this current one.'

'She's going to divorce him,' said Abigail. 'That's what we've been told by Sickert's sister, and Stanford Beckett at the National Gallery.'

'You've met Sickert's sister?'

'Helena Swanwick,' nodded Abigail. 'She was at Ellen Sickert's when we called there earlier.'

'Abigail was at Girton College with her,' added Daniel. 'Ellen Sickert may have the address for Walter in Dieppe.'

'I'm going to see her after I've left you to tell her about O'Tool's murder. I was going to ask her for Sickert's address in Dieppe at the same time, but she's not very conducive to helping the police out, which is why I'm asking you.'

'Sympathise with her. She's got a lot to feel angry about,' said Abigail. 'Anyway, she's not at their house, she's staying with her sister, Jane, at 10 Hereford Square, Kensington. I'm sure she'll be sociable. She was actually quite nice to us when we were there.'

'How was the murder discovered?' asked Daniel. 'Sickert's

not there. Who discovered the body?'

'There's a woman who cleans. Not the rooms, the stairs and passages. She noticed the door to Sickert's studio was open, so she looked in. O'Tool's body was on the floor.'

'Would it be possible for us to get access to Sickert's studio?' asked Daniel.

'You want to check out the scene of the crime?'

'My guess is it's connected to the murders of the two women. I'm wondering if the murderer might have left some clues.'

Feather produced two keys on a key ring, which he put on the table.

'14 Robert Street,' he said. 'I got these from the landlord. The bigger key's the one to the front door. The smaller one is for Sickert's studio, which is at the top of the house. The rest of the house is made up of rooms and flats. When are you going there?'

'It'll have to be tomorrow morning,' said Daniel. 'We have an appointment with some prostitutes at Charing Cross Station, and then our night trip to Smithfield.'

'A busy time,' commented Feather. 'Drop the keys back to me at the Yard in the morning. If Armstrong sees you, officially you've called to tell me what you found out at Smithfield and Charing Cross, and I never gave you those keys.'

'Understood,' said Daniel. He picked the keys up and dropped them in his pocket. 'Is there any chance of examining O'Tool's body while we're at the Yard? I assume it's at the mortuary.'

'Only if the chief superintendent isn't around,' said Feather, getting to his feet and putting on his hat.

* * *

PC Wurzel was waiting for them at the ticket office at Charing Cross Station.

'I've lined up a couple of the women who were closest to Kate,' he told them. 'Jenny Kipps and Dolly Pinn. I'll introduce you to them and then I'll have to get on with my rounds. But if you need anything else, you can always leave a message for me at the station in the Strand.'

They followed him to the Ladies Waiting Room, where two women overdressed in voluminous skirts and blouses, their faces heavily rouged, stood chatting. The two women stopped as they saw Wurzel approaching with Daniel and Abigail.

'Here you are, ladies, the two people I told you about. Mr Daniel Wilson and Miss Abigail Fenton, the famous Museum Detectives.' To Daniel and Abigail he announced: 'That's Jenny Kipps with the red blouse, and Dolly Pinn with the blue hat.'

'Thank you very much for agreeing to talk with us,' said Abigail.

'Thank you for wanting to find the bastard what done poor Kate,' said Jenny venomously. 'She didn't deserve to die like that. No one deserves to die like that.'

'Mr Wilson was one of Inspector Abberline's team during the first Ripper murders, so he's an old hand at this sort of thing,' said Wurzel. 'No better man. If anyone can find the bastard who did this, he can.' Then he added hastily, with an apologetic look at Abigail. 'And Miss Fenton, too, of course. Anyway, I'll leave you together. And, as I said, if you need me, you know where to find me.'

With that he touched the edge of his helmet with his finger, gave a nod, and departed.

'He's all right, is Pete,' said Dolly as they watched him leave.

'He was a bit sweet on Kate. I guess that's why he's keen to catch whoever did it.' She looked at Abigail, a look of curiosity on her face. 'You really a detective, miss?'

'I am,' said Abigail. 'Or, rather, I have been since Mr Wilson and I started working together.'

'In the papers they call you an Egypto . . . Egypt . . . something ologist.'

'Egyptologist,' said Abigail. 'Yes, I do that as well.'

'They say it's stuff to do with the pyramids,' continued Dolly.

'It is,' said Abigail.

'How do you get to do stuff like that?' asked Dolly. 'I mean, you're a woman.'

'I went to university,' Abigail told them.

Both women looked stunned.

'I didn't know women were allowed to go to university,' said Jenny.

'Only one or two universities,' said Abigail. 'But I hope the others will catch up and let women in.'

'We never even went to school proper,' said Dolly.

'But you learnt to read, since you read about us in the papers,' said Abigail. 'That's very impressive.'

Both women looked uncomfortable, and Jenny said: 'We can only read bits. It was Pete Wurzel who read to us about you in the papers.'

'Pete says he'll help us learn to read,' added Dolly. 'He says we can improve ourselves and not do what we do.'

'That's very commendable of him,' said Abigail.

'Yes, he's a good bloke,' said Jenny. 'Anyway, you want to know about Kate.'

'Yes, please,' said Abigail. 'Our big question is, was there anyone among the . . . ah . . . men she knew, who frightened her? Who she might have thought was dangerous.'

Both women shook their heads.

'No, Kate was wise to that,' said Dolly. 'If she thought a bloke might damage her in some way, beat her up or something, she wouldn't go with him. Not that it didn't happen, but not badly.'

'And she wasn't averse to giving 'em a kick in the balls if things got difficult,' said Jenny.

'She wouldn't let 'em tie her up, like some like to,' said Dolly. 'And she wouldn't take it up the arse cos she never wanted them to be behind her, ever since one of 'em tried to strangle her.'

'When was that?' asked Daniel.

'Over two years ago, but she never forgot it.'

'Usually she just gave 'em a hand job, or sucked 'em off, but there were a few she did the whole thing with.'

'Were there any particular people she mentioned as strange?' asked Daniel.

'Not really,' said Jenny. 'There was the toff, as she called him, who was odd, but in a nice way.'

'What way's that?' asked Daniel.

'He used to send his man, his driver, into the station to find her, and they'd go to his carriage, which was outside. Kate said he was lovely. He never did anything, never wanted anything from her, just wanted to talk.'

'About what?' asked Daniel.

'Her,' said Jenny. 'She said he never talked about himself, just wanted to know what she'd been up to, where she lived, what she wanted to do. That sort of thing.'

'And he paid her, same as if they'd actually done something,' said Dolly.

'Did you ever see this man?' Daniel asked.

'No. Just his driver. And we didn't see much of him. He always had a black scarf wrapped round the lower half of his face and a hat.'

'How long had he been coming to see her?'

'He first came about two months ago,' said Jenny after a bit of thought.

'And he just chose her?'

'No. The driver said he was looking for a Kate Branson for his master. He promised her there'd be no funny business. And there wasn't. That's what Kate told us when she got back. No business at all. Just talking.'

'And he came back again?'

Jenny nodded. 'About a fortnight later. Then, a fortnight after that. And then every so often after that.'

'When was the last time he came to see her?'

'About a week ago. When she came back she was all excited, and we both thought they'd finally done it, which would have pleased her because she really liked him.'

'She always said he was a perfect gentleman,' added Dolly.

'And he hasn't been back since?'

'Not as far as we know. Though that last time, when she was all happy after seeing him, she told us she thought things were going to be better for her.'

'Like he'd made a promise of something nice to her,' said Dolly. 'Then this happens. Some bastard rips her apart.'

As Daniel and Abigail walked up Charing Cross Road on their way home, Abigail said: 'You think it's this man, don't you? The toff, as they call him.'

'It's all very suggestive of it,' said Daniel. 'Neither woman was killed at the gallery, where they were found. This carriage sounds ideal for moving a dead body around.'

'We didn't get much of a description of him, or his driver,' said Abigail.

'Kate told Jenny and Dolly she thought the man was in his forties,' said Daniel. 'Well spoken. Upper class. Posh, in her words. And wealthy.'

'But there was no mention of him coming for her on the night she was killed.'

'I expect he'd arranged for her to be waiting at a certain spot, away from the station.'

'Yes, that makes sense,' agreed Abigail. 'But there's nothing for us to identify him.'

'If it is him, we know more than we did before,' said Daniel.

'Very different from your butcher,' pointed out Abigail.

'Unless they're working together,' said Daniel.

'In the way that Sickert was said to be working with Sir William Gull and Prince Albert Victor,' added Abigail. She nodded. 'It's a possibility.' Then she suddenly said: 'By the way, I may have been wrong about Constable Wurzel. His character, I mean. His encouraging Dolly and Jenny to learn to read. Offering to help teach them. It's not what I expected.'

John Feather stood in the drawing room of the house and watched Ellen Sickert and her sister Jane, as they sat straight-backed beside one another on the settee.

'I'm very sorry to tell you that Mr Edwin O'Tool, a friend of your husband's, was found dead at his studio in Robert Street today. He'd been murdered.'

Ellen Sickert gave a shudder and Jane reached out and gripped her sister's hand.

'How?' asked Ellen.

'His throat had been cut. It's believed it happened sometime this morning. Mr O'Tool's body was only discovered by the cleaner when she went into the studio when she noticed the door was open. I'm here to inform you, and also to ask if you have an address for your husband in Dieppe.'

'Why?' asked Ellen.

'So that we can write to him and inform him of what's happened.'

'I'll write to him,' said Ellen.

'We do need to inform him officially,' said Feather.

'You have informed me. I'm his wife, and also the person who pays the rent for his studio in Robert Street.'

'Very well,' nodded Feather. 'When you write to him, would you ask him to make contact with us at Scotland Yard?'

'Why?' she asked again.

'We want to catch the person who murdered Mr O'Tool. We have no information about him, where he lived, his acquaintances . . . anything that can lead us to his murderer. We know that your husband knew him and associated with him from the statements that your household gave to Sir Bramley Petton, and the fact that he was found dead in your husband's studio. Do you know anything about Mr O'Tool?'

'Other than the fact that Walter brought him home that one evening and the two of them got drunk, no.'

'Then Mr Sickert is the only one who can give us any information about him,' said Feather.

'Are we in danger, Inspector? My sister and I?' asked Jane.

Feather frowned.

'Danger, ma'am?'

'Two women associated with Walter, both of whom modelled for him, have been murdered recently. A friend of his – or, at least, a drinking acquaintance – has also been murdered. Whoever is doing these things seems to be concentrating on people close to Walter. So how safe are we?'

Damn! thought Feather. That thought hadn't even occurred to him. It struck him that there was no trace of nervousness or fear in her in what she asked, she was just asking a straight question; and he realised that Jane Cobden was as strong a person as her sister.

'I don't know,' Feather admitted. 'I suggest I arrange for a constable to stay on duty outside your house, and I'll arrange for others to take his place during the night.'

'Thank you,' said Jane. 'That will be a great relief.' She looked at her sister. 'Won't it, Nellie?'

Ellen hesitated, then nodded.

'Yes. Thank you, Inspector. And in return, I'll give you Walter's address in Dieppe. I shall still write to him, but I shall also inform him to expect a letter from you.'

CHAPTER SIXTEEN

Although Daniel and Abigail went to bed at ten o'clock, hoping to get a few hours' sleep before they made their way to Bob Bones' butcher shop in the early hours, neither slept properly. By one o'clock both were still awake. Daniel got up first and went down to the kitchen to turn up the range and add wood and coal to the glowing embers in order to bring the hotplates up to heat, and by the time Abigail appeared, fully dressed, he had the kettle on the hob steaming, and four slices of toast keeping warm on the top.

'We'll need something to keep us going,' said Daniel as he buttered the toast for them. He looked at his much-loved old and blackened cast iron range and said ruefully: 'I suppose we ought to think of something easier for cooking. Possibly a gas oven. I believe that some houses have electric cookers, which everyone says is the way of the future.' He looked at Abigail and asked: 'We really ought to move. This house did me well enough when I was on my own, mainly because as a policeman and then a private investigator I was hardly here. But now, the outside toilet in the yard, where we have to take a candle with us at night so we can see, the gas lighting in the house, the tin bath filled with hot water from the copper in the scullery, you deserve something better. An inside toilet and a proper bathroom, for starters.'

'*We* deserve something better,' she corrected him. 'You're the one who gets up at the crack of dawn to clean the grates and lay the fire in the range and the hot water copper.'

'So it's agreed, then,' said Daniel. 'We move house.'

'We agreed that about a year ago,' smiled Abigail. 'Just like we agreed we'd get married.'

'Then let's stop talking about it and do it,' said Daniel firmly.

'Let me get this trip to Egypt out of the way first,' said Abigail.

Daniel shook his head. 'No, let's sort it out before you go. Once we've agreed on the house, I can arrange things while you're away. Decorate it. Furnish it.'

'I want to furnish it,' protested Abigail.

'You will. We'll choose furniture and wallpaper and everything together before you go, and I can get on with it while you're in Egypt. It'll be ready for you to come back to.'

Abigail thought about it as she sipped her tea. Then she nodded. 'Yes. Let's do it. Get married and move house. Once this case is over.'

It was bitterly cold when they left the house and both wore thick coats, scarves, gloves and hats.

'It's cold enough to snow,' observed Daniel.

As they walked along Plender Street, heading for Camden High Street, Daniel told Abigail about the meat market they were going to. 'There's been a meat market at Smithfield since the tenth century, although at first – and right up to about forty years ago – it was a live cattle market. At least, the animals went in alive.'

'And they were actually slaughtered there?'

'Slaughtered and butchered. It was reckoned about a quarter of a million cattle a year, along with one and a half million sheep, were herded through the streets of the City of London every year.'

'Through those narrow streets? It must have been awful!'

'It was. You think London's bad with all the horses spreading their manure over the roads as they pull wagons, carriages and omnibuses, but that's nothing compared to when that number of sheep and cattle were shepherded through to Smithfield. And it wasn't just the smell from their droppings – butchering adds to the aroma: the smell of blood, of offal. The place was awash with blood and guts.

'In the end, under pressure from numerous petitions, Parliament closed it down in the 1850s and created a new cattle market at Copenhagen Fields while they built a proper market on the site, the one that's there today. It still smells, but it's under control.'

'But we're not going to Copenhagen Fields.'

'No, it's Smithfield for us. And even though they use loads of ice to keep the meat fresh, be prepared: the smell of blood and meat can be quite overpowering.'

Bob Bones was hitching his horse up to his covered van

when they arrived at his butcher's shop.

'Good, you're early,' he said. 'We can get off. And I'm glad you've wrapped up well. When we come back the van will be pretty cold because I'll pick up some ice at Smithfield to keep the meat good.'

At this time of day there was hardly any traffic on the roads, making their journey across London much easier and quicker than their bus journey the previous day, although as they neared Smithfield they got caught up in traffic jams as they encountered more covered vans, all painted, as was Bones's, with the name of a butcher.

Smithfield Meat and Poultry Market itself was an enormous building, bigger than most of London's railway termini, with the main building stretching away into invisibility, despite the gaslight from the street lamps.

'It's huge,' said Abigail, impressed. 'How do you get whatever meat you buy from there to wherever you park your van? I can't imagine carrying one carcass of a sheep or a cow that distance, let alone a few.'

'There's a road that goes through the middle of it. It's called the Grand Avenue and you park near where you know you're going to do business.'

Bones joined the stream of traffic heading towards the entrance, which was a huge, open arch made of cast iron. On either side of the arch were bronze statues of dragons, each clutching a shield decorated with an armorial cross. Behind the dragons, the stone towers that reached up into the night sky were decorated with carvings of griffins.

'A lot of money went into making this place,' said Bones.

'Daniel told me it was built only recently,' said Abigail.

'And it's still being added to,' said Bones. 'The meat and poultry markets are all done, and now the fish market is nearly finished.' He pulled his van to a halt at the side of the road, then got out and hitched the horse's reins to a post. 'This is us,' he said.

Daniel and Abigail got down from the van and walked with Bones into the main market. To Abigail, it looked like a scene from some nightmarish painting of hell: illuminated by gas lamps high up, flayed corpses of cows and sheep hanging from hooks, trolleys laden with kidneys, livers, hearts, intestines and other organs. Men with cleavers and saws, most of them wearing leather aprons, attacked the carcasses. Buckets filled with blood were everywhere.

'Blood for black pudding,' explained Bones, noticing Abigail looking at these buckets warily. 'People love it.'

Each stall was piled high with meat in different forms, and beside each stall was a trolley filled with bones as the butchers cut the flesh from ribs and the long bones of the animals. The heavy smell of blood was everywhere. The blood that covered the long wooden benches on which the butchers worked ran down to the floor, where it was fed into gutters.

'I've pulled up here 'cos this is where most of the Whitechapel butchers gather,' said Bones. 'I chop and change – one week I'll do business with one bloke, then a different one the next. But always the same ones. Most of us trade with the regular people we know. It's a guarantee of quality for the kind of meat you know your customers want.' He looked at Daniel. 'See anyone you recognise?'

'Unfortunately, I only saw his feet,' said Daniel. 'But he had a tattoo on his wrist. I only saw part of it, but it looked like part of the letter L, in blue ink.'

'That might be a help,' said Bones. 'Most of these blokes work with their sleeves rolled up. Which wrist was it? Left or right?'

Daniel struggled to remember, visualising the fist looming into his semi-blocked view.

'The left,' he said.

'Right,' said Bones. 'Let's hope we get lucky. I'll let you two wander around a bit, while I do some business. But I won't be far away.'

Bones walked off, heading for the heart of the market, while Daniel and Abigail stood and studied the men working at the benches. Suddenly one man caught his eye, a young man who was looking at Daniel with uncertain and wary glances.

'See him?' Daniel whispered.

'Who?'

'At that stall with the board over it that says Karl Ramsden.'

Abigail looked. 'Yes. He looks a bit . . . well . . . nervous.'

'Yes, that's what struck me. I wonder if he's got a tattoo on his arm?'

As Daniel headed for the stall, Abigail following, the young man suddenly put down the meat cleaver he'd been wielding, went to another man and muttered something to him, then disappeared through a door at the rear of the stall, taking off his apron as he did so.

Daniel and Abigail arrived at the stall and Daniel gave a smile to the man who the young man had muttered something to.

'Excuse me,' he said.

The man shook his head.

'We don't do sales to the public,' he said curtly.

'No, I'm not here to buy meat,' said Daniel. 'We're with Bob Bones, who's a friend of ours. He's got a butcher's shop in Camden Town and we asked him if we could come with him to Smithfield.'

'Why?' asked the man suspiciously.

'We're writers,' said Daniel. 'We've been asked to write some articles about important places in London, and Smithfield is certainly one of those.'

The man grunted in agreement, then continued smashing his meat cleaver down on the bench, chopping long bones into smaller pieces.

'I was interested in that young man who was here just now. I'm sure I know him from somewhere.'

'What young man?'

'The one who was talking to you just now.'

The man shook his head. 'I don't know what you're talking about,' he said.

'There was a young man with you a moment ago. He took off his apron and left just before we reached here.'

'You must be mistaken,' said the man. He smashed the cleaver down and the bone he was working on snapped in two. 'Now if you don't mind, I need to get on.'

Daniel nodded.

'Sorry to have troubled you,' he said.

He led Abigail away and they went in search of Bob Bones, and found him conducting business at another of the stalls.

'Bob, can you do us a favour?' asked Daniel.

'Sure. What?'

'Over at that stall, Karl Ramsden's, there was a young man

working, but as we approached he left in a hurry. I'm interested in finding out who the young man was, and where I can get hold of him.'

'Karl?' frowned Bones. 'He's a bit of a sourbones. Don't like giving anything away.'

'Maybe if we offered him money?' suggested Abigail.

'No, I don't mean it like that,' said Bones. 'He's not a great one for giving out information. He comes from Whitechapel and they're a bit wary there of who they talk to. They don't like strangers who ask questions.'

'Do you know him?' asked Daniel.

'I've done business with him.'

'Would you mind asking him about the young man?'

Bones gave it some thought, then said: 'I'll give it a try. The worst he can do is tell me to get lost. But I don't think he will. Karl likes doing business too much.'

'Will it help if we come with you?' asked Daniel.

'No. You wait here.'

Bones walked through the crowd of butchers to Karl Ramsden's stall. They saw Ramsden put down his cleaver and listen to Bones for a few minutes, then shake his head. Bones then said something else, and this time Ramsden did reply, not much, but enough for Daniel and Abigail to realise he'd got some sort of answer from the man.

Bones made his way back to them.

'The young bloke who was there, Karl says he only knows him as Joe. He's a casual, comes in and does stuff for Karl on a cash basis some nights. He turns up and asks Karl if he needs anyone, and if Karl does, he gets to work.'

'Does he know where he comes from? Or anything about him?'

'No. My guess is he must be local if he just turns up like that. And as Karl's got his place in Whitechapel, which is just down the road, I'm guessing that's where this Joe will be from.' He regarded Daniel inquisitively. 'You said you were looking for a young butcher from Whitechapel, didn't you? Could be you've found him.'

'Yes, but where do I find him again?' asked Daniel.

'By coming back another night and seeing if he's here,' suggested Bones.

'Somehow, I don't think he'll be back,' said Daniel.

'You might be right,' nodded Bones. 'Listen, now you've found what you want, why don't you go back and wait by the van. I'll join you as soon as I've done my business. Half an hour should see me finished.'

Daniel and Abigail headed out of the market towards where the van was parked, with the waiting horse.

'It's quite possible that Karl Ramsden was lying when he said he didn't know what Joe's second name was, or where he can be found.'

'Yes, the same thought occurred to me,' said Daniel. 'I think it might be worth letting John Feather know. Karl Ramsden may sing a different tune when Scotland Yard start asking him questions.'

'It's possible that this Joe may not be the one who attacked you,' said Abigail. 'There are many other reasons why he acted so shiftily when he saw you. Let's face it, we stick out here, we're obviously not butchers. And maybe he's got a guilty conscience about something else, possibly something criminal, and when he saw you looking at him, he got cold feet.'

'That's all very possible,' agreed Daniel. 'But I'd still like to take a look at his left arm and see if he's got a tattoo. And, for that, John Feather could be our man.'

'Or possibly Sergeant Whetstone might know about him?' suggested Abigail.

'He might, but I think that'll be harder. A young butcher called Joe with a tattoo on his left wrist. I bet you that describes half the men in Whitechapel.'

CHAPTER SEVENTEEN

When Bob Bones dropped Daniel and Abigail off at home, they were both fast asleep within minutes of them falling into bed; but not before Daniel managed to murmur 'I love you, Abigail', and Abigail responded with, 'I know, but not tonight, Daniel.'

The sun was streaming in through the gap in their bedroom curtains when they awoke, and as Daniel started to get out of bed to go downstairs and put the kettle on the range for tea, Abigail reached out and pulled him back. She pulled his head down to hers and kissed him.

'Now,' she whispered, 'I can enjoy it.'

Chief Superintendent Armstrong was waiting impatiently for John Feather when the inspector arrived for work at Scotland Yard. 'Well?' he asked. 'Did you get Sickert's address in Dieppe?'

Feather nodded and took a piece of paper from his pocket,

which he passed to the chief superintendent.

'I must admit, I thought you might have difficulty in getting her to give it to you,' he said.

'Initially she wasn't going to, but when I arranged for a constable to be on guard overnight outside her sister's house where she's staying, she relented.'

'A guard?' asked Armstrong, bewildered. 'Why did you do that?'

'Because she and her sister are both concerned,' explained Feather. 'Two women who used to model for Walter Sickert have been killed, then his drinking companion is also murdered at his studio. They wonder if they might be next.'

'Yes, that's a good point,' mused Armstrong. 'Well done, Inspector.' He looked at the address in Dieppe on the piece of paper. 'And now we know where to get hold of him, if needed. It might even be worth getting in touch with the French police in Dieppe and asking them to keep an eye on him. Do we have anyone in the squad who can write in French?'

When Daniel and Abigail came downstairs they found an envelope on their doormat.

'It's from Sergeant Whetstone,' said Daniel, opening it. 'The address of the tailors in Bethnal Green where Henry Nichols works.'

'So that's our next port of call,' said Abigail.

'No, first I think we go to check out Sickert's studio at Robert Street, the scene of the crime, so we can return the keys to John Feather. At the same time, we can tell him about Karl Ramsden and Joe the butcher. Then we'll go to Bethnal Green.'

Sickert's studio in Robert Street was on the third floor of the tall, narrow building.

'It's similar to the one he had in South Hampstead,' commented Daniel as they unlocked the door of the studio and entered.

There was a strong smell of turpentine mixed with oil paints. Two skylights in the ceiling let in daylight. There were two easels in the studio, each with unfinished paintings on them. One seemed to be of a man sitting at a table with a pint of beer in front of him; the other of a woman bathed in stage lights, her arms aloft as if she was singing out loud.

'I may not like him, but even at these stages, he's got talent,' conceded Abigail.

'Fortunately, the cleaner hasn't got around to mopping up the blood,' said Daniel. 'Maybe she decided she didn't want to,' said Abigail. 'At least, not until she'd arranged for extra payment with the landlord.'

Careful to avoid the patch of blood that had spread across the wooden floor, Daniel took his magnifying glass from his pocket and knelt down to examine the floor. Very slowly, he worked his way from the patch of blood towards the door. Suddenly he stopped.

'There's part of a boot print here,' he said. 'It's just one part of the boot, where the killer must have trodden in the blood.'

'You sure it's a boot and not a shoe?' asked Abigail.

'See for yourself,' said Daniel, offering her the magnifying glass.

She took it from him and looked through it at the red-brown smudge. Yes, there was a clear tread of a boot in the blood, rather than the smooth flat surface to be expected from the sole of a shoe. She peered closer.

'What have you seen?' asked Daniel.

She got up and handed the glass back to Daniel. 'There's a speck of something stuck in the boot print.'

'Yes, I see it,' said Daniel. He took a penknife from his pocket and gently teased the speck out of the blood and examined it closer.

'Have you got a piece of clean paper?' he asked.

Abigail took a notepad from her bag and tore a sheet off.

'Make a kind of envelope from it,' said Daniel.

When Abigail had done that, Daniel dropped the bloodstained speck inside it, closed it and put it safely in his inside pocket.

'What do you think it is?' asked Abigail.

'I think it's sawdust,' said Daniel. 'But I need to check.'

'The man who attacked you?' said Abigail. 'The butcher?'

'We need to get it looked at under a microscope,' said Daniel. 'But not just anyone. We need someone who knows how to identify what this is.'

'We need Sherlock Holmes,' smiled Abigail.

'That's an idea,' said Daniel.

'That was a joke,' said Abigail.

'I know, but your friend, Mr Conan Doyle, must have based Holmes's scientific work on something. I remember there was talk of creating a science lab at Scotland Yard to do exactly that sort of thing. We'll have a talk to John Feather and see if there's been anything like that set up. If so, we'll get them to look at it.'

John Feather was in his office, along with Sergeant Cribbens, when they arrived at Scotland Yard. Cribbens had his faithful pipe going, which gave off a thick, foul-smelling smog, and the sergeant was quick to open the window when he saw the expression of distaste on Abigail's face.

'Sorry about that, Miss Fenton,' he apologised. 'It's my one pleasure, but I'll let it go out while you're here.'

'No, no,' said Abigail. 'This is your office, Sergeant, as well as the inspector's. It would be impolite of me to expect that.'

'Thank you, miss, but allow me to do it. I can soon get it going again after you've gone.'

'Unfortunately,' muttered Feather under his breath. Then he smiled at Cribbens. 'Only joking, Sergeant.'

Daniel took the keys to the Robert Street address from his pocket and put them on Feather's desk.

'Here you are, John.'

'What did you find?' asked Feather, putting the keys into his desk drawer.

'You remember we told you about the man who attacked me, and I said I had the idea he was a butcher in his late teens or early twenties?'

Feather nodded. 'You were going to Smithfield at some unearthly hour this morning to check out young butchers.'

'And we did, and I think I may have spotted him. Or, rather, he saw me and hurried off very quickly.'

'Did you find out who he was?'

'According to the butcher on whose stall he was working, a man called Karl Ramsden, he was just some occasional casual worker called Joe. Ramsden said he didn't know where he lived or anything about him.'

'That sounds like this Ramsden is protecting him.'

'My thought exactly,' agreed Daniel. He produced the

handmade envelope with the blood sample inside it and put it on the inspector's desk. 'While we were at the studio, I found something in a bloodstained boot print.'

Feather opened the envelope and peered inside. 'What is it?' he asked.

'I think it might be sawdust.'

'Your butcher again.'

'Possibly. If so, this could be the man who killed O'Tool, and also possibly Anne-Marie Dresser and Kate Branson. This Joe character is about twenty, and he's from Whitechapel, as is Ramsden, which fits with my theory that the killer may have been a child of one of the Ripper's original victims. I don't think Abigail and I will get anywhere with Ramsden, we have no official authority to demand anything. But you can. And if this Joe character is the murderer, you and Armstrong will get the credit for catching the killer.'

'Yes, I can see the chief super going for this,' said Feather.

'One thing I didn't mention before,' added Daniel. 'If you find this Joe, take a look at his left wrist. The man who attacked me had a tattoo in blue on his left wrist, with a capital L as part of it.'

Feather picked up the envelope and peered inside at the speck in the dried blood inside it.

'The reason I brought it in is because I wondered if anything ever happened about that idea for a science lab here,' said Daniel.

Feather looked at him and smiled. 'Have you been listening at doors?'

'No.'

'I ask because just two weeks ago such a science laboratory was imposed upon us.'

'How?' asked Daniel. 'I have to say I'm delighted, but I

146

thought there was a great deal of resistance to the idea from the senior people here.'

'There still is, but the commissioner was pressurised by the home secretary. Evidence now has to be examined scientifically.'

'The home secretary's been reading Sherlock Holmes stories,' said Abigail, amused.

'You may be more right than you think,' said Feather. 'As you can imagine, the chief super wasn't happy when he was told. As far as he's concerned, all this newfangled stuff takes money away from what he calls "real policing".'

'I'd hardly call science newfangled,' observed Abigail. 'Leonardo da Vinci was carrying out experiments on carcasses hundreds of years ago. And look at the work of Joseph Lister. It's all investigative science.'

'That's what the new man says, Dr Robert Snow.'

'Doctor?' queried Daniel.

'Yes, he's a fully qualified doctor, but he decided he wanted to use his scientific skills to solve crimes rather than treating patients.' Feather smiled. 'It helps that he's also a nephew of the home secretary, so regardless of what Armstrong feels about it, the science laboratory looks here to stay.' He made for the door. 'If you come with me, I'll introduce you to him and we'll see what he makes of this. Hold the fort, Sergeant. If anyone wants me, I'll be with Dr Snow.'

'Right-ho, sir,' said Cribbens, and he picked up his pipe from the ashtray where he'd deposited it and began to blow life into the still-glowing embers.

Dr Robert Snow was a short, thickset man in his late twenties with a mass of unruly ginger hair. The science laboratory was actually a small former storage room in the basement of Scotland Yard whose shelves were now packed with different sorts of chemicals in jars. On a bench were two microscopes, a Bunsen burner, glass retorts and other pieces of equipment more usually found in a chemist's laboratory. Snow greeted Daniel and Abigail with a broad smile of welcome and firm handshakes.

'It's a pleasure to meet you,' he said enthusiastically. 'I've read about your work as the Museum Detectives and your analytical processes. I suppose yours comes from exploring the mysteries of the pyramids, Miss Fenton, and making calculated deductions from the evidence you find.'

'I think you give me too much credit, Doctor Snow,' said Abigail. 'All archaeological expeditions are team efforts where we pool our thoughts.'

'But it's the expedition leader who has the final say, I believe. And that will be you on your forthcoming trip with Conan Doyle to Egypt.'

Abigail shot an accusing look at Feather, who gave her an apologetic smile.

'I couldn't resist boasting about it,' he said. 'I understand a woman leading such an expedition is a first.'

'Almost a first,' Abigail corrected him. 'There have been one or two before me.'

'But I'm guessing you haven't come down here to discuss Egyptology,' said Snow quizzically.

'No,' said Abigail. 'Mr Wilson has a sample from a crime scene.'

'It's a speck of something that was in a bloodstained boot print,' said Daniel, offering the handmade envelope to Snow.

148

'I'd like to know what it is. I think it might be—'

Snow held up his hand to stop him.

'No,' he said. 'If you tell me what you think it is I might be unconsciously influenced to reach that same conclusion. Leave it with me and I'll report back.'

'When?' asked Feather.

'Later today,' said Snow. 'First, I need to leave it to soak in a solution to separate it from the blood.' He opened the envelope and peered at the contents. 'Excellent!' he said happily. 'Real work. So far, most people here at Scotland Yard seem reluctant to involve me in their investigations.'

'It's early days,' said Feather. 'And once you've identified this, who knows – that might influence others to bring you their evidence to be examined.'

Daniel, Abigail and Feather left Dr Snow dealing with the blood-clotted speck.

'He's not going to find it easy,' said Daniel as they walked along the basement corridor. 'Remember, I worked for the Metropolitan Police, I know how hard it can be to introduce new ways of thinking here at Scotland Yard. He's lucky he's got you on his side, John.' He gestured at the sign that said: 'Mortuary'. 'While we're here . . .'

'I know, Edwin O'Tool's body. Let's hope that the chief superintendent doesn't waltz in while we're there.'

'Is he in the building?'

'I believe he has a meeting with the police commissioner and the home secretary at the Houses of Parliament,' said Feather. 'They're both on edge about these murders. I believe the home secretary is on the Board of Trustees of the National Gallery.'

'So, more pressure from the top,' said Daniel wryly.

149

They reached the mortuary and went in. Feather asked for the body of Edwin O'Tool to be brought out for them. The mortuary attendant, a man in his early sixties, looked with doubt at Abigail, and then turned to Feather.

'This is a woman,' he said.

'A woman who has seen many dead bodies before,' said Feather. 'And many of them in a far worse condition than the late Mr O'Tool.'

Reluctantly, the attendant led them to a table where a cadaver was laid out on a table, covered with a cloth. The attendant lifted the cloth away from the face and peeled it down to the middle of the dead man's chest. He then shot a challenging look at Feather and Abigail, prepared to resist removing the cloth completely and exposing the man's genitals. Daniel, Feather and Abigail ignored his looks and concentrated on the wound in O'Tool's neck.

'It's a deep cut done with some force,' said Daniel. 'It's gone through the jugular vein and the carotid artery.' He leant forward and examined the wound closer. 'It's a straight edge, not serrated. A long narrow blade. Very sharp.'

Feather nodded. 'Your butcher again, do you think?'

'Possibly,' said Daniel. He looked at the waiting attendant. 'Thank you,' he said.

The attendant, still with an expression of disapproval on his face, looked at Feather, who nodded, and the attendant replaced the cloth over the dead man.

They left the mortuary and Abigail commented: 'He's not very fond of having women in his territory, is he?'

'As we said about Dr Snow, some attitudes can be hard to break down. Where are you off to next?'

'Bethnal Green. One of the sons of one of the original Ripper's victims is working for a tailor there.'

'You still think one of their children might be responsible? As with this butcher of yours?'

'It's a possibility,' said Daniel.

'And tailors use very sharp shears,' added Abigail.

'By the way, I put a guard on Jane Cobden's house last night after I visited Ellen Sickert there,' said Feather.

'Why?' asked Daniel, puzzled. 'Has something happened?'

'Two women dead, both of whom were models for Walter Sickert. A friend of Sickert's has his throat cut in Sickert's studio. The two women were both concerned that whoever's behind it is targeting people close to Sickert, and there's none closer than they.'

'You really think they're in danger?' asked Abigail, alarmed.

'I hope not, but they believe they might be,' said Feather. 'And that's what matters.'

CHAPTER EIGHTEEN

'It never occurred to me that Ellen Sickert and her sister might be in danger,' Daniel admitted unhappily as they left Scotland Yard.

'If we're right that the killer wants Sickert blamed, then they should be safe since he's currently known to be abroad,' said Abigail. 'Surely O'Tool was killed in the hope that the police would think that Sickert could have been responsible, because at the time of O'Tool's murder, Sickert was still in this country. At least, he was preparing to get his train at Victoria.'

'I hope you're right,' said Daniel. 'But I'm glad John put a police guard on them, just in case.'

'Can we get to Bethnal Green by underground train?' asked Abigail suddenly.

'You like that way of getting around?'

'I find it preferential for longer distances rather than sitting on a variety of buses for half the day.'

'In that case, the answer's yes. The Circle Line goes to Liverpool Street. It's no distance from there.'

Ellen Sickert rose from the settee where she'd been reading a magazine as her sister returned from checking the post that had just been delivered. 'Is there anything from Walter?' she asked.

'No,' replied Jane. 'It's mostly political stuff for me.' She looked at the return addresses printed on the envelopes. 'The Congo Humanitarian Aid Society, Ireland, The Liberal Party.'

Jane had been elected as one of two women councillors to the Liberal Party at the inaugural London County Council in 1889, in spite of the fact that women were actually barred from sitting as county councillors. Legal action had been taken against the other woman who'd been elected, Margaret Sandhurst, and she'd been forced to stand down as councillor, but Jane had invoked a clause in the election law that said that anyone elected, even if illegally, could not be challenged at the council for a period of twelve months. As a result, she stayed away from all council meetings until February 1890, when she took her seat, to the fury of her political opponents. Jane had not stood for re-election at the 1892 elections, but remained a firm member and organiser of the Liberal Party.

'I'm going out to meet Tom at his office,' said Jane. Thomas Unwin was Jane's husband, the avant-garde publisher of Nietzsche, Ibsen and H. G. Wells. She had adopted the surname of Cobden Unwin. 'Would you like to come? It will make a refreshing change to staying here all day. Otherwise, this house will start to feel like a prison.'

'What about the police constable outside the front door?' asked Ellen.

'He can come with us, if he likes,' said Jane. She smiled. 'Although I don't think he'd care for the company. Tom is meeting a new young author he's thinking of publishing. Somerset Maugham. He'd like me to cast my eye over him and tell him what I think. You can do the same. Tom values your opinion.'

'Yes,' said Ellen. 'I could do with a break from all this dreadful business.' She went to the coat rack and pulled on her outdoor coat. 'What sort of person is this Somerset Maugham?'

'Never met him,' said Jane. 'All I know is he's in his early twenties and Tom thinks he's got talent.' She gave a wicked smile. 'Perhaps we can get the policeman to walk behind us all the way to Tom's office. That would set the cat among the pigeons when we arrived. Mr Maugham would think we were either spies being arrested, or a pair of streetwalkers being kept under observation.'

Jonas Barrowman's tailor shop was in a narrow street in Bethnal Green, alongside another tailor's, a hatmaker, two shoemakers and a shop that sold ties and handkerchiefs.

'Everything for the well-dressed gentleman,' remarked Abigail.

They pushed open the door of the shop and a bell attached to the top of door rang. A young man about twenty years old appeared from the back of the shop. In his hand was a large pair of tailor's shears. He stopped and studied them for a second, then said: 'If you're looking for Mr Barrowman, he's out.'

'No, we're looking for Henry Nichols,' said Daniel. 'Would that be you?'

'It might,' replied Nichols warily.

'I'm Daniel Wilson and this is my partner, Miss Abigail Fenton. We've been engaged by the National Gallery to investigate two murders that have taken place there recently.'

Nichols shook his head.

'Can't help you,' he said curtly. 'I ain't never been there. And I don't know anything about no murders. So you can bugger off.'

Daniel and Abigail exchanged looks that said: *We didn't expect this.*

'Mr Nichols—' began Daniel politely.

'Oh, it's Mr Nichols now, is it?' the young man sneered. 'I know who you are. I recognised you as soon as you came in from all them years ago, when you and that Abberline were in Whitechapel after my mum and them other women got killed by the Ripper. Asking questions, being seen to do all the right things, before you got bought off.'

Daniel bridled.

'We were never bought off,' he said, doing his best to keep his temper.

'Oh no? Everyone knew it was the Queen's grandson and her doctor, along with that painter bloke, but did they get nabbed? Did they hell! You and the others just let it go to one side until they died. At least, until two of 'em died. Now that painter bloke – Sickert – is doing it again, on his own this time, according to the papers. But they let him go again! Still being bought off.'

'Mr Nichols—' Daniel attempted again, but Nichols cut him off.

'No! I ain't talking to you! It was a waste of time talking to you nine years ago. And now it's coming back to bite you. So, like I said, you can bugger off.' He held the sharp point of the shears menacing towards them. 'Before I show you how people down here deal with people like you.'

'Very well, if that's how you feel,' said Daniel. 'But we'll be back. And next time with a Scotland Yard detective and you can show him how handy you are with those shears, which looks just the right sort of implement for the damage that was done to the two women who were killed.'

'Oh no you don't!' snarled Nichols. 'You ain't pinning that on me. I'm as clean as a whistle. But I am telling you that if you keep poking your nose into my business you're liable to get it cut off. Now get out!'

Daniel doffed his hat towards Nichols, then he and Abigail left the shop, the bell above the door tinkling as they did so.

'A very angry young man,' observed Abigail. 'He's obviously angry about Sickert. Do you think he's capable of carving up those women to try and get revenge on him?'

'I don't know,' admitted Daniel. 'I still think the butcher is the more likely candidate.'

'They both come from the same area. Both are about the same age, and with the same burning anger of injustice. Maybe they're working together.'

'It's possible,' said Daniel. 'When Joe attacked me, he had a companion with him. Another man who held me down.'

'Nichols?' suggested Abigail.

'Maybe,' said Daniel. A grim expression came over his face. 'I can't get over what he said about me and Abberline being bought off. It's virtually the same accusation that the butcher made when he attacked me.'

'They were both children at the time,' said Abigail.

'So they're repeating what the adults around them said at the time.' He shook his head, angry. 'I can't believe that's what the people of Whitechapel thought of us. We spent every waking hour on the case. We followed up every lead, however flimsy it seemed. We pulled in for questioning everyone whose name came up.'

'Not everyone would have thought that about you,' said Abigail. 'Sergeant Whetstone certainly doesn't.'

'I expect they thought he was in it with us!' burst out Daniel. Then he turned to Abigail. 'I'm sorry,' he apologised. 'I didn't mean to lose my temper like that.'

Abigail slipped her arm in his and drew him to her.

'I know you didn't,' she reassured him. 'And I'd have acted the same if someone said the same thing about me.'

'I can't get over the fact that for the past nine years, Henry Nichols has believed that I was crooked. Taking bribes to let Gull, Sickert and the prince go free.'

'Don't let it get to you,' said Abigail. 'In fact, when we get home I'll give you a special treat which will cheer you up.'

'I doubt if even sex will make me feel better,' said Daniel sourly.

Abigail removed her arm from his and looked at him disapprovingly.

'I was going to suggest pie and mash,' she said primly.

Daniel gave her a sheepish smile. 'Perhaps with sex afterwards?'

'Don't push your luck, Daniel Wilson,' said Abigail. She took his arm again. 'You are such a peasant.' Then she grinned at him. 'But I like that about you.'

* * *

157

Chief Superintendent Armstrong scowled as he entered Scotland Yard, and he continued scowling as he walked up the wide marble staircase towards his office. He noticed that the officers he passed took care to stay away from him, those he passed on the staircase giving him a wide berth and doing their best to avoid eye contact with him in case he barked at them for some misdemeanour. Everyone at Scotland Yard knew of the chief superintendent's temper.

He considered going to Inspector Feather's office and demanding what progress had been made on the murders – 'The National Gallery murders' as some of the papers were calling them, while one or two insisted on describing them as 'The New Ripper strikes'. In the end he decided against it. The inspector would only ask him how he'd got on with the police commissioner and the home secretary, and the truth was it had been a painful experience and one he'd prefer to forget.

They'd blamed *him* for the lack of progress. The home secretary, particularly, had not been impressed.

'The National Gallery is an iconic place,' he'd said. 'It is more than a building, it is at the heart of our culture. It has been defiled, and not just once, but twice. It was reported in the press that Walter Sickert had been arrested, but the next thing we learn is that he has been released and allowed to go to Venice. This is a disaster, Chief Inspector! To arrest and publicly name one of this country's greatest artists, to libel him, and then be forced to backtrack with no apology, makes us a laughing stock.'

'With respect, sir, we had information naming him.'

'Information? A scrap of paper from some illiterate who obviously holds a personal vendetta against Sickert.'

'We were just following procedure, sir.'

'Well in this case the procedure was stupid and ill-advised and badly carried out. And what's this I read about these Museum Detectives, Wilson and Fenton, being brought in? This doesn't look good for the Metropolitan Police, Chief Inspector, if the National Gallery prefer an investigation by these amateurs over that of the official police. As a trustee myself of the National Gallery I am outraged, and I have written to Stanford Beckett demanding to know why the National Gallery has taken this decision without consulting the Board.'

'I believe it was Mr Sickert's doing to engage them, sir, rather than the National Gallery itself.'

'Why? Was that because he wanted to revenge himself on Scotland Yard after the public humiliation of his arrest, or because he feels that Wilson and Fenton are more capable of finding the murderer of these two women than the official police?'

'With respect, sir—' began Armstrong, but he was cut off by the home secretary banging his fist down impatiently on his desk.

'Damn your respect, sir!' he raged. 'We are talking about the reputation of Scotland Yard and the Metropolitan Police. The nation's guardians! You will find and charge the person who carried out these hideous and heinous crimes and you will do it before the so-called Museum Detectives. Is that clear?'

'Yes, sir,' Armstrong had replied.

But how? he wondered as he sat in his office, an air of gloom hanging over him. And though neither the home secretary nor the commissioner had put it into words, the threat was implicit. His job was on the line.

When Daniel and Abigail got home, they found a letter waiting for them.

'It's from Fred Abberline,' said Daniel, pleased. 'He wondered if we might be in touch. He looks forward to seeing you, as does Emma. She says she'll do you lunch. He asks when we plan to call.' He looked at Abigail. 'When shall we go?'

'The sooner the better,' said Abigail. 'How about tomorrow?'

'Excellent,' said Daniel. 'I'll go to the post office and send him a telegram telling him we'll call on them tomorrow morning.'

'And while you're doing that, I'll make for the pie and mash shop and have it ready for when you get back.' She kissed him on the cheek, then whispered in his ear: 'And afterwards, a little extra delight.'

He gathered her in his arms and whispered back: 'Or, perhaps, put the pie and mash in the range to keep warm for afterwards.'

She grinned at him and said: 'I'm glad it doesn't take much to put the smile back on your face.'

CHAPTER NINETEEN

Stanford Beckett arrived for his day's work at the National Gallery just after nine o'clock to find his chief security guard, Ian Millen, waiting for him in the reception lobby, looking so agitated that alarm signals sounded in Beckett's head.

'What's the matter, Ian?' he asked.

'I'm afraid there's been a tragedy here during the night, Mr Beckett,' said Millen.

Beckett stared at him, horrifying images filling his mind as he asked: 'Not another murder?'

'No, sir, but almost as bad.' He walked off, Beckett following him, dreading what he was about to see.

Millen went through into the modern British gallery and stopped in front of Sickert's portrait of Anne-Marie Dresser.

'There, sir,' he said.

Beckett gasped in horror. The canvas had been slashed with

what appeared to be a sharp knife and the image of Anne-Marie hung down in shreds.

'My God!' he burst out.

'I didn't know whether I should call the police, but I decided to wait for you to arrive.'

'No police,' said Beckett firmly. 'We've already had enough bad publicity with these dreadful murders, I'm surprised the public keep coming.'

'It's the ghoulish side of them, in my opinion, sir. They want to see the spot where the bodies were put.'

'Yes, but this happened *inside* the gallery. Can you imagine how people will react if they feel there's a knife-wielding madman at large inside the gallery? No one will come!'

'What do you want me to do, sir?'

'Send a messenger to my office. I'll write a note to Mr Wilson and Miss Fenton and he can take it to their address. In the meantime, remove the damaged painting and take it to my office, and clean up the area here. When that's done, we'll open to the public as normal. But no word about this must get out, is that understood?'

Frederick and Emma Abberline lived at 41 Mayflower Road, Clapham. Daniel remembered the house from the times he and his then chief inspector had shared a cab or a police van heading back to Whitechapel during the Ripper investigations. Now, as their bus rolled along Stockwell Road, he and Abigail were on the final leg of their convoluted three-bus journey to his old boss's home.

'How long is it since you've seen Abberline?' asked Abigail.

'Five years ago. 1892, when he retired from the police force.'

'And you've not seen him since, even though he's just across the river from you?'

'No. Like I told Sergeant Whetstone, at first I got the impression Fred was happy to stay away from police business, and what else was I going to talk to him about if I called on him? And we were never great social people with one another, not like some coppers who spend all their time with one another.'

'What was he like? As a boss?'

'Excellent. Intelligent. Honest. He was a teacher as well as a detective. He taught us how to look at things, at the whole picture, not just small parts. The police force would have been a better organisation if he'd been given the promotion he merited. He did make chief inspector, but he deserved chief superintendent, or higher.'

'What's his wife like?'

'Emma? Very nice. They always seemed to me to be a very devoted couple. She's actually his second wife.'

'What happened to his first wife?'

'Martha. She died in 1868, just two months after they married.'

'Two months!'

'He mentioned it to me only once, so it's not something we talked about. He and Emma married in 1876, so they've been together a good many years now.'

Inspector Feather left the local constable on duty outside the butcher's shop in Whitechapel, while he walked in to talk to Karl Ramsden. The five customers waiting in the shop took one look at Feather before exchanging glances and mouthing the word 'copper' silently at one another. Two of the men waiting immediately left the shop. The middle-aged man behind the counter wearing a long white coat spotted Feather and gestured for him to come to the front of the waiting customers.

'Copper, eh,' he grunted.

Feather produced his warrant card and held it out to the butcher.

'Inspector Feather from Scotland Yard,' he said. 'Are you Karl Ramsden?'

'I am,' said Ramsden.

'I believe you have a butcher who works for you called Joe. About twenty years old.'

'Who says I have?' demanded Ramsden.

Sensing trouble, the remaining three customers made their way out of the shop and into the street, though Feather noticed they didn't go far but congregated on the pavement. Feather gave the butcher a steely look.

'Mr Ramsden, we can do this the easy way, or we can do it the hard way. The hard way is where I take you to Scotland Yard for questioning, and I have your shop locked up while you're there. And there's no way of knowing how long that could be. An hour. A day. Two days. Or the easy way is where you answer my questions straightforwardly, and I go away and leave you alone. The choice is up to you.'

The rattled and unhappy Ramsden studied the inspector.

'What's all this about?' he asked plaintively. 'What's so important that you threaten my livelihood?'

'We're investigating a murder,' said Feather. 'Two murders, in fact.'

The butcher stared at him, shocked. 'Not those women at the National Gallery?'

'At the moment we're just following some enquiries, talking to people.'

'Not Joe!' burst out Ramsden passionately. 'He couldn't do a terrible thing like that. He's a nice bloke. A good family man. Married, and proper. Two lovely kids him and his missus have got.'

'I'm not saying he's guilty of anything. We just want to talk to him. So he does work for you?'

'Only casual, like – some nights when we're at Smithfield. He comes and gives me a hand. He's got his own job the rest of the time.'

'Where?'

Ramsden hesitated, then said reluctantly: 'Higgins butchers in Cable Street.'

'And what's Joe's surname?'

'Wallace,' muttered Ramsden.

'Next, do you have an address for him?'

'Number 10, Nelson Place,' said Ramsden, even more reluctantly. 'It's one of the turnings off the Commercial Road.'

'Thank you, Mr Ramsden,' said Feather. 'One last question, does he have a tattoo on his left wrist?'

Ramsden shrugged.

'No idea,' he said. 'I don't pay him that much attention. Just so long as he works hard. Which he does.'

Walter Sickert sat on the sea wall overlooking Dieppe's pebbled beach. Beyond the beach was the Channel, and beyond that, England. He read Ellen's recently arrived letter through again. Edwin O'Tool dead, killed in his studio. And now there was a police guard on Jane's house in Kensington. Sickert shuddered.

Whoever had killed Anne-Marie, Kate and poor Edwin was now after them. And therefore, it followed logically, Sickert himself. He was the one person that connected the other victims, and the potential victims.

Why? Who was doing this? Who hated him so much to want to destroy everyone in Sickert's life, the people that he cared for and was close to? And when would they come for him? After they'd killed Ellen and Jane, and heaven knows who else?

When he'd stood on the platform at Victoria, he'd announced that he was heading for Venice. Was that where his would-be assassins were at this moment? Searching for him to dispose of his body in the maze of canals?

Or were they here in Dieppe? Had they followed him? Were they watching him even now, waiting for the moment to strike?

Nervously he looked at the people on the beach, families with children playing, a group of men playing boules. Were those men really playing boules – or, more precisely, *pétanque*, in which the balls were thrown, as opposed to *bocce*, the other version of boules, where they were rolled? The men looked genuine enough, typical Normandy peasants and fishermen. Or were they using the game as a way of keeping watch on him?

He put Ellen's letter back in the envelope, got up and began to walk back into the town towards the small house and studio he kept there. He threw a quick glance over his shoulder. The men seemed intent on their game of pétanque, no one seemed to be following him. But then again, they didn't need to. Most people here in Dieppe knew him by sight, and they knew where he lived.

I need to move, he decided. But where?

* * *

166

Neither Abberline nor Emma had changed much in the five years since Daniel had last set eyes on them. Abberline, now in his mid-fifties, still sported his familiar moustache that curled along his cheeks to join his bushy sideburns, giving him a sporting air.

Emma had grown slightly plumper since Daniel had last seen her, but she still seemed to have the same happy air about her.

Daniel and Abberline shook hands, and Emma gave Daniel a peck on the cheek, before giving Abigail a hug of welcome and shepherding them into the front parlour, where they settled themselves down on the comfortable, florally cushioned armchairs.

'It's a pleasure to meet you, Miss Fenton,' smiled Abberline.

'Call me Abigail, please. Daniel's told me so much about you I feel I already know you.'

'Abigail,' nodded Abberline. 'I'm referring particularly to your work in Egypt. The pyramids and that. It was Emma who spotted an article about you in one of her magazines.'

'It had photographs of you at some of these places. In one of them you were holding a shovel.'

'They don't call them digs for nothing,' smiled Abigail.

'So you do the work as well?' asked Abberline. 'You don't just give orders?'

'The only way to find out things is to get your hands dirty,' said Abigail.

'Sounds like life in the police force,' chuckled Abberline. 'Right, Daniel?'

'But in a much hotter climate. Abigail's off to Egypt again in a few months. This time she's actually leading the expedition.

167

It's being set up by Arthur Conan Doyle.'

'The Sherlock Holmes man?' Abberline looked at Abigail, impressed. 'You certainly move in exalted company, Abigail.' He turned to Daniel. 'As I said, in a way I was half-expecting you to get in touch, once the newspapers said you were looking into the murders for the National Gallery.' He chuckled. 'I bet that upset old Armstrong.'

'Everything we do seems to upset him,' said Daniel ruefully. 'What I wanted to ask you about were the original Ripper's victims.'

'You know their names as well as I do, Daniel.' He ticked them off on his fingers. 'Mary Ann Nichols. Annie Chapman. Elizabeth Stride. Catherine Eddowes. Mary Jane Kelly.'

'What I'm looking for is if any of them had nephews or cousins or any family who were children at the time who might have gone into the butchery trade.'

'Butchery?'

Daniel nodded.

'We've got a lead that our suspect may be a butcher. Aged about twenty. And I think he might have been connected to one of the original victims in 1888. Which would make him about ten when the original murders happened.'

'A butcher,' said Abberline thoughtfully. 'None of the five women who were murdered had anyone in their family in the butcher trade, as far as I know. And you know, Daniel, that in working-class areas, kids tend to follow their parents into whatever trade they're in.' He gave a grin. 'Whether it's legal or not. Pickpockets. Burglars. Sons learning the trade from their dads and uncles, same as if it was butchery or driving a wagon.'

'The other lead we had was with the second victim.'

'Kate Branson,' nodded Abberline. He smiled when he saw their expressions of surprise. 'Like I said, I've been following the case in the papers. Anne-Marie Dresser the first one, Kate Branson the next. Both prostitutes?'

'Yes, although they also worked as models for artists, notably for Sickert. The thing is that Kate Branson seemed to have one particular client who she called "the rich toff". He used to pick her up at Charing Cross in his carriage and then just talk to her, nothing more. But he still paid.'

'Different people have different needs,' commented Abberline. 'You know that, Daniel, from talking to people during the Ripper investigation.' He looked thoughtful. 'So you're looking at the sons of the Ripper's victims, that one of them may be behind these latest killings. Why?'

'It's because of Sickert. There's feeling in Whitechapel that Sickert, along with Sir William Gull and the prince were the ones who did the killings, but that they got let off because of who they were. Now it's just talk on the street . . .'

'But talk on the street carries weight,' finished Abberline. 'More weight than whatever facts may have been.'

'Perhaps one of them wants revenge now he's older. Gull and the prince are dead but Sickert's still alive. Everything so far looks as if whoever's doing it is trying to frame Sickert. We've looked at the children of the victims, and so far none of them fit. Which is why we're looking at relatives.'

Suddenly, Abigail asked: 'Were there any other victims apart from the five that were reported? Women who were killed around the same time who *might* have been Ripper victims, but weren't listed as such.'

Abberline looked at her with new admiration, then at Daniel.

169

'That's good thinking,' he said. 'I'm surprised you didn't think of that, Daniel.'

Daniel looked uncomfortable at this, and Abigail said smoothly: 'I'm sure Daniel has, he just hadn't said it yet.'

Abberline chuckled. 'No, I know Daniel. You were ahead of him in that thought, Abigail. There were other women who disappeared about that time, or were killed – but not mutilated in the same awful way – that some people said the Ripper was responsible for as well. But because the injuries were very different, sometimes just a cut throat or a battering, they weren't included.' He sat in thought for a moment, then asked Daniel: 'Did you keep your old notebooks?'

'I did,' said Daniel.

'So did I,' said Abberline.

Abberline got up and headed out of the room.

Higgins' butchers in Cable Street had the same smell about it and the same sawdust spread over the floor as Ramsden's. It also had the same sort of customers, who looked warily askance when Inspector Feather entered, and two of the men waiting decided to leave.

I don't think I look like a copper, thought Feather. I'm in plain clothes, but somehow they know.

There were two butchers behind the counter, a middle-aged stout man with a bald head and ginger mutton-chop whiskers, and a younger and slimmer version of the same, down to the ginger mutton-chop whiskers. Father and son, thought Feather. The older man gestured for Feather to come forward to one side of the counter, keen to get rid of him.

'Inspector Feather from Scotland Yard,' he introduced

himself, showing his warrant card. 'I'm looking for Joe Wallace, who I believe works for you.'

'He does, but he didn't turn up this morning. Nor yesterday. He must be sick.'

'Does he often not turn up?' asked Feather.

'No. He's usually reliable. Like I said, I can only think he's sick.'

'No word from his family?'

'No.'

'Well, if he comes in, will you give him this and ask him to get in touch with me?' And Feather handed over a card with his details on.

Higgins nodded and put the card in a drawer below the counter. All eyes followed the inspector as he walked out of the shop.

'No luck, sir?' asked the constable waiting outside.

'No,' said Feather. 'Not that I expected him to come out if he was there, I just wanted to see what the reaction was.'

'D'you think he was hiding out the back?'

'It's possible.'

'Do you want me to go round the back and take a look?'

Feather shook his head.

'No, it's enough to let him know we're looking for him. Next, we'll go to his home and stir things up there. Once he realises we're looking to flush him out, he'll have to make a bolt for it.'

Abberline returned carrying two notebooks.

'Here we are,' he said. 'The key ones from 1888. You can borrow them, but promise me you'll send them back when you've finished.'

'I promise,' said Daniel, and he carefully placed a book in each of the big pockets of his coat. 'By the way, do you know a Catherine Heppenstall? We heard she came from Clapham.'

'As a matter of fact, we do,' said Abberline. 'Although Emma knows more about her than me.'

'Catherine Watts, as she was,' nodded Emma. 'Not that we actually *know* her. More like we know *of* her. She was a well-known performer here, and when she married Mr Heppenstall it was big news in the local paper. Clapham singer marries top London surgeon.'

'Did you know they'd parted?'

Emma looked shocked. 'No. Why?'

'Apparently Mr Heppenstall discovered that Catherine had a romantic entanglement with Walter Sickert.'

'The painter again,' murmured Abberline.

'The very same. We were wondering what happened to her. If she returned to this area.'

Emma shook her head. 'Not that I heard of, and if she had come back people would have known about it. She wasn't one for hiding her light under a bushel.'

Abberline looked at Daniel and Abigail and asked: 'Do you think something's happened to her?'

'We don't know,' said Daniel carefully. 'We'd just like to know where she is.'

'Perhaps her family knows,' said Emma. 'They still live in Clapham. Not that I know them,' she added hastily. 'But I know where they live. When Catherine married Mr Heppenstall, they put her family's address in the article.' She got up. 'I've still got the paper somewhere. I used it to line the larder shelves.'

She bustled out of the room.

'Are you thinking Mr Heppenstall may have . . . done something to her?' Abberline asked. 'And then killed these women to frame Sickert for the affair with his wife?'

'I don't know,' admitted Daniel. 'It would help if we could find out if Catherine Heppenstall was still alive.'

'One thing intrigued me when I was reading about the case,' said Abberline. 'First, Sickert gets arrested, then he's freed. Then the latest I read, he's off to Venice.' He looked at Daniel inquisitively. 'I sense Armstrong's hand in all this. What's he up to?'

'It wasn't all Armstrong's doing,' explained Daniel. 'Yes, arresting Sickert after the first woman was killed was his doing, but then he had to let him go. He wanted to keep him in England after the second woman was murdered, but then something happened to change it all.'

Emma Abberline re-entered, holding a page from the local newspaper. 'Here it is,' she said, handing the page to Daniel. 'That's their address there. Pulver Street. Fred can give you directions, if you wanted to talk to them.'

'Yes, I think that's a good idea,' said Daniel. 'Thank you.'

'You were saying that Armstrong wanted to keep Sickert in England, but then something happened to change that,' said Abberline, intrigued.

'Daniel was attacked,' said Abigail.

'Attacked?' echoed Emma, shocked.

Daniel told them about the attack on him, and the threat to Abigail. 'So it seemed to me the best way to ensure Abigail's safety was to get Sickert out of the country.'

'Yes, clever thinking,' nodded Abberline in approval. 'If he's not here, they wouldn't kill any more women thinking they could frame him for them.' He smiled at his wife. 'I told you Daniel was a clever one, Em.'

'You're living very dangerously, with some very dangerous people,' commented Emma, concerned.

'It goes with the job,' said Abigail, trying to appear casual.

'It may do, but that's why we didn't have women detectives in the police,' said Abberline.

'Do you ever miss it?' asked Daniel. 'The job?'

'I do, but I don't miss the Yard and all the politics,' said Abberline. 'That Cleveland Street business did it for me, the people at the top protecting their own.'

'Have you ever thought of setting up on your own?' asked Abigail. 'Like Daniel and I?'

Abberline looked at Emma, and when she gave a shrug and a nod, he turned back to them, lowering his voice to a whisper as he said, 'It's funny you should mention that, because recently I've been approached by a private firm about working for them.'

'Oh? Who?'

Abberline smiled. 'I shouldn't say, but I think I can trust you to keep it to yourselves. They're quite a large outfit.' He gave a proud smile as he whispered: 'Pinkertons.'

'Pinkertons,' whispered Daniel in awe, forcing himself not to utter the famous name out loud. 'My God, Fred, they're the biggest there is!'

Abigail looked puzzled.

'Who are Pinkertons?' she asked.

'Surely you've heard of Pinkertons?' said Daniel, shocked.

'No,' she said. 'We've never come across them in our investigations.'

'That's because our investigations were in Britain,' Daniel

explained. 'The Pinkerton Agency are American. They first came to fame protecting Abraham Lincoln.'

'Not very successfully,' observed Abigail.

'Pinkertons weren't looking out for him when he was assassinated,' said Abberline. 'And they're not just big in America. They're in continental Europe. Australia. They'll be here soon, you mark my words.'

Walter Sickert sipped at his brandy as he contemplated his half-completed letter to Ellen. What could he say? That he was sorry? He'd said that already; too often, he admitted regretfully. He'd heard nothing from his sister, Helena, which was ominous, suggesting that Helena's appeals to Ellen not to go ahead with the divorce had been unsuccessful.

He looked around the small bar. The rest of the clientele seemed to consist of rough-looking men, fishermen and farmers. Most of them ignored him, he was a familiar figure in here, but he noticed that three men sitting at a table on the other side of the bar were watching him, and their expressions were not friendly. In fact, they were looking at him with serious hostility, and muttering in low tones – presumably about him.

Fear struck him. Were they here to kill him, as Anne-Marie, Kate and Edwin had been killed? Their faces gave them away as being Normandy locals, but what was to say that they hadn't been contacted by someone from London and hired to kill him? Sickert had noticed a few English in Dieppe these last few days. Perhaps one of them had been the messenger of evil intent. Money had changed hands and now these three men were here, watching him, waiting to make their move.

Sickert put his half-finished letter back inside his pocket, drained the last of his brandy, rose and made for the door to the street. Out of the corner of his eye, he noticed the three men also get to their feet. Yes, they were definitely coming after him.

As soon as he was outside, he quickened his pace, half-walking, half-running. The police station, he decided. It was only a small local commissariat, but he would be safe there. Fortunately, over the many years he'd been coming to France he'd learnt to speak and understand the language, although the dialect of Normandy was different from Parisian French. He'd tell the local gendarmerie that three men were after him with murderous intent and he needed protection. The police might even be able to force the men to tell them who had hired them, and he'd be able to pass this back to London, and the police would be able to arrest the people behind them, who obviously were also behind the killings of Anne-Marie, Kate and Edwin.

Suddenly he heard the sound of running boots on the cobbled road surface behind him, and he shot a quick glance over his shoulder and was terrified to see two of the men from the bar closing on him, one a large, burly, bearded man, the other small and wiry.

His chest hurting with running, Sickert desperately tried to accelerate away from them. He wasn't far from the police station now, if he could just reach it and stagger in through the door . . .

Suddenly another man appeared in front of him, emerging from a narrow lane to his left. It was the third man from the bar, and as Sickert tried to dodge past him the man's fist lashed out and crashed into Sickert's face, sending him tumbling to the ground.

'No!' he yelled in fear. '*Non! Au secours! Au secours!*'

Then a kick from a boot smashed into his back and he screamed out in pain.

CHAPTER TWENTY

Lily Wallace stood in the doorway of the narrow terraced house in Nelson Place, a sleeping baby in her arms and a little girl of about two hanging onto her skirt. The little girl looked up at Inspector Feather and the uniformed police constable with undisguised curiosity, her mouth open in wonder. Perhaps she'd never seen a police constable up close before. The police in Whitechapel tended to keep away from narrow streets and lanes unless there was a call for help or an alarm raised.

Lily Wallace shook her head. 'No, Joe ain't here.'

'Do you know where he is?'

'At work, I expect.'

'He's not at Ramsden's or at Higgins',' Feather told her.

She shrugged. 'I expect he's gone somewhere else, then. Joe works casual. Different places, different people. There's loads of butchers in this part of London. Everyone wants meat.'

Feather nodded.

'Thank you, Mrs Wallace. Will you tell Joe I called looking for him?'

'What's it about?' she asked.

'Just a few questions,' said Feather blandly. 'We're interested in someone Joe might know.'

'Who?'

'I'm afraid we can't say at the moment, but hopefully Joe will be able to help us. I've left my card at Higgins in Cable Street for him.'

He doffed his hat, then he and the constable walked off.

Lily Wallace shut the door then walked through the house and out into the backyard and the outside toilet. She banged on the wooden door.

'It's all right, Joe,' she said. 'They've gone.'

She heard the bolt inside being drawn back, then the door opened and Joe Wallace peered out nervously.

'What did they want?'

'They didn't say. Just said they wanted to talk to you about some bloke you might know.'

Wallace gave a sarcastic laugh and stepped out of the outhouse. 'Yeh, right!'

'He was from Scotland Yard. Called himself Inspector Feather. Said he'd left his card for you at Higgins.' She looked at him suspiciously. 'What's going on, Joe?'

'Nothing, Lil. It's all a mistake. Someone's been spreading lies about me.'

'About what?'

'About nothing.'

'It ain't nothing if the police are calling!'

'Don't worry, I'm going to get this sorted out.'

'How?'

'There's a bloke I know. He'll sort it out for me. I'll go and see him.'

'Where?'

'Up west.'

'Is this that rich bloke who keeps coming round?'

'What rich bloke?' asked Wallace uncomfortably.

'Oh, come on, Joe! I'm not an idiot. Twice now you've said you had some private work to do, and both times this carriage pulls up at the end of the street. Don't think I haven't seen it.'

'Have you been spying on me?'

'I've got a right to know what you're up to when you go off like that. After the first time I wondered if it might be some fancy woman.'

'Don't be daft. And I bought money back with me, didn't I?'

'Yeh, but I wondered what for.'

'Lil, how can you think that about me? It was a butchery job. A private one. This bloke wanted some meat cut up in a special way at his place.' He looked at her suspiciously. 'How did you know it was a rich bloke?'

'With that carriage?'

'Yeh, but how did you know it was a bloke?'

'Like I said, in case you were up to something with some woman, I went after you when it happened again the second night, and I heard his voice when you opened the door of the carriage.'

Wallace shook his head. 'I never thought you'd do something like that, Lil. Follow me. It means you don't trust me. You never follow me when I do a night shift at Ramsden's.'

'That's different, I know Karl Ramsden. Who is he, this bloke?'

'It's secret, Lil. Private work. He's . . . eccentric.' He looked at her, worried. 'You sure they've gone?'

'Yeh.'

'Still, just in case they're watching the house, I'll go over the back wall. Go and get my coat for me, just in case they're looking in through the windows.'

Lily regarded him, uncertain.

'You're really sure there's nothing going on?'

'Nothing, Lil! On my word! I swear! I'll be back as soon as I've got this sorted.'

She hesitated, then turned and headed back towards the house, the little girl still clinging to her skirt.

Daniel was scowling as they left the Abberlines' house. 'I am such an idiot,' he castigated himself. 'I should have thought of that! About other possible victims.'

'I'm sorry,' said Abigail. 'I didn't mean to embarrass you in front of your old boss.'

'You didn't embarrass me. *I* embarrassed me.'

'I should have said something to you first,' said Abigail apologetically. 'It was just the idea popped into my head and I just said it.'

'And I'm glad you did, otherwise Fred wouldn't have lent us his notebooks.' He patted his pockets where he'd put them. 'When we get home, we'll compare his with mine and fill in any blanks.'

Abigail suddenly came to a halt and held Daniel's arm. 'I have a suggestion,' she said.

Daniel looked at her, intrigued.

'You obviously have a great deal of respect for Fred Abberline, and he for you. You obviously worked well together in the past. How do you feel about bringing him into our investigation?'

Daniel stared at her, stunned.

'Working with us?'

'Why not? We work with John Feather.'

'Yes, but . . .' Daniel faltered.

'We can ask Ellen Sickert if she'll agree to add Mr Abberline to our team. If she doesn't agree, we'll hire him and pay him part of our fee.'

As Daniel frowned, thinking this over, Abigail added: 'You've said yourself, Whitechapel is at the heart of this. Fred Abberline was an inspector there for nine years, and right at the centre of the Ripper investigation. You believe these murders are linked right back to those original deaths. What better man to work with us on this than the one who led that original investigation?'

Slowly, hesitantly, Daniel nodded. 'Yes,' he said. He turned and headed back towards Abberline's house.

'Where are you going?' asked Abigail.

'To ask Fred if he'll join us.'

'But we haven't got approval from Ellen Sickert yet,' Abigail pointed out. 'It was only a suggestion.'

'And an excellent one. And, as you've suggested, if she says no, we'll pay him from our fee.' He grinned. 'This is like the Ripper investigation all over again.'

Abberline looked at them in surprise when he opened the door to their knock.

'I thought you'd gone.'

'We had,' said Daniel. 'But we've got an offer to make you. Would you work with us on this case? Paid, of course.'

'Paid?'

'In your role as a consulting detective.' Daniel grinned. 'If you're good enough for Pinkertons, you're good enough for us.'

'Are you sure?' asked Abberline doubtfully. 'You weren't always enamoured of me when I was your boss, Daniel. Sometimes I knew you thought I pushed too hard.'

'I was young and learning,' said Daniel. 'And you wouldn't be the boss in this case.'

'No, I'm aware of that,' said Abberline. He suddenly smiled and nodded towards Abigail. 'She is. And yes, count me in.'

'Thank you,' said Abigail.

'I think the next move will be for you to come to the National Gallery and meet Stanford Beckett,' said Daniel. 'He's the curator there.'

'And he's the one paying for your investigation?'

Daniel hesitated, then said: 'No. That's Walter Sickert.'

'Sickert?'

'To be exact, Ellen Sickert, his wife, is the one who's paying for everything.'

'I can't see her agreeing to my joining you,' said Abberline doubtfully. 'She was quite angry when she realised we were questioning Sickert. In fact, very angry.'

'But she's hired us, and I was your sergeant at that time,' Daniel pointed out. 'We're fairly confident she'll agree.'

'And if she doesn't, we'll pay you from our fee,' said Abigail. She smiled. 'We'll simply increase our charge.' Then she became serious as she added: 'She is very determined to have Walter proved innocent of these crimes, which means discovering the real culprit.'

'Very well,' said Abberline. 'If you're sure.'

'We're sure,' said Abigail. 'And she will be, too.'

'So, when can you be free to meet Mr Beckett?'

'The sooner the better,' said Abberline.

'How about tomorrow? Will one o'clock tomorrow afternoon be all right for you?'

'Make it two,' said Abberline. 'Emma likes us to sit down for lunch at twelve.'

'Two o'clock it is,' said Abigail. 'We can show you where the bodies were dumped.'

'And tonight we'll go through your old notebooks and see if there's anything we need to ask you about them,' added Daniel.

'You think it's this butcher?' asked Abberline.

'I do,' said Daniel.

'Where does this rich bloke, Kate Branson's toff, fit in?'

'I'm not sure,' Daniel admitted. 'If it wasn't for the fact this butcher is in the frame, the toff would certainly have been a candidate. He's got a carriage in which he could move the bodies. But so, I assume, has this butcher. When we were at Smithfield, all the butchers had vans to transport their meat.'

Sickert sat at a table in the small police station while a woman summoned from a local cafe bathed the cuts and bruises on his face with water from an enamel bowl. His yells and those from some local bystanders had brought the local gendarmes running from the station and they'd soon overpowered the three men, who were now locked in a cell. The sergeant in charge returned to Sickert after questioning them about the attack, and now he sat down at the table with the English painter.

'The big one with the beard is called Charles Dresser,' he

told Sickert. 'He is the uncle of Anne-Marie Dresser, who used to live here before she went to London. The other two men are shipmates with him. He works on a fishing boat. He'd been away at sea, and when he got back to shore, he read the paper that his niece had been killed in London. Murdered by the Ripper, it said. The New Ripper. The paper said that a Mr Walter Sickert had been arrested for her murder, which is why he was shocked to see you walking free here in Dieppe. All he could think of was that you had escaped and fled England.

'Unfortunately, the more he thought about it, the more he drank, and the more he drank, the angrier he became.'

'I didn't kill her,' said Sickert. 'The police in England let me go because they had evidence that I couldn't have killed her.'

The sergeant nodded. 'Yes, we found a later edition of a newspaper that said that. We've told Charles Dresser and that he made a mistake. So I ask you now, do you wish to press charges against these men?'

Sickert weighed up the question. He was still not convinced that the men were innocent, but the sergeant and other officers at the station had assured him that they knew the men, that they were genuine fishermen.

'Did they have weapons on them?' he asked. 'Knives?'

'No,' said the sergeant. 'Which is unusual for fishermen, but M'sieur Dresser and Jerome, one of his comrades, had both got in trouble before for getting into a fight when they were drunk and producing their knives. So they had decided that thereafter they would always leave their knives at home so nothing like that could happen again.'

'Very well,' said Sickert. 'In that case, I don't wish to press charges against them. But warn them that if they come after me again, I will. And, again, do repeat to them that I did not kill Anne-Marie. I am completely innocent of her death.'

Pulver Street had terraced houses on both sides of the street, their red brick and roofs stained with dark smoke smudges from the railway line that backed on to it. A woman in her late fifties looked out anxiously when she opened the door to Daniel's knock.

'Mrs Watts?' asked Daniel. When the woman nodded, he said: 'We're here about your daughter, Catherine.'

'You've got news of her?' asked the woman, suddenly eager. She turned and called into the house: 'Charlie! There's people here with news of our Cath!'

'Actually, I'm afraid . . .' began Daniel apologetically, but before he could finish a man in shirtsleeves and braces appeared from a nearby room, his face showing the same eagerness as that on his wife's.

'You've got news of Cath?' he burst out excitedly. Then, when he saw the awkward looks on their faces, his whole manner changed: he stumbled back and fell against the wall of the passage. 'It's not . . . ?' he stammered.

'No,' said Daniel quickly. 'It's not bad news. In fact, we have no news of her at all. We came here in the hope you might have.'

'Who are you?' demanded Watts, and he glared at them aggressively.

'We're private enquiry agents,' said Abigail. 'My name's Abigail Fenton and this is Mr Daniel Wilson, formerly a detective sergeant with the Metropolitan Police. We've been hired by Mr Walter Sickert, an artist, to ascertain the whereabouts of Mrs

185

Catherine Heppenstall, which we understand is her married name.'

'Who's this Sickert?' demanded Watts.

'I remember now,' said Mrs Watts. 'Catherine wrote to us about a year ago and said he was painting her portrait. She was very proud. She said he painted all the great ladies. All the top people.'

'Yes, that's true,' said Abigail.

'Why's he want to know where she is after all this time?' demanded Mr Watts, suspiciously.

'We're not sure,' lied Abigail. 'He just hired us to find her. We assume it's something to do with the portrait.'

'Did he finish it?' asked Mrs Watts.

'We're not sure,' Daniel told her. 'And I'm afraid we can't get hold of Mr Sickert to ask him at the moment. He's in Venice.'

'Venice?' frowned Watts. 'Where's that?'

'Italy,' said Abigail. 'He's gone there to paint.'

Watts and his wife exchanged puzzled looks, then Mrs Watts said to her husband in appeal: 'Let's talk to them, Charlie. They might know something.'

Still looking cross, Charlie Watts gave a reluctant nod. 'You'd better come in,' he said. He looked at his wife. 'Take 'em into the parlour, Edie. I'll put on my jacket and join you.'

Daniel and Abigail followed Mrs Watts along the narrow passage to the parlour. It was a small room, one that looked as if it wasn't used often with its highly polished dark brown furniture and immaculate floral-decorated armchairs. She gestured them to sit, then seated herself, and Charlie Watts appeared, now wearing a jacket.

'We're very sorry to trouble you,' said Daniel. 'We wondered if Catherine had been in touch with you recently?'

186

Watts shook his head.

'We haven't seen her for over two years,' said Mrs Watts. 'Not since she went up west. She moved there because she said she had more chance of getting better singing jobs at the top places in London. We used to get letters from her when she was first there, telling us how she was doing, and what places she was appearing at.'

'She's a singer,' grunted Watts. 'Good, too.'

'Then one day we got a letter from her telling us she was married to this top doctor.'

'A surgeon,' Watts corrected her. 'That's more than a doctor.'

'Edmund Heppenstall,' said Mrs Watts. 'She sent us a photo of the wedding.' She gestured at the sideboard. 'I keep it in the drawer to look after it. It's the last one we had of her.'

'May we see it?' asked Abigail.

Mrs Watts got up and went to the sideboard and took a framed photograph from the drawer, which she handed to them. It showed a couple, he in top hat, frock coat and tails and she in a long white bridal dress, standing in a garden somewhere. Another couple were in the photograph, the man standing to attention next to Heppenstall, the woman next to Catherine.

'You weren't at the wedding?' asked Abigail.

'No,' said Watts sourly. 'We weren't good enough.'

'Charlie!' his wife rebuked him. 'That's not right. She knew it would be hard for us to get up from Clapham.'

'She's ashamed of us,' said Watts bitterly. 'That's why we weren't invited.' He looked aggressively at Daniel and Abigail. 'I'm just a labourer. I work on the railway. She didn't want the likes of me and Edie mixing with her new toff friends, embarrassing her.'

'That's not fair, Charlie,' protested Mrs Watts.

'No? Then why didn't she write and let us know she was getting married before they did it? I'll tell you why. She was worried we'd want to be invited, or we might even have just turned up.'

'You said she wrote and told you she was having her portrait painted by Mr Sickert,' said Abigail. 'Did she write again after that, to tell you how it went?'

Both the Watts shook their heads. 'No,' she said. 'That was the last we heard from her.'

'I wrote to her after we hadn't heard anything to ask her what was happening to the painting,' said Watts. 'But I never got a reply. Not a word. So I wrote again. And again, nothing. So I wrote again, saying this time that I'd be coming up west and I'd call on her.' He looked shamefaced as he added: 'I wasn't really going to, but I wanted to provoke her into giving me the decency of a reply. Instead, I got a letter from that husband of hers, saying "I have to inform you that your daughter is no longer at this address, and I have no way of contacting her".' He scowled. 'Bastard! He dumped her.'

'Do you know that for certain?' asked Daniel.

'No, not for sure, but what other explanation is there? He obviously found himself someone else, someone posher than our Cath, someone more *appropriate* to his social standing.'

'And you haven't heard from Catherine since?'

'No. Nothing.' He hesitated, then said, very reluctantly: 'I even went to their house to find out what had happened to her.'

'He did,' nodded Mrs Watts.

'This butler opened the door and I told him I was Mrs Heppenstall's father, and I wanted to know where she was.

Heppenstall came to the door when the butler told him who I was and what I wanted. He stood there looking down his nose at me like I was something disgusting that had turned up on his doorstep and told me he had no idea where Catherine was and that he had no interest in knowing her whereabouts. He also told me in no uncertain terms that if I bothered him again, he'd have the police on me. And then he shut the door in my face.'

'Charlie was so upset when he came back,' said Mrs Watts.

'I was,' nodded Watts angrily. 'To be treated like that, like I was the lowest of the low.'

'Did you make any further enquiries about her?' asked Abigail.

'Who from?' asked Watts. 'We knew nothing about her life in that circle. We knew her address and the name of her husband, and the fact she was having her portrait painted by this artist bloke Sickert. There was no one to ask about her.'

'You could have sought out Mr Sickert,' suggested Abigail.

'Where?' asked Watts. 'I had no idea where he lived. I'd never heard of him. The only person who might know where I could get hold of him was Catherine's bastard of a husband, and he'd made it clear he wanted nothing to do with me.'

'And you're sure you haven't heard from Catherine since?' asked Daniel.

'Nothing,' said Watts sadly.

'How did the announcement about Catherine's wedding to Mr Heppenstall get into the local paper here in Clapham?' asked Abigail.

'That was Edie,' said Watts. 'She went in and told them.'

'I wanted those people who looked down on Catherine to know how well she'd done, marrying a real toff in London, a top doctor.'

'Surgeon,' Watts corrected her again.

'There were people here who said bad things about her, saying she was a low person because of the places she appeared in here in Clapham,' said Mrs Watts. 'It's not easy for a singer who's just starting out to get engagements, so she often used to appear in local pubs, many of them not the best of places. That's the reason she went up west, to really get her career going at decent places. I wanted those people who said bad things about my girl to choke on their words when they saw that piece in the paper about who she was marrying.'

CHAPTER TWENTY-ONE

On the bus on the way back home, Daniel and Abigail decided to share their suspicions with Feather about Heppenstall and Catherine.

'For one thing, Scotland Yard have got the resources to mount a search for her.'

'If she's still alive.'

'Exactly. And if she can't be found, that will suggest she's dead and her body's been disposed of.'

'Not necessarily,' Abigail cautioned. 'It may mean she doesn't want to be found. She could well have taken on a new identity, and be anywhere. Liverpool. Manchester. Glasgow. She's a performer, she can go anywhere.'

'Yes, I suppose you're right,' agreed Daniel reluctantly. 'But I'd still like to find out.'

When they arrived home, an envelope marked 'urgent' was

waiting for them on their doormat. Abigail opened it.

'It's from Mr Beckett,' she said. 'He asks if we can call to see him at the National Gallery immediately.'

'Not another murder, surely?' said Daniel. 'If that was the case there'd also be a note from John Feather waiting for us.'

'John's not in the habit of leaving notes,' Abigail pointed out.

In view of the urgency expressed in the note, they caught a hansom cab to the National Gallery, where they found an agitated Stanford Beckett eager to see them.

'I'm sorry we didn't come sooner,' said Daniel. 'We've been in Clapham. Your note said it was urgent. We assume something bad has occurred?'

'Dreadful,' said Beckett in anguish. 'Not as bad as the murders, of course, but for the gallery it's appalling. Last night someone managed to get into the gallery and slashed a painting, absolutely ruining it.'

Daniel and Abigail exchanged puzzled looks. 'Surely that's a matter for the police,' said Daniel.

'No, absolutely not,' said Beckett firmly. 'The gallery's reputation has already been badly damaged enough by these appalling murders. It might frighten the public off completely from coming here if it gets out that some madman with a knife might be prowling around here. And I believe the slashing of the painting might be connected to the murders.'

'How?'

Beckett walked over to where a cloth was draped over a framed picture leaning against the wall of his office, hiding it. He removed the cloth, and they recognised Sickert's portrait of Anne-Marie Dresser. The canvas had been slashed from top to bottom repeatedly.

'Was the other portrait of Anne-Marie damaged?' asked Daniel. 'The one by Degas?'

'No,' said Beckett. 'Thankfully, that was spared.'

'Then this attack was aimed at Sickert,' said Abigail.

'But why?' appealed Beckett. 'For the same reason the victims were chosen, to incriminate Walter?'

Daniel shook his head. 'This is different. Those women were killed and their bodies transported here and dumped at your door calculatedly in cold blood. This attack was carried out in a passionate frenzy. Who hates Sickert with such intensity, apart from the killer?'

'Simon Anstis?' suggested Abigail.

'Simon?' echoed Beckett, shocked. 'Surely not!'

'How did the intruder get in?' asked Daniel. 'Were any windows broken, or locks forced?'

'No,' said Beckett. 'It looks as if the intruder managed to get hold of a key to let himself in.'

'Have there been any reports of keys being stolen from your staff?' asked Daniel.

'No,' said Beckett.

'Then it's someone with an intimate knowledge of the gallery who's been able to get hold of a key by some means, and knew which key opened which door, and where the painting was he wanted to attack.' He looked at Abigail and nodded. 'I agree with Miss Fenton, Simon Anstis is a very likely candidate.'

'But there's no proof!' burst out Beckett.

'No, but there's no harm in us talking to him and gauging his reaction,' said Daniel.

'You can't accuse him,' warned Beckett nervously. 'If you're wrong, he'll sue the gallery for defamation, and the resultant publicity will be a disaster for us!'

'Leave it to us,' Daniel told him reassuringly. 'We won't be accusing him of anything, merely asking him if he knows who might have done it in order to help us in our enquiries in case it's associated with the murders. He came across to us as a very fragile person, his reactions to our talking to him will be interesting.

'Also, the reason we were in Clapham was to pay a call on Mr Abberline, formerly my inspector in the original Ripper investigations. We sought his help because we think the latest murders are connected in some way to the Ripper murders.'

Beckett stared at them, horrified.

'You mean . . . he's back?'

'We don't think it's the same killer, but it's someone with an association with that original case. Possibly a relative of the victims. You recall that Sickert was a suspect at the time, and we feel that whoever's doing this is aiming it at Sickert in order to get revenge on him. That's why we'd like to bring in Mr Abberline.'

'Bring him in?' repeated Beckett, not fully comprehending.

'There's no one who knows more about the original Ripper case than Abberline. He's already lent us his original notebooks from that time. We feel the key to this is going back to the original Ripper case, and for that we'd like him on board with us.'

'We're going to call on Ellen Sickert to see if she'll approve him joining us,' added Abigail. 'She is the one paying for the investigation, after all.'

'And if she says no?'

'In that case we'll pay him out of our fee,' said Daniel. 'But we are sure, with his help, we can solve this case and identify the murderer.'

Beckett sat, thinking this over. Finally he said: 'Very well. If you think it will bring this dreadful situation to an end but Ellen says no to him, I'll talk to the Board and see if they will cover his costs.'

'Thank you,' said Daniel. 'But we hope that won't be necessary. We've arranged to meet him here at two o'clock tomorrow afternoon. We'll see Mrs Sickert before then.'

'If she says no, I won't have an answer from the Board by tomorrow.'

'That doesn't matter. As we said, if they refuse, we'll bear the cost of Mr Abberline ourselves.'

Simon Anstis was in his studio working on the portrait of Anne-Marie when Daniel and Abigail arrived.

'I can't help myself,' he explained mournfully. 'I'm trying to capture the perfection of her.' He let out a painful sigh. 'Have you caught the maniac who killed her? Is that why you're here? To tell me his name?'

'I'm afraid not,' said Abigail. 'We're sorry to trouble you with this, but there's been an incident at the National Gallery, which we feel might be connected to the recent tragedies.'

'An incident?' Anstis repeated nervously.

'It seems that a painting was damaged during the night.'

'A painting?'

'Yes, the portrait of Anne-Marie by Walter Sickert.'

Anstis swallowed nervously and demanded: 'Why have you come to me?'

'We're actually talking to everyone with a connection with

the gallery,' said Daniel in reassuring tones. 'Especially those who knew Anne-Marie.'

'Sickert knew her!' burst out Anstis. 'You say it's his picture of her. He's a violent man. Talk to him.'

'Sickert isn't in the country,' said Abigail. 'He left for Venice a couple of days ago. His departure was reported in the newspapers.'

'I don't interest myself in what the newspapers say,' said Anstis stiffly. 'But I can assure you that it wasn't me who damaged the picture.'

Daniel smiled reassuringly at him. 'Not to worry, Mr Anstis, we'll know soon enough who did it. Have you heard about the new science of fingerprints?'

Anstis looked bewildered. 'No. What is it?'

'Various people believe they are the best method of identifying those responsible for crimes. Francis Galton, a cousin of Charles Darwin, produced a book about it. According to Galton, a person's fingerprints are unique to them. Some years ago, a chief police officer in Argentina created the first method of actually recording fingerprints, and he was able to use this method to discover a murderer. We're going to do the same with the damaged painting of Anne-Marie at the National Gallery. We've arranged for someone to come in tomorrow with the necessary equipment and dust the frame of the picture for fingerprints. Once we have those prints, we shall be comparing them with people we think might be people of interest. Not just you, but everyone at the gallery. We're sure you won't mind.'

'I didn't do it! It wasn't me!' burst out Anstis.

'Then you have no reason to fear. The science we are introducing will bear that out and will point us to the true culprit.'

'But how can they do anything with the frame? Surely if the portrait's damaged it's been removed.'

'From where it hung, but it's now in Stanford Beckett's office waiting to be examined.' He smiled. 'Thank you for your time, Mr Anstis. We'll be in touch.'

As they walked away from the house where Anstis had his studio, Abigail asked: 'What was all that stuff about fingerprints? Did you just make it up on the spur of the moment to unsettle him?'

'Not at all, it's a new science that is very real. Dr Henry Faulds, a Scottish surgeon, was one of the first to put forward the idea in about 1880 while working in a Tokyo hospital. His theory was that people had their own particular fingerprints, which were unique to them. He came up with the first classification and how to identify different prints. When he returned to England in 1886 he was in touch with Scotland Yard and offered them his system. They refused.'

'So it's not really being used as a system of detection.'

'Not in England, but it is elsewhere. Dr Henry Faulds passed his information to Charles Darwin, who in turn passed it to his cousin, Francis Galton, who published a book about it called *Finger Prints*. This chief police officer I mentioned, Juan Vucetich, set up a fingerprint bureau in Argentina in 1892 after he'd read Galton's book. I read a report about the first case in which Vucetich used the method. A woman was found in a house with injuries to her neck, along with her two sons, whose throats had been cut. She accused a neighbour of the crime, but Vucetich and his inspector found a bloody thumb print on a doorpost at the scene of the crime. When they compared it to the woman's, it matched.'

'She could have touched the doorpost after she'd got stained with blood from her dead sons.'

'She could, but when they presented the evidence of the thumbprint to her, she was so shocked that she confessed that she'd carried out the murders. Reading that report convinced me that fingerprints could be the way forward in detection. The trouble is, for it to work you need a massive amount of fingerprint details, with names and addresses, to compare any fingerprints found at the scene of a crime with. And at the moment, Scotland Yard still aren't interested.'

'So telling Simon Anstis about them was a ruse.'

'It was. You saw how rattled he was when I mentioned them to him. My guess is he'll try and get in to the gallery tonight and rub down the frame with polish or something to get rid of his fingerprints.'

'And we'll be waiting for him?'

'We will,' said Daniel.

Joe Wallace had been sitting in The Flower Pot pub for over an hour, making one pint of beer last, and the barman was watching him warily. Mind, in the pub everyone watched people warily. And not just in this pub but in the whole of Seven Dials.

Seven Dials was in the heart of Covent Garden, so called because of the sundial on a post at the crossroads, the junction of seven streets, with seven dials, one for each of those streets. He was told that once upon a time, hundreds of years ago, it had been planned to make this an upmarket area to house the rich. Whether that was true, Joe didn't know. What he did know, as did everyone else in London, was that Seven Dials was one of the worst slums in London, even worse than any in the East End. Every crook, every crime, every vice could be found here. There was no chance of the police coming in and checking on people, no police officer felt safe here. Joe didn't feel safe here, he only felt safe on his home turf of Whitechapel. And he didn't like the way the barman kept looking at him. Sooner or later he'd either have to leave or buy another drink, and he was short of money.

Where was his man? Joe had put a note through the letter box of the address he'd been given, with strict instructions only to make contact in an extreme emergency. Well, having the police chasing him all over Whitechapel, from Ramsden's to Higgins', and then to his own home, counted as an emergency in Joe's book. And not just the local police, but Scotland Yard!

Suddenly he was there, looking down at Joe.

'Where have you been?' demanded Joe. 'I've been here hours!'

'I've been busy,' said the man. 'What's so urgent that you felt the need to contact me? I told you, only in an extreme emergency.'

'That's what this is,' said Joe. 'The police are after me. I've got to get away. I need money. They know what we've been doing.'

'Sssh!' snapped the man sharply. He jerked his head towards the door. 'We'll talk outside.'

Joe finished the remains of his pint, got up and walked after the man, who'd already left the pub and gone out into the street. *I can't leave without the kids and Lily*, he decided. *I need enough money to get us all safe. If he don't cough up, I'm talking. That's what I'll tell him.*

* * *

In his office at the National Gallery, Stanford Beckett stared at Daniel and Abigail, bewildered.

'Fingerprints?' he said.

'They're a scientific reality, but at the moment it's a ruse to see if Simon Anstis returns to the gallery tonight to do something about them.'

'You really think he was the culprit?'

'We do,' said Abigail. 'At least, Daniel does, and I trust what he calls his policeman's nose.'

'So what do you plan?'

'When the gallery closes, we shall situate ourselves here in your office with the door closed. If, as I suspect, Simon Anstis arrives to try and rub the frame of the damaged picture down and remove the telltale fingerprints, we shall apprehend him.'

Beckett looked unhappy at this. 'If it was him, last night he used a knife. Who's to say he won't be carrying a knife again?'

'I don't believe he will, but just in case, do you have a night watchman patrolling?' asked Daniel.

'No,' said Beckett. 'So far there's been no need for one.'

'Is there anyone on your security staff who might agree to do some overtime tonight?'

'There's Ian Millen,' said Beckett. 'He's a former soldier. He's a bachelor who lives on his own, so he has no family to explain why he'd be needed.'

'I'm sure he won't be actually needed,' said Daniel. 'But just in case I'm wrong, can you arrange for Mr Millen to join us?'

'What will you do with Simon if he does turn up?' asked Becket anxiously.

'Yes, that's a difficult one,' said Daniel. 'If we just let him go there's no knowing what he might do.'

'You mean he might carry out another attack here at the gallery?'

'It's possible,' said Daniel. 'You have other paintings by Sickert here, don't you?'

'Yes.'

'Then my advice is to have him arrested and for him to spend the night in a police cell. That should frighten him off doing anything like it again.'

Beckett shook his head.

'The National Gallery can't afford the bad publicity such an arrest would have. Everyone would know about what had happened.'

'Only if the National Gallery pressed charges,' said Daniel. 'If, as I suspect, you won't, then there's no reason for the case to come to court, and so no publicity of any sort about it. But I'm pretty sure it will put Mr Anstis off doing anything like it again.'

'You can stop him being prosecuted?' asked Beckett.

Daniel nodded.

'I can arrange with Inspector Feather for a constable to join us tonight. If Anstis comes in, the constable can take him to the local police station in the Strand and put him in a cell. We can go in to see him in the morning and tell him that the National Gallery have decided not to press charges, providing he promises not to repeat the act. After a night in the cell, I have no doubt he'll agree. He'll be released and the story ends with no publicity for the gallery.'

'You're sure?' pressed Beckett.

'Absolutely,' said Daniel.

'Very well,' said Beckett.

Daniel gestured around at the office. 'It will also mean Abigail and I can be in here while Mr Millen and the constable are in the room opposite, ready to rush in when we call. Otherwise, there's not going to be much room for all of us while we wait for what could be hours.'

Beckett got to his feet.

'Thank you,' he said. 'You've taken a load off my mind. If you come with me, I'll introduce you to Mr Millen.'

Ian Millen was a man in his early fifties, who looked every inch the former soldier: stiff-backed, a broken nose indicating he'd seen action, and very keen to get to grips with – as he described him – 'the vandal who ruined that painting'.

Daniel and Abigail outlined their plan, that they'd return to the gallery just before it closed to the public at seven o'clock that evening and take up their positions in Mr Beckett's office, while Millen and a constable waited in the room opposite.

'It will give you a companion while we wait,' smiled Abigail.

'You really think he'll come back again?' asked Millen.

'We hope so,' said Daniel. 'Let's say, we've baited the trap.'

CHAPTER TWENTY-TWO

After leaving the gallery, they made their way to Scotland Yard to see John Feather.

'We could be in for another night without sleep,' said Abigail. 'First Smithfield, now the National Gallery.'

'You don't need to come,' said Daniel. 'I'm sure that Mr Millen and I can deal with Simon Anstis, if it is him and he does take the bait.'

Abigail looked at him, affronted.

'Oh no you don't. You're not leaving me out of tonight's escapade.'

'As Mr Beckett pointed out, he might come armed with a knife,' said Daniel.

'In which case three of us will be better placed to deal with the situation than just two.' She looked at Daniel. 'Shall we tell John about the attack on the painting?'

'I think we have to,' said Daniel.

'Despite Mr Beckett not wanting the police involved?'

'He doesn't want word about it to get out and create more bad publicity for the gallery. We'll tell John what we're planning and ask him to keep it to himself for the moment. But just in case I'm wrong and it *is* connected with the murders, John needs to know.'

John Feather was in his office at Scotland Yard, packing up to go home when Daniel and Abigail arrived.

'I wondered if I might see you today,' said Feather. 'I got the report from Dr Snow. You were right about the speck in the blood. It was sawdust.'

'So, the butcher.'

'Yes. And, as you asked, I went looking for your young butcher while you two were off gallivanting heaven knows where.'

'We went to Clapham to see Fred Abberline,' Daniel told him. 'He's joining us in the investigation.'

'You're still convinced these killings relate back to the original Ripper murders?'

'I am. And Fred's given us his notebooks from then to go through. How did you get on with the butcher? Did you find him.'

'No. His name's Joe Wallace and he seems to have vanished.'

'When you say vanished . . . ?' asked Abigail.

'I called at Karl Ramsden's, then at Higgins' the butchers in Cable Street where he works, and also at his home. No one's seen him.'

'Do you think something's happened to him?'

'I don't know. I think it's more likely that, if he is our killer, he got scared when he saw you at Smithfield, and when people started asking questions about him, he did a runner.'

'In my experience, people like that don't run far, they like to feel safe and secure in a patch they know,' said Daniel.

'So you think he's hiding out somewhere in Whitechapel?'

'That's my guess,' said Daniel.

'Yes, it makes sense,' nodded Feather. 'I'll get the local force to start poking around. It may stir things up and flush him out into the open. One thing, he doesn't seem to have his own van.'

'But all butchers have vans,' said Daniel. 'We saw them at Smithfield. It was packed with them.'

'Maybe, if they're butchers who've got their own shops. Joe Wallace is a jobbing butcher, a casual who picks up work here and there working for other butchers.'

'So he couldn't have moved the bodies about,' mused Abigail thoughtfully.

'Unless he borrowed a van.'

'I think that's unlikely,' said Daniel. Then he looked at Abigail and exclaimed: 'The toff!'

'Yes!' said Abigail.

'Who's the toff?' asked Feather.

'Remember we told you we'd met Helena Swanwick, Walter Sickert's sister?'

'Who was at Girton with Abigail,' nodded Feather. 'I remember.'

'Well, she told us that Walter had had an affair with the wife of a top London surgeon called Edmund Heppenstall. Sometime after Heppenstall discovered the affair, Mrs Heppenstall vanished. As far as we can make out, Heppenstall says she left him. But there's been no trace of her. She was originally from Clapham and she came to the West End to get on in her career as a singer. Usually, when people leave, they often go back to their roots to get themselves together. But Catherine Heppenstall just vanished.'

'We went to see her parents while we were in Clapham and they told us they'd heard nothing from her for over a year,' added Abigail. 'Heppenstall wrote to them and told them she was no longer living with him. Her father went to see Mr Heppenstall to ask about her, and Heppentsall told him to leave or he'd set the police on him.'

'What are you thinking?'

'Say Heppenstal lost his temper when he found out about her affair with Sickert, and something happened which resulted in his wife's death. In his mind the person responsible for all this is Walter Sickert.'

'And you're thinking that this Heppenstall butchered the two women to try and get Sickert implicated?'

'He'd have the skill to do what was done to the women,' said Abigail.

'So would this butcher, Joe Wallace.'

'And Heppenstall and Wallace could be working together.'

'That's a bit of a leap,' said Feather doubtfully.

'When we talked to the prostitutes at Charing Cross Station, they told us about this rich man who used to come and pick Kate Branson up in his carriage,' said Daniel. 'She called him the toff. Say Edmund Heppenstall and this toff are one and the same.'

'Some rich surgeon and a butcher from Whitechapel killing women together just to get some kind of revenge on Walter

Sickert?' Feather shook his head. 'That's really clutching at straws.'

'All I'm saying is it's another possibility. We'd be able to remove Heppenstall from the list if we could find his wife and talk to her. If she's alive . . .'

'It wouldn't change things,' said Feather. 'He would still feel as resentful against Sickert even if she'd just walked out on him.'

'Yes, but it would show he hadn't done something serious like kill her,' said Abigail. 'Killing her would make his feelings against Sickert far worse.'

Feather shook his head, unconvinced.

'It all seems a bit far-fetched, to be frank. Joe Wallace seems a much more likely candidate. Especially as he's vanished, which is always suspicious. It's just a question of finding out if he borrowed anyone's van on the night the murders were done.'

'But is there any way a search can be made for Catherine Heppenstall? Notices sent out to police forces across the country?' asked Abigail.

Feather shook his head. 'I can't see the chief superintendent agreeing to that. At the moment it's only your theory that Heppenstall may have bumped off his wife, there's no evidence to support it. And he's an eminent surgeon. A notice like that going out will be sure to come to his attention. For the moment, let's concentrate on trying to bring Joe Wallace in.'

'All right,' said Daniel resignedly. 'There is something else that's happened. At the National Gallery.'

'Oh?' said Feather, intrigued. 'What?'

'They had two paintings of Anne-Marie Dresser on display, one by Sickert and one by Degas.'

'Who's Degas?' asked Feather.

'Edgar Degas,' said Daniel. 'A French artist. Very famous.'

'I didn't know you knew anything about artists, Daniel,' commented Feather. 'I suppose it's to do with hanging out at the National Gallery.'

'No, Abigail told me about him,' admitted Daniel. 'Anyway, last night someone got into the National Gallery and attacked Sickert's painting of Anne-Marie with a knife. Slashed it to ribbons.'

'The National Gallery didn't tell us about it,' said Feather, annoyed.

'No, they want to keep it under wraps for the moment. They're worried about the impact some knife-wielding maniac might have on their attendance figures.'

'Yes, I can see that, but we should have been told. It could be connected to the murders.'

'It could be, but we've got a hunch it isn't. We think it's a rival artist called Simon Anstis who was – and still is – intensely jealous of Sickert because of his relationship with Anne-Marie,' said Abigail. 'He hates Sickert and this picture of a nude Anne-Marie must drive him mad.'

'We'll bring him in for questioning,' said Feather. 'What's his address?'

'No,' said Daniel. 'We've got another idea.' He outlined the trap they'd baited for Anstis using the possibility of fingerprints being discovered on the picture frame. 'So tonight, we're going to lie in wait for him and hope he turns up.'

Feather looked at them, concerned.

'If he was armed with a knife last night, what makes you so sure he won't be armed tonight, if he does call?'

'If I'm right, all Anstis will have on him will be polish and a cloth.'

'And if you're wrong?'

'We'll have the assistance of an ex-soldier who works as security for the National Gallery. But it would be useful to have a constable as well, if you can arrange one. The plan is that the constable will take Anstis to the nearest police station, which is the Strand, and tomorrow morning Abigail and I go and see him there and tell him that the National Gallery have decided not to press charges providing he promises not to do such a thing ever again.'

'So preventing any bad publicity for the gallery.'

'Exactly.'

Feather took a sheet of notepaper headed Scotland Yard Detective Division and wrote a few words on it before passing it to Daniel.

'Take this to the Strand,' he said. 'It's my authority for them to assign you a constable.'

Their next port of call was Kensington, and Jane Cobden's house. A uniformed police constable was on duty outside and, recognising them, he saluted them as they walked to the front door.

Ellen Sickert and Jane Cobden were in the sitting room, as before, and they looked apprehensively at Daniel and Abigail as they entered.

'You have news?' asked Ellen.

'Some, but nothing conclusive, I'm afraid,' said Daniel. 'I see your police guard is still in place.'

'Yes,' said Jane. 'Inspector Feather arranged it.'

'He's a good man,' said Daniel.

'I wrote to Walter to tell him about Mr O'Tool. I haven't

had a reply yet, but post between England and the Continent is always slow.' She looked enquiringly at them. 'You say you have some news? Does it point to the person who's behind the killings?'

'So far, the evidence points to the killer possibly being a butcher, a young man of about twenty. Inspector Feather and the police are searching for him but they haven't been able to locate him yet.'

'Who is this man? Where does he come from? And why is he trying to implicate Walter?'

'His name's Joe Wallace. He comes from Whitechapel. We believe he's the son of one of the victims of the original Ripper.'

Ellen leapt to her feet. 'This is to do with the rumours that were circulating at the time. That Walter was involved in a conspiracy that led to the deaths of those women.'

'Yes,' said Daniel. 'That's what we believe.'

'But why now? After all this time?'

'We think there's a possibility that he's been encouraged in his murderous actions by another man, a rich man, who may have reasons to want revenge on your husband.'

Now it was Jane's turn to leap to her feet and she turned to her sister accusingly. 'It's some angry husband! I told you, Nellie, but you wouldn't listen. I told you that Walter would never change.'

Ellen Sickert crumpled to the settee.

'Yes, you did,' she said sadly. She looked up at Daniel and Abigail, an expression of anguished appeal on her face. 'Is that what this is about? Walter having an affair with a married woman?' Her tone bitter, she added: 'Another of his society sitters?'

'It's possible,' said Abigail carefully. 'Although, at this stage, it may be just rumour and gossip.'

'It's never just rumour and gossip!' said Jane derisively. 'Walter is a serial philanderer, but Nellie closed her eyes and ears to his misdeeds.'

'We'd like to bring Frederick Abberline into the investigation,' said Daniel.

'What?!' said Ellen sharply. 'Why? Abberline was no friend to Walter. It was his hounding of him that's led to this current situation.'

'We never hounded your husband, Mrs Sickert,' said Daniel politely. 'We followed information received, as we were supposed to do. We talked to many men at the time. Over a hundred. The fact that no charges of any sort were ever brought against your husband shows that Mr Abberline dismissed the idea of him as the Ripper.'

'But the fact that no one was ever charged left a cloud hanging over Walter!'

'That's why, in this case, we feel it important to catch the murderer and lay any idea that your husband may have been involved to rest. And, in my opinion, there is more chance of doing that if we bring in Mr Abberline. As I've said, we feel it's connected to the original Ripper crimes, and there's no one who knows more about them than he.'

Ellen Sickert fell silent, then she paced around, wringing her hands in obvious torment. Finally, she said: 'Very well. Bring him in. But I'll never forget what that man did to Walter, humiliating him. I'll make sure you and Miss Fenton are paid for your work, but if there's no outcome, I'll be damned if I'm going to pay that man one penny.'

'Thank you,' said Daniel. 'And I promise you that will be the case, if we don't catch the murderer.'

As they left the house, Abigail said: 'If we don't catch the killer, we'll be out of pocket.'

'If we don't catch the killer, we'll lose more than money,' said Daniel. 'After all the publicity with this case, our reputation will be gone. No more Museum Detectives.'

CHAPTER TWENTY-THREE

PC Wurzel and Ian Millen sat in the small storeroom directly opposite Stanford Beckett's office. A shout from the office would bring them rushing the few steps across the corridor. In the meantime, while they waited, they played cards, using a small upturned wooden crate as a card table. The gas lamp had been lowered, but there was still enough illumination for them to see the cards they were playing.

'I'm a vital part of this investigation,' Wurzel told Millen proudly. 'Them Museum Detectives sought me out to take 'em to Charing Cross and introduce them to friends of the last one that died, poor Kate Branson.' He watched Millen lay down the eight of clubs and studied his own hand. They were playing rummy because Millen had insisted he did not gamble. 'Money's too hard earned to throw away on the turn of a card,' he'd said when Wurzel had produced the pack of cards and suggested a few hands of poker. Wurzel hesitated, then picked up the discarded eight of clubs and added it to his own hand before putting down a three of hearts in its place.

'I'm wondering if this bloke we're laying in wait for will be armed,' continued Wurzel. 'I mean, he slashed that picture up pretty badly with a knife. Who's to say he won't try the same with us?'

Millen lifted a leaded stick from beside his chair.

'If he does, he'll regret it,' he said.

'Well, yeah,' agreed Wurzel, and he produced his police truncheon, which he put on the crate. 'This'll do the trick as well. But say he's alerted to the fact we're here?'

'He won't be, so long as we keep quiet,' said Millen pointedly. 'No talking. Let's just play cards.'

In Stanford Beckett's office on the other side of the corridor, Daniel and Abigail pored over the two notebooks Abberline had loaned them. Each had taken one of the notebooks and Daniel had left his own notebook on the table between them so each could refer back to it and cross-check details. As was the case with the two men in the storeroom, they'd lowered the gas lighting, with the additional precaution of pulling the heavy curtains shut to keep the light from being seen by anyone outside in the street. Both kept their ears alert for any sound in the corridor that would indicate an intruder, and when they did speak, they spoke in whispers, as now.

'He's got more details about the murders in his notebooks than you had in yours,' whispered Abigail. 'Listen: Mary Ann Nichols (née Walker) was killed on 31st August 1888. She married William Nichols in 1864 and had five children. After William had an affair, the couple separated in 1880. Mary became an alcoholic with a taste for gin. She became a prostitute. living in casual lodging houses. According to her friend, Ellen Holland, who Nichols shared a bed with in a lodging house in Thrawl Street, on the evening of 31st August the deputy at the lodging house turned her out because she did not have the four shillings lodging fee. At 2.30 a.m., Holland saw Nichols at the corner of Brick Lane and Whitechapel High Street. She was drunk and hardly able to stand. At 3.40 a.m. two carmen, Charles Cross and Robert Paul, discovered her body at the entrance to the stableyard in Buck's Row.'

'Fred was always very good on details,' nodded Daniel.

'And this about Elizabeth Stride, who was killed in the early hours of 30th September,' continued Abigail 'On 30th September, PC 425H William Smith saw Stride talking to a man in Berner Street at 12.30 a.m.. At 12.45 a.m., James Brown saw a man and a woman talking at the junction of Fairclough Street and Berner Street.

'Also at 12.45 a.m., Israel Schwartz saw a man walk up to Stride in Berner Street and argue with her, then throw her down to the ground. At 1 a.m., a street jewellery hawker and also a steward of the International Working Men's Education Club, discovered Stride's body in Berner Street.

'He then goes on to Catherine Eddowes, who was also killed in the early hours of 30th September: at 1.35 a.m., Joseph Lawende, Joseph Levy and Harry Harris saw Eddowes talking to a man at the corner of Church Passage. At 1.45 a.m. PC 881 Edward Watkins of the City Police discovered the mutilated body of Eddowes in Mitre Square.'

'I agree he's got more details than I had in mine, but as I said, I'd only joined Abberline's squad six months before the

Ripper enquiries,' Daniel defended himself. 'I'd only recently been made a detective sergeant. I was lucky that Abberline had noticed me when I was a detective constable and thought I had potential and so he had me added to his team. To a great extent, I was still learning my way. '

'You learnt from Abberline?'

'I did. As you've just seen from those reports, he was very precise. A great man for recording every last detail so he could compare notes later and see where they might lead. You'll see he even entered the autopsy reports on each victim so he could compare the injuries they'd suffered, look for any common denominator.'

Abigail turned to the autopsy reports, all neatly copied out in Abberline's precise handwriting.

'"Autopsy report on Mary Ann Nichols by Dr Rees Ralph Llewellyn",' she read.

'"Five of the teeth were missing and there was slight laceration of the tongue. There was a bruise running along the lower jaw and the right side of the face. This might have been caused by a blow from a fist or pressure from a thumb."' There was a great deal more about bruising and cuts to the face and a description of cuts to her throat and neck which had 'severed the tissues right down to the vertebrae', before she came to: '"There were no other injuries about the body until just about the lower part of the abdomen. Two or three inches from the left side was a wound running in a jagged manner. The wound was a very deep one and the tissues were cut through. There were several incisions running across the abdomen. There were also three or four similar cuts running downwards on the right side, all of which had been caused by a knife".'

Abigail then turned to the autopsy report on Annie Chapman, this one by a Dr Phillips. As with Mary Ann Nichols, there was bruising to the face and, as with Annie Chapman, the knife cuts to her neck had been so deep her throat had been severed. Dr Phillips then went on to detail: 'the injuries to the abdomen. The abdomen had been entirely laid open and the intestines severed from their mesenteric attachments, which had been lifted out. From the pelvis, the uterus and its appendages with the upper portion of the vagina and the posterior two-thirds of the bladder had been entirely removed.'

Abigail then tuned to the autopsy report by this same Dr Phillips on Elizabeth Stride.

'Elizabeth Stride's body wasn't mutilated like the others,' said Abigail.

'No, but the injuries to her face were the same,' said Daniel. 'The suggestion was that, with all the people around, the killer abandoned the idea of mutilating her; but he was able to carry that out shortly after on the body of Catherine Eddowes.'

Abigail turned to the autopsy report on Catherine Eddowes, and after a few moments said: 'My God, what sort of monster was he? He cut out her vagina and her rectum, along with her intestines.'

'He was the worst I've ever known,' said Daniel. 'Especially because it all seemed so calculated, and at the same time pointless. What was he after?' He hesitated, then said: 'If I were you, I'd avoid the autopsy report on Mary Jane Kelly. The others were bad, but this was by far the worst. He had more time with Mary Jane than with the others. All the others were killed and eviscerated in the open. Mary Jane was killed in her room. The killer had all the time he wanted to do what he wanted.'

Abigail nodded, closed the notebook and pushed it away. 'Yes. I've had quite enough pain and misery from the first ones.' She opened the notebook again. 'But I can cope with Mr Abberline's notes about events leading up to her death. As you say, comparing what he did to the other women.'

She read Abberline's notes, which informed her that Mary Jane Kelly was killed on 9th November in her room at 13 Miller's Court.

'At 8.30 a.m. on that morning, Caroline Maxwell met and spoke to Kelly at the corner of Miller's Court. Maxwell said that Kelly was very drunk. At 10 a.m., Maurice Lewis, a tailor of Dorset Street, says he saw Kelly drinking in the Britannia pub at the corner of Commercial Street and Dorset Street. Later that morning, Thomas Bowyer of 37 Dorset Street called at Kelly's place to collect the rent on behalf of the landlord, John McCarthy, and discovered Kelly's mutilated body.'

She put the notebook down and looked at him, overcome by the horrific details. 'I can't imagine how it must have been for you being involved in all this,' she said.

'About the same as it is for both of us right now, looking into these two killings at the National Gallery,' said Daniel ruefully.

'No, it's different,' said Abigail. 'Those two women were killed and mutilated to try and incriminate Sickert because of some real or imagined hurt. These women were killed for – what? Pleasure?'

'Who knows?' sighed Daniel. 'We were desperate to catch him and stop him before he killed more. But then, he seemed to stop.'

'Why?'

'Some suggested he'd died. Others said he'd fled abroad.

Certainly, there were reports of similar murders in America within the year of them ending in England.' Suddenly he exclaimed in a note of triumph, 'Here we are! Good old Fred!'

'What have you found?' asked Abigail.

'The names of other potential victims, all murdered in the same area but questions remained as to whether they were actual victims of the Ripper or of someone else.'

He pushed the open notebook to her.

'Emma Elizabeth Smith,' read Abigail. 'Martha Tabram. Alice McKenzie. Mary Bigwell, Jane Turner, Barbara Willen.'

'Look at Barbara Willen's address,' urged Daniel keenly. 'The Shambles.'

'An old name for a butchery,' said Abigail.

'We need to talk to Sergeant Whetstone again,' said Daniel. 'This time with Fred.'

Suddenly he put his finger to his lips as he heard a shuffling noise outside in the corridor. Abigail heard it, too. They got up and moved silently to take up positions behind the door. Slowly, the door opened and a hooded figure stepped into the office. The intruder hesitated, then saw the damaged painting leaning against the wall opposite and went to it, lifting up.

'Stop right there,' said Daniel, 'Put that picture down and raise your hands in the air.'

Suddenly the figure whirled round and hurled the painting at them, at the same time rushing for the door, but before he could reach safety the door of the storeroom opposite was jerked open and the burly figure of Ian Millen leapt out and thrust his leaded stick hard into the intruder's stomach.

The intruder collapsed to the floor with a yelp of pain, and the wiry figure of PC Wurzel entered the action, dropping on the fallen figure with a force that brought another cry of pain.

'Got him!' exulted Wurzel triumphantly.

Daniel stepped forward and removed the hood from the intruder's face, revealing the anguished features of Simon Anstis.

'Don't hurt me!' begged Anstis, shielding his face with his hands and arms.

'Constable Wurzel, this is Mr Simon Anstis,' said Daniel. 'Would you please take him into custody and charge him with burglary and criminal damage.' He turned to Ian Millen. 'Mr Millen, would you be kind enough to accompany PC Wurzel to the Strand police station when he takes Mr Anstis in, just in case Mr Anstis decides to be difficult.'

'I won't!' Anstis promised. 'I've never hurt anyone! It's not in my nature.'

Millen hauled Anstis to his feet.

'It will be my pleasure,' he said. He leant in to the cowering Anstis and growled menacingly: 'I'll teach you to deface the paintings in my care.' He produced his leaded stick and poked it at Anstis. 'Give me just one excuse and you'll feel this again, laddie. And harder next time.'

'Thank you,' said Daniel. 'We'll wait for your return so that you can lock up.' He looked at Anstis and held out his hand as he added: 'And we'll have the keys that you used to get in.'

Anstis took two keys on a ring from his pocket and passed them to Daniel. Then his arms were gripped by both Millen and PC Wurzel and he was escorted out.

'Now,' said Daniel, sitting down at the desk. 'I think we'll return to Fred's notebooks until Mr Millen comes back.'

CHAPTER TWENTY-FOUR

Daniel and Abigail left it until nine o'clock the following morning before they went to the Strand police station. They were taken to the holding cell where Simon Anstis was being held. The artist cut a forlorn sight, his clothes crumpled from having slept in them on the cell's hard bench. Not that he looked like he'd had much in the way of sleep.

'We assume you stole the keys to the gallery,' said Daniel.

His head bowed, Anstis nodded. 'One of the attendants,' he said. 'He'd left them on a hook.'

'And you got in and slashed Sickert's portrait of Anne-Marie.'

He looked up at them, his face anguished and despairing.

'I couldn't bear Sickert using that to show off his relationship with Anne-Marie. Rubbing what he had with her in my face. But I swear, I never killed her. Or damaged her in any way.' He slumped back against the wall. 'What will happen to me? Will I go to prison?'

'Fortunately, Mr Beckett at the National Gallery has decided not to press charges,' said Daniel.

Anstis looked at them, a spark of hope coming into his face, which then vanished as his head dropped again.

'What does that mean?' he asked plaintively.

'It means you're a very lucky man,' said Daniel.

'You mean I won't go to prison?'

'Thanks to Mr Stanford Beckett.'

Anstis leapt to his feet.

'I must go and see him and thank him,' he said.

Daniel stopped him.

'No,' he said. 'At this moment you won't be welcome at the National Gallery. I suggest you stay away from it, and refrain from contacting Mr Beckett or anyone connected with the gallery.'

'He'll want to see me,' insisted Anstis. 'I have to apologise to him.'

'He has instructed us that he doesn't want you going to the gallery. Not at the moment. That may change.'

'When?'

'When some time has passed and you've shown that you can be trusted by staying out of trouble.'

'But how will he know that I've been of good behaviour if I can't see him?' begged Anstis.

'He has asked us to keep an eye on you,' said Daniel.

'From a distance,' added Abigail. 'We will be reporting to him on the way you conduct yourself. Behave as a responsible citizen, causing no trouble to anyone – and I stress *anyone*, and that especially includes Mr Sickert and his family and his works of art – and *perhaps* you will be allowed back in.'

'I'll be good,' said Anstis fervently. 'I promise!' He looked about him at the confines of the cell. 'How do I get out of here?'

'Mr Beckett has given us the authority to sign for your release,' said Daniel. 'Once that's done, you're free to go.'

Anstis fell to his knees and took hold of Daniel's coat. 'Thank you!' he sobbed.

'You can thank us by keeping to the straight and narrow,' said Daniel, lifting Anstis to his feet.

'So Simon Anstis is back on the street,' said Beckett. 'Do you believe he's safe?'

'We do,' said Abigail.

'There's nothing like the night in a police cell to make someone consider their situation,' added Daniel.

'Mr Millen told me about Simon being apprehended last night,' said Beckett.

'Do pass on our grateful thanks to Mr Millen. He was invaluable.'

'I think he was quite proud to have taken part in the arrest of the person who damaged the painting.'

Daniel fished the two keys he'd taken from Anstis out of his pocket and put them on Beckett's desk. 'These belong to one of your attendants. That's how Anstis got in.'

'What about the damage to the painting?' asked Abigail. 'Is there no way to recover it?'

'It was so seriously damaged, I have my doubts about that. But restorers can do wonderful things. Fortunately, the canvas was only slashed top to bottom, not side to side as well. I'll ask the restorers to look at it and give a report.'

'In the meantime, we've decided to take positive action to try and restore the gallery's image, move away from the murders.'

'Oh? How?' asked Abigail.

'When William Turner died in 1851, he bequeathed the entire contents of his studio to the National Gallery. There were a great many finished paintings, far too many for us to show at the same time. In fact, there were 300 oil paintings, 30,000 sketches and watercolours, and 300 sketchbooks.'

'My God!' exclaimed Abigail. 'You'd need a Turner Gallery on its own to show all of them.'

'Exactly,' said Beckett. 'Fortunately, Turner stipulated in his will that two of his paintings – *Dido Building Carthage* and *Sun Rising Through Vapour* – be displayed alongside two works by Claude: *Landscape with the Marriage of Isaac and Rebecca* and *Seaport with the Embarkation of the Queen of Sheba*.'

'Claude?' asked Daniel.

'Claude Lorrain, a French painter who died in 1682 at the advanced age for those times of 80. Or possibly 81. Or even 79. No one's sure of the year of his birth. In the art world he's generally only referred to as Claude. Turner greatly admired his works, especially his landscapes.

'In view of the recent tragedies, and the resultant bad publicity for the gallery, the Board feels now is a good time to change the display, with two not-often-seen works by Turner, along with the two by Claude. We hope it will bring the public in.'

'Is that not in breach of Turner's will?' asked Abigail.

'It appears not. Turner made his first will in 1829 when he was 54; and it was that initial will that specified *Dido* and *Sun Rising Through Vapour*. He amended his will in 1848, adding all of his works to his bequest. According to our lawyers, that later amendment means we can display any two others alongside the Claudes.

'We will be hosting a special unveiling on Monday afternoon. We'd be honoured if you could attend.'

'We'd be delighted,' said Abigail.

Beckett gave a sly smile as he added: 'There is an ulterior motive in my invitation to you. You asked before about people who might have feelings of resentment towards Walter Sickert, whether personal or professional jealousy. Most of them will undoubtedly be present at the unveiling of the new Turners and the Claude. It will give you the chance to meet some of these potential suspects in person.'

'An afternoon listening to artists and art critics,' groaned Daniel as they left the National Gallery.

'It's a good opportunity to meet people who hate Sickert.'

'From what we've heard about him so far, I'd think there's no building large enough to accommodate the number of people who loathe Walter Sickert,' grumbled Daniel. 'I still think we should concentrate on our hunt for the butcher, Joe Wallace.'

'And the rich toff that Kate Branson spoke about?'

'Heppenstall,' said Daniel. 'It's got to be him.'

'I agree we have evidence linking the butcher, but Heppenstall is still speculation. He's a rich man who has a good reason for hating Sickert.'

'And he may have killed his wife.' Daniel looked thoughtful, then he said: 'I think it might be a good idea to shake Mr Heppenstall up a bit.'

'Upset him?'

'In a subtle way,' said Daniel. 'Just enough to see if we can provoke a reaction, watch how he behaves.'

'When? Now?'

'No. Let's wait until Abberline has joined us. He was always good at reading people. And his name still carries weight. Let's see how Heppenstall reacts when he realises that the scourge of the original Ripper is on his tail.'

'What about Henry Nichols?' asked Abigail. 'We haven't checked him out since that first difficult encounter with him.'

'I'm not sure if we can consider him as a suspect,' said Daniel. 'He's neither rich, nor involved in the butchery trade.'

'Yes, but he could be involved in some way. He's certainly angry enough and determined to get vengeance on Sickert.'

'Yes, that's true,' said Daniel. 'We'll look into him.'

As they approached their house, they saw a horse and police van parked outside it and a large, bulky man putting something through their letter box.

'Sergeant Cribbens!' exclaimed Daniel. 'Sergeant!' he called out.

'Mr Wilson. Miss Fenton!' beamed the sergeant. 'I was just leaving a note from Inspector Feather, but it's even better you're here. There's another body and he wants you to take a look at it with him.'

'Another woman?'

'No, this one's the butcher he's been looking for. Joe Wallace.'

'Dead?'

Cribbens nodded as they climbed into the police van. 'It looks like he cut his own throat. At least, a cut-throat razor was found beside his body. Admission of guilt, do you reckon? He knew he was being looked for and he decided to top himself.'

'Where's the body?' asked Daniel as the van rolled along the cobbled road.

'Seven Dials.'

Daniel looked at the sergeant, puzzled. 'Seven Dials in Covent Garden?'

'That's the one,' nodded Cribbens. 'The inspector's with the body now. He was hoping you might be in. I get the idea he thinks it's odd.'

'It certainly is!' said Daniel. 'A man comes all the way from Whitechapel to Seven Dials to commit suicide? And he brings a razor with him to do the job? If he's going to kill himself, surely he'd do it nearer home? When was the body found?'

'About an hour ago, but the inspector reckons he was killed much longer ago than that. It was in a pub privy. The door to the privy had been tied up to stop it being used. That often happens when a privy gets blocked. This morning some bloke wanted to use it urgently, so he kicked the door in and found Wallace's body inside.'

'Have the family been informed?'

'The inspector sent a carriage to Whitechapel to tell his wife. She might already be there now. They went to get her not long before I was sent to find you.'

'Seven Dials,' sighed Daniel.

'What's Seven Dials?' asked Abigail.

'Of course, you've never had cause to go there,' said Daniel. 'Fortunately.'

'Indeed, miss,' contributed Cribbens. 'It's one of the worst rookeries in London.'

Abigail looked towards Daniel for a translation.

'A slum area where the buildings are so crammed together

you can travel through it without once stepping on the ground. In and out of upstairs windows and over roofs. It's inhabited by criminal gangs and the poor people they live off, and there's little the police can do about it because it's too dangerous for the police to venture into it, unless they're in force. And when that happens, the criminals simply disappear into the surroundings.'

'So if Joe Wallace was there, it suggests he was meeting with some criminal,' said Abigail.

'Which still doesn't make sense,' said Daniel. 'Criminals are very territorial. Whitechapel criminals usually stay in the East End. It's where they know they're safe. It can be dangerous to trespass in another gang's area.' He looked out of the window. 'Here we are. I'm guessing we'll have to walk from here.'

'As you say, sir,' said Cribbens. 'The streets and lanes are too tight to get a carriage down them.'

He opened the door and Daniel and Abigail disembarked with the sergeant and followed him through narrow twisting cobbled lanes with open sewers at each side. The stench of urine and human faeces was overpowering.

'My God!' said Abigail recoiling. 'I thought the tanneries of Egypt were bad, but this is even worse.'

The presence of the police had brought out some locals as onlookers, keen to find out what was going on. Abigail noticed that most of the people milling around were women and children.

'I assume the men disappeared when the police arrived,' she said to Daniel.

Daniel nodded. 'It's a tradition round here. A large police presence means questions being asked. The men are here, but out of sight.'

Sergeant Cribbens stopped by a pub with a faded sign outside, which identified it as The Flower Pot. They followed him down a narrow alley that ran beside the pub. Inspector Feather was standing beside a privy talking to a woman who appeared to be in her forties, although as they approached they realised she was much younger, just in her twenties. The woman was angry and was jabbing her finger at Feather's face. 'I tell you, that's not his!' she stormed.

Feather stepped back from her to greet Daniel and Abigail.

'You were in,' he said. 'Thank heavens for that. This is Lilly Wallace, Joe's wife.'

'His widow, now!' snapped the young woman. She glared at Daniel and Abigail. 'Who are you?'

'Daniel Wilson and Miss Abigail Fenton,' said Daniel. 'We're private investigators hired by the National Gallery to look into recent events there.'

'You're the two who've been chasing Joe!' said the woman accusingly, and now she turned her anger on them. 'You drove him to this!' Then suddenly she subsided and muttered: 'Or you would've, if he'd topped himself. But I don't believe it. For one thing, that razor ain't his.'

'You're sure?'

'Of course I'm sure. He never needed one. He was a butcher. He used a knife to shave. He said if it could shave bristles off a pig, it could get them off his chin.'

They were interrupted by the door of the privy opening and an elderly doctor stepping out, carrying his doctor's bag.

'You can have him now, Inspector,' he said to Feather. He doffed his hat towards Lily Wallace. 'My condolences, Mrs Wallace,' he said.

'He didn't do it!' burst out Lily. 'He wouldn't have killed himself and left me and the kids. Someone did him.'

'When was the time of death, Doctor?' asked Feather.

'At least a day ago, as far as I can make out, from the advanced state of rigor mortis.'

'Yeh, that was when I last saw him,' said Lily. 'He said he was going up west.' She looked accusingly at Feather. 'That was right after you called, looking for him.'

'So he was in the house?' said Feather.

'Yes, hiding. Scared. What did you expect me to do, peach on him?'

'One other thing,' said the doctor. 'There's a wound on the back of his head. He might have hit his head against something when he fell, or . . .'

'Someone bashed him!' said Lily firmly. 'I told you. Someone did this to him.'

'I'll leave you now, Inspector, and examine the body formally later at the Yard,' said the doctor, and with that he departed.

'Why was Joe going up west?' Daniel asked Lily.

'He was going to see some rich bloke. He said it was this bloke's fault the police were looking for him and he was going to get it sorted.'

'Is that what he said? It was this rich bloke's fault?'

'Well, not in so many words. But this rich bloke had called for him twice in a carriage. Joe said it was to do private work for him, but I don't know what sort of private work it was. Joe said it was butchery work.'

Feather exchanged looks with Daniel and Abigail, then said to Lily: 'Mrs Wallace, this is no place to talk. Would you mind coming to Scotland Yard with me?'

'Yes I would!' she snapped at him. 'I ain't going to no Scotland Yard. I've got the kids waiting for me at home. They're with a neighbour.'

'In that case, can we drive you to Whitechapel and we'll talk there?'

She hesitated, uncertain. Then nodded towards the privy. 'What about Joe? We can't leave him there.'

'I'll have Joe sent to Scotland Yard. I'm afraid we'll need to examine his body, but we'll help you make arrangements for his funeral.'

'Funeral?' she barked angrily. 'It'll be a pauper's funeral.'

'Would you mind if I examined the scene?' Daniel asked.

'That's what I was hoping you'd say,' said Feather, relieved. 'That's why I sent for you.'

'While you're doing that, perhaps Mrs Wallace wouldn't mind if I accompanied you to Whitechapel, Inspector,' said Abigail. 'It would save her the distress of having to undergo further questioning again later.'

Lily Wallace nodded. 'Yeh,' she said. 'It won't seem so bad if I arrive home and there's another woman with me, instead of just the police.'

Feather turned to Sergeant Cribbens and said: 'I'll let you take Mr Wilson back to the Yard, Sergeant. Miss Fenton and I will join you there after we've seen Mrs Wallace home.' To Daniel, he said: 'I left the razor where it was. Can you bring it with you when you're ready?'

With that, Feather and Abigail walked with Lily Wallace to the carriage that had brought her from Whitechapel, and Daniel and Sergeant Cribbens walked into the privy.

Daniel's detailed examination of the body and the crime

scene confirmed the doctor's conclusion: that Joe Wallace had been struck on the back of the head. Daniel took out his magnifying glass and studied the open razor that lay beside the body. As he'd hoped, there were the impressions of fingerprints in the blood on the handle.

'You don't reckon he did it, do you, Mr Wilson?' remarked Cribbens.

'It seems unlikely. Why would a man travel all the way from Whitechapel to Seven Dials to cut his own throat? And do it with a razor that wasn't his, according to his wife?' Very carefully he laid a handkerchief down beside the bloody razor, then took a pair of tweezers from his pocket and lifted the razor, laid it on the handkerchief and wrapped it carefully. 'If I'm right, these fingerprints will tell us whether Wallace killed himself or someone else did it.'

'I've heard the chief superintendent talk about this fingerprints business,' said Cribbens doubtfully. 'He don't believe in them.'

'Then we're lucky the chief superintendent isn't here,' grinned Daniel.

CHAPTER TWENTY-FIVE

As the carriage rattled over the cobbles, John Feather questioned Lily Wallace while Abigail kept notes of her answers in her notebook.

'You said that Joe was going to see some rich man,' said Feather. 'How did you know he was rich?'

'Because it had to be the same bloke who picked Joe up a couple of times. He had a carriage, a proper one, real money.'

'Do you know who this man was?'

'No. I never met him, just saw the carriage he was in. He used to park at the end of the street when he wanted Joe for a private job. That's what Joe called it. Private work.'

'Butchering for him?'

She nodded.

'How do you know it was a man in the carriage? It could have been a woman?'

She gave a harsh laugh. 'That's how I know. I thought he

233

might be seeing some woman, so after the first time he went out, I followed him. The door of the carriage opened and I heard the bloke talk to Joe.'

'What about?'

'Just, "get in". But that's how I knew it was a bloke.'

'What sort of voice did he have?'

'Well, like I said, I didn't hear him say much. But it was a posh voice. With that and the carriage, that's how I knew he must be rich.'

'How old did this man sound? Young? Old?'

'I couldn't tell, not from just two words.'

'And Joe never told you what sort of butchering work he was doing for this man?'

She shook her head.

'How many times did this man pick Joe up?'

'Twice. Like I say, it was the second time I went out after him.'

'Can you remember the dates?'

'I'm not much good with dates,' she admitted. 'To be honest, every day's pretty much the same as the others, except for Christmas and birthdays.'

'Which days did the man come to collect him? Two days ago? Three? Last week?'

She frowned, thinking hard.

'The last time he went out with this bloke was Wednesday night. The 17th. And the time before was Sunday 14th.'

Abigail made a note of the days, which she underlined: Sunday 14th February; Wednesday 17th February. The two bodies had been discovered outside the National Gallery in the early hours of Monday 15th and Thursday 18th.

* * *

Daniel and Sergeant Cribbens arrived back at Scotland Yard and had the body of Joe Wallace taken from the police van and despatched to the mortuary. They then went to Inspector Feather's office and found Feather and Abigail already there.

'It was him,' said Abigail. 'Joe Wallace, working with this mysterious rich man.' She looked at her notes. 'Joe went out with him on the night of Sunday 14th February to do some private butchery work, as he told his wife. The body of Anne-Marie was found outside the National Gallery the following morning.

'Joe went out with this same man again in his carriage on the night of Wednesday 17th, and Kate Branson's body was found the next morning.'

'So, did he kill himself, or did someone do the job for him?' asked Feather.

'If he decided to kill himself, why go all the way to Seven Dials to do it?' asked Daniel. 'My guess is he went there to meet someone, and they killed him.' Daniel produced the razor wrapped in his handkerchief. 'This will tell us. There's a perfect set of fingerprints in the blood on the handle. If they don't belong to Joe Wallace, someone killed him. Which is what I'm pretty certain happened. And his wife feels the same.'

'The chief superintendent doesn't believe in this fingerprint business,' Feather reminded him.

'John, this is scientific evidence,' stressed Daniel.

'To his mind it's all hogwash.'

'Did anyone see Wallace at Seven Dials, before he died?' asked Daniel.

'We got the local bobbies asking questions. One old woman offered them information in exchange for gin.'

'Doesn't sound as if it would be very authentic,' commented Abigail.

'Everything has to be taken with a pinch of salt,' agreed Feather. 'But she has a pitch selling matches on the corner not too far away from it, so she could see who went in and out. She's a people-watcher.'

'Did she see him come out?'

'No. But over an hour later she saw this toff, as she called him, go in. The toff came out again about a quarter of an hour later and went off.'

'That's our man!' exclaimed Daniel. 'Did she describe him?'

'No. She said he had a long coat on, and a white scarf wrapped round the lower part of his face, and he was wearing a top hat. So, it's a good description of his clothes, but not of him. We still don't know what he looks like or whether he's young or old.'

'The privy's out the back of the pub so he must have taken Joe out the back door.' He looked at Feather. 'Have you talked to the barman at the pub?'

'Not yet,' said Feather. 'I was going to bring him in once I'd reported everything to the chief superintendent, in case he wanted to handle the questioning. He's very hands on with this case because of the pressure he's under from the top.'

The door opened and they all turned to look at Chief Superintendent Armstrong. He looked at Daniel and Abigail with a scowl.

'What are you two doing here?' he demanded.

'We had some information we wanted to share with Inspector Feather.'

'What information?'

'About the National Gallery murders.'

Armstrong's eyes narrowed suspiciously, then he turned to Feather. 'Someone said you've got the man who did them.'

'Yes, sir,' said Feather. 'Joe Wallace. A butcher from Whitechapel.'

'I hear he's dead. Killed himself. Cut his throat.'

'Yes, sir. But we're not sure if he did it, or if he was murdered.'

'Who'd want to murder him?' demanded Armstrong.

'His accomplice,' said Daniel.

'What accomplice?'

Daniel gestured to Feather to reply. 'It would seem that this Joe Wallace was working with someone else, a rich man. This fits with what we've been told about a rich man who used to pick up Kate Branson in his carriage. Apparently, Wallace met with this rich man at the pub in Seven Dials shortly before he died. There's suspicion that this rich man killed Wallace to silence him.'

Armstrong held up his hand to stop him.

'No,' he said firmly. 'Let's not confuse the issue. You've got evidence to bear out the idea that this Wallace killed the women?'

'He may not have killed them,' said Abigail. 'Although we're fairly sure he did the butchery.'

Armstrong shook his head. 'Wallace did it. Now he's topped himself. He must have felt the law was closing in on him.' He looked at Feather. 'Is that right, Inspector? I understand you've been making enquiries about him.'

'Yes, sir. That's correct.'

'That's it, then. Good, dogged police work. Case closed. I can tell the commissioner we've solved it.'

'You're forgetting about the rich man,' said Abigail. 'His accomplice. Joe didn't have a van, so they must have used his carriage to pick up the women and move their bodies about.'

Armstrong shook his head.

'No,' he said, even more firmly than before. 'If this rich man, as you call him, was Wallace's accomplice, Wallace might have gone to meet him to ask for help. Money to get him out of the country, or something. The bloke turned him down. For Wallace that was the last straw. He'd done the killings. He butchered the women and dumped them. Now, as the net closed in on him, he killed himself. That's all we need.'

It was almost one o' clock when Daniel and Abigail arrived at the National Gallery to inform Stanford Beckett of the death of Joe Wallace, and the decision by Chief Superintendent Armstrong to declare the case closed.

'So this Wallace did the murders?' said Beckett.

'The chief superintendent seems to think so, but we're not so sure,' Daniel told him. 'We believe Wallace was working with someone else, a mystery rich man. Wallace may well have carried out the butchery on the victims, but they may have been dead already, killed by this other man.'

'But the main thing is that Walter is exonerated,' said Beckett.

'Indeed,' said Daniel. 'We shall go and see Mrs Sickert later today and tell her.' He sighed. 'And now we have to meet Mr Abberline and tell him that the investigation is officially ended. At least, we assume that's what Mrs Sickert will decide when we tell her the news. We're fairly sure that Chief Superintendent Armstrong is currently producing a press release that will go out to the newspapers telling the public that the reign of terror of the New Ripper is over and the killer is dead.'

As Abigail and Daniel left Beckett's office, Abigail noticed the grim expression on Daniel's face. 'You're not happy with the decision.'

'No, I'm not,' said Daniel. 'Are you?'

'No,' said Abigail. 'But I can't see what we can do to change it. If the chief superintendent declares the case closed and that Wallace was the killer, that's it. No one's going to pay us to carry on the investigation.'

'No, but I can't just leave it as easily as that. To satisfy us, I need to talk to the barman at The Flower Pot. He must have seen this rich man.' He turned to Abigail and said: 'Can you wait here in case Fred turns up early while I go to Seven Dials? I won't be long, but I need to see if the barman knows anything.'

'If he does, he won't talk,' warned Abigail. 'That's the impression I get.'

'And you're right,' admitted Daniel ruefully. 'But I just need to go there for my own satisfaction.

Chief Superintendent Armstrong looked at the words he'd written. He was trying to make sure his press release had impact. The journalists would rewrite it to suit their own particular readers, he knew that, but he wanted them to be excited by it. And, most importantly, to be aware that the case had been solved as a result of meticulous work by Scotland Yard's detectives under the personal direction of Chief Superintendent Armstrong. London was safe again. The killer was dead by his own hand, despatching himself when he became aware that Scotland Yard were closing in on him. But as he read the piece, doubt nagged at him. Who was this mysterious rich man that Wilson and Fenton had mentioned? Wallace's accomplice, they'd said. And they insisted this rich man had actually killed Wallace, cut his throat to silence him. Was that possible? If so, this mystery man was still at large. Which meant that danger still stalked the streets.

He reread his words again, and gave an inward groan. These were the words of a politician doing his best to assure the public that everything was all right and they were safe again. Yes, it was a sad fact that a man in his position had to be part-politician to deal with the press, the commissioner, the home secretary and Uncle Tom Cobbley and all. But first and foremost he was a policeman. His job was to keep London safe by *solving* crimes, not by pretending they'd been solved because some miscreant had killed himself. Or, worse, been murdered. If another murder happened, another woman butchered like the previous two, there'd be an outcry, claims of 'foul' against him for claiming the case was solved.

With a sigh of resignation he crumpled the piece of paper and dropped it in his waste basket. Then he got up and walked along to Inspector Feather's office, coughing as he went in as a result of the thick acrid smoke from Sergeant Cribben's infernal pipe.

'I've changed my mind, Inspector,' he announced as Feather looked enquiringly at him. 'Send a note to Wilson and Fenton. Tell them to come in. Just in case there is anything in this business of this mystery rich man.'

'Yes, sir,' said Feather, reaching for a piece of paper and pencil. 'When do you want them to come in?'

'Today,' said Armstrong. 'Tell them we'll be here all day.'

'We, sir?'

'You're included, Inspector. You seem to have a rapport with them.' He turned to Cribbens. 'You're not included, Sergeant. It's bad enough having to endure the foul fog you create in here, I don't want it contaminating my office.'

The barman at The Flower Pot regarded Daniel suspiciously as he entered the pub and came to the bar. He knows I'm a copper, thought Daniel. Public or private doesn't matter, the crooks recognise us straight away.

'Remember me?' asked Daniel. 'I was here this morning when the body was discovered in your privy.'

'Nothing to do with me,' grunted the man. 'I never saw the bloke before.'

'That's strange,' said Daniel, 'because we spoke to someone who said the dead man was in your pub for quite a while on his own before the man he was due to meet turned up. A rich toff, he was described as.'

The barman shook his head. 'I never saw him. Whoever told you they was in here was seeing things. I never saw either of 'em.' He looked at Daniel with suspicious hostility and demanded: 'Anyway, who are you? You're not a regular copper.'

'Private investigator, hired to find Joe Wallace. The dead man in your privy.'

'Well, you found him.'

'And the rich toff he was meeting in here yesterday.'

The barman glared angrily at Daniel.

'You ain't the police, so you've got no power here. I've told you, I didn't see anything and that's an end to it.'

Daniel met the man's glare with a cool look of his own.

'As I see it, you've got a choice. You can talk to me, or you can be hauled in to Scotland Yard and they can put you through the wringer. I can make that happen. I used to be a detective sergeant with the Yard and we still work together, which is why they brought me in this morning.'

The man produced a leaded stick from beneath the counter, which he slammed down menacingly on the bar.

'And you've also got a choice,' he said. 'You can walk out or be carried out with a broken head. And no one's taking me to Scotland Yard.'

Daniel looked at the leaded stick, unimpressed.

'You're making a big mistake,' he said calmly. 'You're looking at a charge of being an accessory to murder. That's a hanging matter. Now whatever this rich bloke's paying you isn't enough to stop that happening.' He reached into his pocket and took out one of his business cards, which he laid on the bar. 'If you change your mind, get in touch. The name's Wilson. I'll be at the National Gallery for the next hour. That address is where you can get hold of me if I'm not there. If I'm out, leave a note and I'll come back. I'll give you till four o'clock today to think about it, and then I tip the wink to the boys at Scotland Yard. It's up to you.'

With that, Daniel left, aware of the barman's eyes burning into his back. Yes, Scotland Yard had been an empty threat now that Armstrong had decided the case was closed; but Daniel hoped the barman wouldn't know that. It now depended on how quickly the chief superintendent issued his statement to the press. Usually, the earliest the statement would appear in the press would be first thing tomorrow morning, but if Armstrong worked fast, it might even be in tonight's late editions. He

242

could only hope the barman made his mind up in the next few hours, before the late editions came out.

When Daniel returned to the National Gallery, Abigail was outside the main entrance, waiting for Abberline.

'How did you get on in Seven Dials?' she asked.

'Not well,' he admitted. 'I tried a bluff on the barman of the pub in the hope it might persuade him to tell us about the rich man.'

'Did it work?'

'I don't know. We'll find out in the next couple of hours.'

'Here's Fred,' said Abigail.

Daniel turned and saw Abberline arriving.

'Here I am,' he said. 'What's our first move?'

'Our first move is to sit on this wall while we tell you it looks as if the investigation is at an end,' said Daniel ruefully.

He directed Abberline to the nearby decorated concrete wall that edged the entrance area. They sat, and Abberline regarded them with puzzled eyes. 'At an end?' he asked.

Daniel told him about Armstrong's decision to declare the case closed. 'The butcher we told you about, Joe Wallace, was found dead this morning. His throat had been cut and a bloody razor was found beside the body.'

'The way you say that suggests you don't think it was suicide.'

'No, I don't – we believe he was murdered by his accomplice. But all the evidence pointed to Wallace having been involved in the murders, and the butchering of the bodies. So, as far as Armstrong is concerned, that's the end of it. Wallace was the guilty party and he killed himself when he realised the net was closing in on him.'

'Have you told your client yet? Mrs Sickert?'

'No, but we're fairly sure she'll say that's the end of it. All she wanted was for her husband to be proved innocent of these latest killings. Whatever statement Armstrong puts out will do that.'

Abberline gave a sigh.

'So, I've had a wasted journey.'

'We'll make sure you're paid for today,' said Daniel.

Abberline shook his head.

'Forget it. I haven't done anything.' He got up. 'I think I'll have a look around the shops, get something for Emma. We don't get up to town much. And since I'm here, perhaps you can give me my old notebooks back. I don't trust the post. Too many things disappear.'

'They're at home,' said Abigail. 'We didn't expect this kind of news. We're not far away. Come home with us and we'll have some tea and cake.'

'What sort of cake?'

'Fruit cake,' said Abigail.

Abberline's eyes lit up. 'I love fruit cake.'

Abigail gestured towards the entrance to the gallery. 'Do you want to look around the gallery, as you're here?'

'No,' said Abberline. 'If it's a choice between art and fruit cake, I'll take fruit cake every time.'

Abberline elected to walk to Camden Town rather than take a bus. 'I've had enough of buses today to last me,' he said. 'And I still like a good walk. It's the best way to see a city.'

'It is,' agreed Daniel.

Their journey home took them longer than usual because Abberline was keen to stop at different shops in Charing Cross

Road, and then Tottenham Court Road. 'We don't have shops like these in Clapham,' he explained.

Daniel and Abigail were happy to humour him in his window-shopping. They both felt deflated at having the case ended, for them, unsatisfactorily. The killer, the 'rich toff', was still out there.

When they arrived home, they found a plain buff envelope on their doormat.

'That could be from the barman at The Feather Pot,' said Daniel eagerly.

'No, this is John Feather's handwriting,' said Abigail as she picked it up. She opened it and read the note inside, and a smile lit up her face. 'It looks like Chief Superintendent Armstrong has had second thoughts. The case isn't closed, after all. We're summoned to a meeting with him to discuss the continuation of the investigation.'

Daniel and Abberline exchanged puzzled and suspicious looks.

'What's his game?' asked Abberline warily. 'Armstrong never does anything except in self-interest.'

'Perhaps there's been another murder?' suggested Daniel.

'We'll soon find out,' said Abigail, putting the letter in her handbag. 'You'll come with us to Scotland Yard, won't you, Mr Abberline? It looks as if we're still on the case, and it will be good for you to hear what the chief superintendent has to say.'

'No thank you,' said Abberline, tight-lipped. 'I never liked the man, and he never liked me. I've no interest in sitting listening to him praising himself. I'm a citizen, now, not one of his employees, so I'll pass.' Then he smiled at them as he added: 'But I'll meet you afterwards and you can tell me what he says, and what happened at this meeting, and where we stand. Is Freddy's still open?'

'It is,' said Daniel.

'Then that's where you'll find me. First, I'll take a wander round the shops and see what I can get for Emma. Then I'll see you at Freddy's.'

CHAPTER TWENTY-SIX

The barman from The Flower Pot slipped the note through the letter box at the address he'd been given. 'But no personal visits,' he'd been warned. 'Leave a note if you have information. I'll get in touch.'

This ought to be worth something, the barman thought as he walked away. All he had to do if this Wilson bloke carried out his threat and brought the Yard in was hold his nerve. Keep denying everything. He hadn't survived in Seven Dials all these years by grassing to the law about anyone, and he wasn't going to start now.

Daniel and Abigail were still unsure of the purpose behind their being invited to Scotland Yard, particularly because the chief superintendent's manner was not exactly welcoming. He sat behind his desk, glowering unhappily at them. John Feather, sitting at one side of the desk, kept his facial expression bland and non-committal. Something's happened to force Armstrong to change his mind, but he's not happy about it, realised Daniel.

'May I ask, Chief Superintendent, what prompted you to change your mind?'

'Who said I'd changed my mind?' demanded Armstrong defensively. 'It's just that since then I've discussed the case with Inspector Feather, and he told me that Lily Wallace mentioned some rich man who collected Joe Wallace in a carriage and took him out on the two nights that the women were killed.'

'That's right,' said Abigail. 'I was with the inspector when she said it.'

'Have you got any idea who this rich man is?' asked Armstrong.

Daniel and Abigail exchanged wary glances, then Daniel said: 'We suspect it might be a man called Edmund Heppenstall.'

Armstrong frowned.

'Who's Edmund Heppenstall?'

'A very important surgeon, and someone with a deep hatred of Walter Sickert.'

'Why?'

Daniel and Abigail told the chief superintendent the background they'd discovered, Catherine Heppenstall's affair with Sickert and her subsequent disappearance, and their suspicion that Heppenstall may have killed his wife, at which Armstrong snorted contemptuously: 'Rubbish! Men of that social standing don't kill their wives.'

'I'm afraid they do,' said Daniel. 'And, because of their social standing, most of them get away with it. We were about to talk to Mr Heppenstall before you told us the case was closed.'

'If you talk to this Heppenstall, it's absolutely without my permission,' said Armstrong firmly. Then he asked: 'Have you got any other suspects for this supposed rich man?'

'Not at the moment. However, we have brought Fred Abberline in to help us.'

'Abberline!!' exploded Armstrong. 'Why?'

'Because he was always a good detective, and his knowledge of Whitechapel and the original Ripper killings is second to none. And we're convinced they're connected. Joe Wallace was a child during the original Ripper killings, and we think it's likely he was related to one of the victims. The word in Whitechapel is still that Sickert was involved in the original killings, along with Sir William Gull and Prince Albert Victor . . .'

'It may be the word in Whitechapel, but I'll have no such things said in here!' shouted Armstrong, banging his desk. 'Nor to anyone else. You're talking rumour and gossip intended to smear the Queen! I won't have it!'

'I'm just repeating what they say in Whitechapel. We heard it again from someone else who was a child of one of the Ripper's victims, and Joe Wallace said it when he attacked me.'

'I don't care!' raged Armstrong. 'I won't have that kind of treasonous muck repeated.'

'It's why Joe Wallace did what he did to those women,' said Daniel.

'That's speculation!' said Armstrong hotly.

Daniel shrugged. 'Very well,' he said resignedly. 'We'll concentrate our efforts into trying to find out who this mystery rich man is.'

'With Inspector Feather,' said Armstrong sternly. 'I want everything you find out shared with us at Scotland Yard.'

Daniel and Abigail nodded. 'Everything we find out, we'll share,' said Daniel. 'One thing we'd like is your permission to check the razor that was found by Joe Wallace's body for fingerprints,' said Daniel.

'Fingerprints?' said Armstrong scornfully. 'Stuff and nonsense.'

'It can't do any harm,' persisted Daniel. 'And it will at least confirm that Wallace didn't kill himself.'

Armstrong fell silent and they could see he was racked with indecision. Finally, he said reluctantly: 'If you want to waste your time on it.' He looked at Feather. 'Where is this razor?'

'I've got it,' said Daniel.

Armstrong whirled round to glare at him.

'You?'

'I picked it up at the scene of the crime,' said Daniel. 'I brought it to give to Inspector Feather, but after you said the case was ended, I forgot to hand it over.' He tapped his inside pocket. 'I brought it with me now. I'd like to take it to Dr Snow.'

'Dr Snow!' said Armstrong, his voice once again heavy with scorn. 'It's all just poppycock, all this so-called science. Mumbo jumbo. Wasting time and money that could be spent on proper policing. Men on the beat.'

'Nevertheless, I'd like your permission to have Dr Snow examine the fingerprints on the razor and compare them with Joe Wallace's.'

Armstrong looked sour, but said grudgingly: 'I've already said you can.'

'Thank you.'

'And everything on this investigation goes through us,' stressed Armstrong.

'In that case I think you ought to pull in the barman at The Flower Pot pub where Joe Wallace's body was found,' said Daniel. 'Wallace was in that pub yesterday with this rich man.'

Armstrong looked aggressively at Feather. 'You didn't tell me that.'

'With respect, sir, I was going to, but you'd declared the case closed with Wallace dead.'

'Well do it,' said Armstrong. 'Bring him in.' He turned back to Daniel and Abigail and said sternly: 'And Scotland Yard are in charge of this case. Is that clear?'

'Absolutely,' said Daniel. He looked at Abigail, who nodded. 'Absolutely,' she echoed.

Abberline was waiting for them in Freddy's, a cup of coffee before him on the table, along with one of his old notebooks.

'How did you get on?' he asked as Daniel and Abigail sat down.

They filled him in on their meeting.

'So what's Armstrong after?' asked Abberline.

'The credit when we solve the case,' said Abigail.

'And you're all right with that?'

'So long as the man who killed those women and Edwin O'Tool is brought to justice, we're content,' she told him.

Abberline nodded, then tapped the open notebook in front of him. 'I've been thinking about this butcher, Joe Wallace, and I went back to my old notes after you said about other women who might have been victims of the original Ripper, and any children they might have had – especially any who might have gone into the butchery trade.'

'Yes, we saw one that made us think,' said Abigail. 'A woman who lived at The Shambles, which is an old name for a butcher's.'

'Barbara Willen,' nodded Abberline. 'She was never included in the official list of Ripper's victims, but the locals all believed she should have been. I checked out The Shambles at the time. It's where they used to prepare the offal. Her husband – actually, her common-law-husband – worked there. His name was Ben Wallace.'

'As in Joe Wallace?' asked Daniel eagerly.

Abberline nodded. 'Right. He was Joe's father.'

'And Ben Wallace was a butcher?'

'More of a butcher's labourer, as I recall,' said Abberline. 'He was a drinker. When he had taken drink he wouldn't have been the safest person to be wielding a sharp knife, so he got given the messy jobs. Washing the heads and the intestines. But it's quite likely that Joe followed his dad into the business.'

'It's a pity we didn't get hold of him before he went in search of his mystery accomplice the other day, who obviously killed him,' sighed Daniel.

'You sure he didn't kill himself?'

'Certain,' said Daniel. He tapped his pocket where he still had the razor. 'Joe's wife, Lily, said this razor that was used wasn't Joe's. The razor's got fingerprints on it in the blood. If we check those with Wallace's fingerprints and they're different, then we know he didn't kill himself.' He frowned. 'There are three men we're looking for: this mystery rich man who quite possibly killed Joe, the driver of the carriage, and whoever was with Joe when he attacked me.'

'Perhaps the man who was with Joe when he attacked you was this rich man? Or the carriage driver?' suggested Abigail.

'Maybe,' said Daniel. 'But it could have been a pal of Wallace's from Whitechapel.' He nodded towards Abberline's half-empty cup of coffee. 'When you've finished that I suggest we go and see Dr Snow at Scotland Yard's new science department.'

'Science department?' said Abberline, bemused. 'My word, there have been changes. Don't tell me that Armstrong's bringing in modern methods.'

'No, it's happened in spite of Armstrong, not because of him,' said Daniel. 'He doesn't approve. But he's given us permission to take the razor in to be examined. So I suggest we go and do just that before he changes his mind.' He regarded Abberline cautiously. 'If you're all right with that? Coming in with us, I mean.'

'Armstrong knows I'm here?'

'He does.'

'How did he react?'

Daniel gave a wry smile and looked at Abigail, who said, 'Let's just say he didn't bar you. Which makes a change. Daniel and I keep being barred from Scotland Yard on his instructions.'

Abberline picked up his cup and drained the rest of his coffee. 'Right,' he said. 'Let's go and see this Dr Snow.'

Dr Snow examined the bloody handle of the razor under his microscope.

'Fascinating!' he said. 'I see what you mean about the patterns of the fingerprints. They're very clear.'

'The whole idea behind fingerprints is that for every one of us the skin at the tips of our fingers and thumbs is raised just a bit,' said Daniel. 'It's called the friction ridge, and it makes patterns: loops, whorls and arches of skin. And everyone's prints are unique to them, so that no two people have exactly the same patterns in their prints.'

'I've read about them, but I've never had the chance to examine any up close before,' said Snow. He gave a rueful sigh. 'Sadly, no one has brought anything like this to me to look at.'

'They will, in time,' said Daniel. He produced a sheet of paper on which were small round prints in black ink. 'I went to the mortuary and got impressions made of Joe Wallace's fingertips and thumbs so we could compare them.'

Snow put the sheet of paper beneath a second microscope and looked at the patterns.

'They're different,' he said.

'May I have a look?' asked Abberline.

Dr Snow stepped back and Abberline studied the imprints in the blood on the razor handle and those on the sheet of paper. 'Fascinating!' he said.

Abberline then stepped aside to allow Abigail to study the images, followed by Daniel.

'This could catch on,' said Abberline. 'But you'd need a vast collection of fingerprints if you want to use this to actually catch criminals.'

'I'm sure that will come,' said Daniel. 'But, for the moment, it's enough to show that someone else other than Joe Wallace wielded this razor.'

The door opened and the burly figure of Chief Superintendent Armstrong appeared. He stopped short when he saw Abberline.

'Abberline,' he grunted.

'Armstrong,' responded Abberline curtly.

'You must take a look at this, Chief Superintendent,' said

Dr Snow enthusiastically. 'The fingerprints on the razor are completely different to those of the deceased, Mr Wallace.'

Armstrong wavered, then said: 'I'll look later. I came down here because the mortuary attendant reported that you'd been in and put ink on the fingers of the dead man.'

'I did,' said Daniel. 'If you remember, you gave me permission to investigate the fingerprints on the razor. This test proved conclusively that Wallace did not commit suicide. He was murdered.'

'By this rich man?' glowered Armstrong.

'That's where the evidence seems to be taking us,' said Daniel.

Armstrong hesitated, then he said: 'You tell us everything you find out. *Everything*. Is that understood?'

With that he left the laboratory.

'He's quite rude, isn't he?' commented Dr Snow, showing his annoyance.

'Trust me, that's him in a good mood,' said Abberline.

The chief superintendent entered Inspector Feather's office and without preamble burst out: 'Lily Wallace saw the carriage this rich bloke picked her husband up in, didn't she?'

'Yes, sir,' said Feather.

'Did she describe it?'

'No, sir. But then, it was dark when he was picked up, and I didn't notice a street lamp at the end of the street where she lives.'

'Bring her in,' said Armstrong. 'I want to know everything about this carriage, marks on it, did it have curtains, everything there is. We find this carriage, we find this mysterious rich man, and our killer.'

'What about bringing in the barman from The Flower Pot?' asked Feather. 'Which do you want done first?'

'Lily Wallace,' said Armstrong. 'She's liable to do a flit. We know where the barman is and we can pick him up at any time.'

CHAPTER TWENTY-SEVEN

Abberline had decided to catch a train to Clapham. 'I don't usually, but at this time of day the buses take for ever,' he told them. They walked with him to Victoria Station to talk about their next course of action on the way.

'I think tomorrow we should call on Edmund Heppenstall and very subtly put the cat among the pigeons,' proposed Daniel. 'See how he reacts.'

'You don't think warning him might be counter-productive?' asked Abberline thoughtfully. 'He might not do or say anything, but start covering his tracks.'

'And we can watch him do it,' said Daniel.

'Difficult because we don't know where those tracks are,' continued Abberline. 'And the only way to do that would be to mount a 24-hour watch on him, which means we're not looking into any other possibilities.'

'What other possibilities?' asked Abigail.

'Well, for one thing, I agree that this Heppenstall character seems a strong candidate, but have you checked on his movements for the nights when the two murders were committed? Does he have alibis that can be checked?'

Abigail and Daniel stared at one another, stunned.

'My God!' said Daniel. 'That's one thing we never checked. I was so sure that Heppenstall was the toff that Kate Branson talked about.'

'He may still be,' said Abberline. 'But let's check first if he's got an alibi for the two nights.'

'The hospitals,' said Daniel. 'Helena Swanwick told Abigail that he's highly thought of as a surgeon. She might know which particular hospitals he works at.'

'I'll ask her,' said Abigail.

'Do that,' said Abberline. By now they'd arrived at Victoria. 'This is where I leave you. Shall we say ten o'clock tomorrow at the National Gallery? It'll give me a chance to meet this Stanford Beckett, now we're back on the case.'

After Abberline had left them to catch his train, Abigail could see that Daniel was in a very grim mood.

'I'm starting to wonder if I'm in the right job,' he said sourly.

'What do you mean?'

'Twice now I've messed up, and both times in front of my old boss. First, I missed the idea of checking on the families of women who might have been victim of the original Ripper, you thought of that.'

'Oh, come on, Daniel. You'd have thought of it once we started going through Abberline's notebooks.'

'Not necessarily. And my biggest blunder was not checking

if Heppenstall might have had an alibi for the nights of the murders. I was so convinced he was involved, working with Joe Wallace, that I didn't do a very basic piece of police work. And both times I messed up in front of Abberline. What must he think of me?'

Abigail put her arms around him and hugged him close.

'He's not your boss any more,' she said. 'You don't need to impress him.'

'Yes, but I don't want to show him I'm a failure.'

Abigail stepped back from him and looked at him, and he saw real anger in her face.

'How dare you!' she snapped. 'You are not a failure. You never were. For God's sake, you came out of the workhouse, completely alone in the world at twelve years old, and battled your way up to be a distinguished officer in Scotland Yard's elite detective division, and now you're applauded by all and sundry and in demand as a private detective by all the great museums.'

'But—' he began.

'There are no buts about this,' she told him firmly. 'Yes, you overlooked a couple of things, and one of them – the business of Heppenstall's alibi for when the murders took place – could be important. We'll soon find out. It could be we discover that Heppenstall *wasn't* working at any hospital on the night the two women were killed and has no alibi for when the murders were committed.'

'But he might!'

'And if so, yes, you made a mistake. *We* made a mistake. Who doesn't make mistakes? When I was studying at Cambridge, one of our lecturers said to us: the person who never made a mistake never made anything. No one gets everything right. If

I listed the mistakes I made when I was at archaeological digs in Egypt and Rome, wrongly classifying some objects, I might think I'd never work again. But we all make errors. The major thing is to learn from them, put them right, and not make the same mistake again.'

'But the business of checking Heppenstall's alibi was so elementary!'

'You think you're the only one who's made a basic mistake? I bet you Abberline made a few during his career.'

'Yes, he did,' admitted Daniel.

'And did you think any less of him because of it?'

'No. Because the ones he made were few and far between, and he always owned up to them and didn't try to pretend they were someone else's fault.'

'And the same could be said of you. And me. And everyone else who's ever achieved anything.'

Daniel fell silent, then gave a sigh and nodded. 'Thanks,' he said. 'I deserved that.'

'I'm also not going to let this business of whether Heppenstall has an alibi wait till tomorrow,' added Abigail. 'We need to find out. *You* need to find out. So we'll go to see Helena now and ask her which hospitals he works at.'

'Mr Heppenstall is in private practice, but he also works as a consultant for University College Hospital and the Middlesex,' Helena told them when they called on her. 'They call him in if there's a patient with a condition that's too much for them to deal with. And also, I believe, he goes in when there's an emergency. Usually those seem to happen at night. I remember someone telling me that the human body is at its lowest ebb

260

during the night.' She looked at them inquisitively. 'Do you suspect him of being involved in the killings? Only, as I said, I can't believe that, not from what I've heard about him.'

'No, no,' Abigail assured her. 'It's about another aspect.' Then, as an apparent afterthought, she said: 'But coming back to the killings, as you know, we're considering the idea that the person behind them may be someone Walter hurt by his actions.'

'Like the business with Catherine Heppenstall?'

'Yes. We were wondering if there were any other rumours and gossip about people who'd suffered because of . . . Walter's indiscretions.'

'That's a very tactful way to put it,' sighed Helena. 'Yes, I do know of another case. But Walter was completely innocent, despite the fact that the affair had a tragic outcome. Although there wasn't actually an affair,' she added hastily.

'What happened?' asked Daniel.

'I don't know if you recall the newspapers reporting on the death of Lady Powbry about a year ago?'

Daniel looked at Abigail, who shook her head. 'No,' she said. 'How did she die?'

'She killed herself.'

Abigail looked puzzled. 'But how did that involve Walter? You said there was no affair between them.'

'That's what's so ridiculous. She became absolutely enamoured of him, but he didn't respond. At least, not in the way she wanted.'

'Why ever not? Didn't he find her attractive enough?'

'Oh, she was attractive. Very much so. But Walter told her no.'

'Why? With no disrespect to your brother, Helena, but I can't imagine him saying no to any woman.'

'I agree, but from what I can gather at that time he had such a tangled love life it was causing him all sorts of distress, and he was sure Nellie was on the point of finding out just what was going on with him and other women, so he backed off.'

'And she killed herself?'

'Yes. She took poison. It was terrible. Awful. But Walter was not responsible.'

'In a way he was, because he rejected her.'

'He would have had to reject her anyway, he couldn't bear Nellie finding out. And Dorothea Powbry made no secret about her love and desire for Walter.'

'How did her husband react? Lord Powbry?'

'To be honest, I don't know, I only heard about the situation second-hand. I never actually spoke to him after the event.' She looked at Abigail. 'Actually, you know him. Or, rather, you did. He was at Cambridge at the same time we were. He was at Trinity.'

Abigail frowned. 'I don't remember any Lord Powbry.'

'Oh, he wasn't Lord Powbry then. He was James Dowsett. He only became Lord Powbry when his father died and he inherited the title, and also his mansion in Oxfordshire and his rather grand town house in Knightsbridge.'

'James Dowsett!' exclaimed Abigail. 'My heavens, I recall him as a rather weedy little chap. Secretary of the Egypt Society, which is why I remember him. They put on a few events, which we classical students attended.' She smiled. 'Although there were always mutterings of protest from some of the more conservative-minded members of the Egypt Society who thought the university was no place for women. Fortunately,

James was not of that mind. As I recall, he was always broke.'

'Yes, his father kept a tight hand on the purse strings; which in a way turned out quite well for James because he's now absolutely loaded.'

'He must have taken his wife's death hard, though,' said Daniel. 'To have your wife take poison that way would shatter most husbands.'

'Yes, you'd think so, but I never heard. And I didn't send a card of condolence because by the time I heard about it she'd been dead for a couple of months, and I didn't want to revive bad memories for him.'

'And you haven't seen him since?'

'No.' She sighed. 'Mr Heppenstall and James; two men whose wives have their portraits painted by Walter, both with tragic outcomes.'

Lily Wallace sat at the bare wooden table in the interview room in the basement of Scotland Yard. Across from her, on the other side of the table, sat Chief Superintendent Armstrong. Next to him sat the inspector who'd brought her in from Whitechapel, under protest, Inspector Feather.

If the chief superintendent had thought this basement interview room and the two burley police constables who stood grim-faced at either side of the door would intimidate Lily Wallace, he was mistaken, reflected Feather. This was a woman who'd been through the mill of grinding poverty, street violence, early pregnancy, born and brought up in an area where gangsters and drunks and truly terrifying people ruled the streets; this basement room held no terrors for her, as was obvious in the disdainful scorn on her face as she looked at the two senior police officers.

She's not going to give us anything, thought Feather. All this does is tell her that anything she knows about Joe and his association with the mystery rich man is valuable; and that means valuable to her. It means money.

'This carriage that Joe was picked up in?' asked Armstrong, fixing what he hoped would be an intimidating glare on the young widow. 'Describe it.'

'I already have,' said Lily. She jerked her head towards Feather. 'I told him.'

Armstrong tapped a stubby finger at statement Feather had written out from Lily following their journey back to Whitechapel with Abigail.

'There's no details,' he said.

'It was dark,' she said.

'How many horses?'

She thought, then said: 'One.'

'How many wheels? Two or four?'

'Four,' she said.

'Tell us about the driver.'

She shrugged. 'He was the driver.'

'What did he look like?'

'I only ever saw him sitting on his driver's box, so I don't know if he was tall or short.'

'His face,' scowled Armstrong.

'I never saw it. He had a scarf pulled up right over his nose. And a hat on his head.'

'What sort of hat?'

Lily frowned thoughtfully for a moment, then she said: 'A top hat.'

'Did the carriage have any emblems on it?'

'Any what?'

'Signs. Crests. Sometimes the doors of carriages have shields or feathers or things painted on them.'

She shook her head. 'If it did, I never saw them. I had my eyes fixed on Joe.'

'Tell me exactly what you saw that night when you followed Joe.'

'I've already said,' Lily pointed out, and again she nodded towards Feather. 'To him.'

'And this time you tell me. Every detail. From the moment the carriage arrived at your door.'

'It didn't arrive at our door,' Lily corrected him. 'There was this knock at the door and Joe went to answer it. I heard voices, Joe's and another man. That turned out to be the driver.'

'What did the driver say?'

'I didn't hear properly. It was more of a grunt. Then Joe came back in the kitchen and said he had to go out. Private work, he said. He took his coat and his bag of butcher's tools and left. I followed him.'

'Why?'

'Because, like I've already told this other bloke, your inspector, I thought he might be meeting some woman.'

'Had he gone off with other women before?'

'No, but that didn't mean he wouldn't. My dad was always going off with other women. It's what men do. I bet you do.'

The chief superintendent bridled and snapped: 'Watch your mouth. I can have you arrested.'

'What for?' demanded Lily. 'Telling the truth?'

'What happened next?' growled Armstrong.

'Joe got to the carriage and the door opened and I heard this bloke say "Get in".'

'What sort of voice? Old? Young?'

'I couldn't tell. But it was a posh voice. Then Joe got in, the door shut, and the carriage went off.'

'And when Joe got back?'

'I was asleep. I didn't hear him come in. I guess he slept on the sofa downstairs because that's where he was when I got up in the morning to sort the kids out.' She glared at the chief superintendent. 'Is that it? Can I go home now? I've got a husband to bury.'

'So, another suspect,' said Daniel as they left Helena Swanwick's house. 'Your old friend, James Dowsett, now Lord Powbry.'

'He wasn't actually a friend of mine,' said Abigail. 'I only really knew him because of the Egypt Society events. Apart from that, he was just someone who was part of the crowd. Although on the fringes of the crowd, really, because, as I said, he was always desperately short of money. And, at the moment, Mr Heppenstall is surely in pride of place.'

'Only if he has no alibi for the nights when the murders were committed,' said Daniel.

'I know someone at the UCH,' said Abigail. 'Adam Parks. Someone else who was at Cambridge at the same time as me. He's an administrator there, which would make him the perfect person to ask if Heppenstall was at the hospital on the nights of the 14th and 17th February.'

'How will you ask without raising suspicions about Heppenstall?'

'I'll think of something,' said Abigail.

'And I'll do the same at the Middlesex,' said Daniel.

'You have a contact there?'

'Not in such an elevated position as yours. Charlie Desmond is the head porter and he knows the comings and goings of everyone at the hospital.'

Lily arrived back in Whitechapel. At least that inspector had been good enough to arrange for her to be taken back, even if it was in a police van. That horrible fat one, the chief superintendent, he'd have made her walk. Rather than set tongues wagging at her being seen getting out of a police van she got the driver to stop well short of her house. As she walked to Mrs Whatmores', the neighbour who'd taken care of her two kids while she was off with the police, she thought about the interview she'd just had. This rich bloke was the key. Him and Joe had been up to something and, although she hated to admit it, it had to do with those dead women whose bodies they'd found at that art gallery in the West End. And Lily was fairly sure that this rich bloke was the one who'd killed Joe, to silence him, worried that Joe might talk. That had to be what happened. Joe was all edgy before he set off, and he'd told her he was going to see this bloke and he'd see him right. That meant money, maybe so him and Lily and the kids could get away. But instead, Joe had been killed, his throat slashed. Either the rich bloke or his driver had done it.

With Joe dying she was left without a penny to support herself and the kids. There was a way to raise money, of course, there always was, but she'd never gone down that road and she wasn't going to now. No, she was going to find out who this rich bloke was and get him to cough up. And not just a pound or two to keep her quiet, big money. And if he tried to do her the way he'd done Joe, she'd be ready for him. She'd always carried a knife in case of trouble. It was a way of life in Whitechapel. The thing was now to find out who this rich bloke was. Joe's mates were the answer. One of them *must* know who he was.

Charlie Desmond was a short, round, balding man in his late forties. Daniel had known him when he'd been with Scotland Yard's detective division and often had cause to call at the Middlesex Hospital to question a victim of crime, or sometimes the alleged perpetrator. In his time as a private investigator since he'd left the Metropolitan Police, Daniel often had occasion to call on Desmond for information about a patient, or a member of staff, to establish whether they might have been culpable in whatever case he was investigating, but so far he'd never called to check on anyone as high up the scale as a consultant surgeon.

'Edmund Heppenstall' queried Desmond when Daniel asked about him. 'What's he supposed to have done? Nothing criminal, I'd stake my life on that. You won't find a more decent gent anywhere in London. And beyond, I'm proud to say. He's a credit both to his profession, and to humanity as a whole.'

'No, no, he's not suspected of anything,' Daniel hastily reassured him. 'It's someone else we're looking into who may or may not have involved Mr Heppenstall in something. To help us eliminate him from our enquiries, we need to find out if he was working here on the nights of Sunday February 14th and Wednesday February 17th.'

Desmond thought it over for a moment, running those dates through his mind, then shook his head.

'No, definitely not. I know because I was on night duty myself both those dates, and I always know if Mr Heppenstall's here. The nurses and the sisters always seem to have a happier air to them when he's in the building. They know how good he is, and whatever comes up he can deal with.'

'According to my contact at the Middlesex, Edmund Heppenstall is a paragon of virtue, worthy of sainthood,' Daniel reported to Abigail when they met up to exchange notes. 'But he wasn't working at the Middlesex on either of the two nights in question, so that means he's still in the frame.'

'I'm afraid not,' said Abigail. 'Adam checked the records for both nights. Edmund Heppenstall was called in to carry out an emergency operation on the evening of Sunday 14th. After preliminary tests and preparations, he was in the operating theatre from nine o'clock at night until four in the morning. The operation was successful. And there are plenty of witnesses to back it up.'

'What did he do after four in the morning?' asked Daniel. 'He could have still gone in search of Anne-Marie.'

'After he finished the operation, he went to one of the rest rooms they have set aside for surgeons. He slept there until eight o'clock.'

'So he couldn't have killed Anne-Marie.'

'No.'

Daniel gave a deep sigh. 'So tomorrow I'll have to eat humble pie to Fred Abberline.'

'It's lucky we found out before we went charging in and accused him,' commented Abigail.

'I was never going to accuse him,' said Daniel. 'I was going to be subtle.'

'Subtle?' Abigail laughed gently. 'Daniel, I love you very dearly and you have many wonderful attributes, but subtlety is not one of them. You are direct. You wear your heart on your sleeve and your feelings on your face. And I love you for that.'

CHAPTER TWENTY-EIGHT

'Did you talk to this barman?' Inspector Feather asked Sergeant Cribbens. They were travelling in a police van to Seven Dials, along with a uniformed constable, to pick up the barman from The Flower Pot pub.

'I did,' said Cribbens. 'His name's Jake Walker. He said he didn't see either Joe Wallace, nor this rich-looking bloke.'

'You think he was lying?'

'Absolutely,' said Cribbens firmly. 'It's Seven Dials. They lie by nature. I was going to suggest taking him back to Scotland Yard, but we only had the van and the carriage; and I was using the van to take Mr Wilson and the body back to the Yard, and you and Miss Fenton were taking Lily Wallace back to Whitechapel. And then, when we got to the Yard, the boss told us the investigation was over, so there didn't seem much point in asking any further questions.'

'Yes, good point,' said Feather. 'But now the chief superintendent's changed his mind, we've got orders to pull him in.'

'He won't talk,' predicted Cribbens. 'They never do.'

'He might if we throw the fear of God into him,' said Feather. 'Or, more exactly, the fear of the scaffold. Daniel suggested he might be guilty of conspiracy to aid a murderer.'

'Worth a try, I suppose,' said Cribbens, not sounding very convinced.

The van drew up as near as it could get to The Flower Pot, and Inspector Feather, Cribbens and the constable got out and made for the pub. They were surprised to see a crowd outside the pub, and as they neared it a man in a stained apron detached himself from the crowd and hurried to greet them.

'That was quick,' he said. 'We only just sent for a bobby.'

'What was quick?' asked Feather.

'You. Scotland Yard,' said the man. 'I recognised you from this morning when the other bloke was found dead. Luckily, Jake didn't get done in the privy.'

Feather and Cribbens exchanged puzzled looks.

'Our barman,' said the man impatiently. 'Ain't that why you're here? Jake getting killed.'

'Where is he?' asked Feather, pushing his way through the crowd to get into the pub.

'In the storeroom out the back,' said the man with the apron.

'And you are?'

'Eddie Mason. I'm the potman and general washer-upperer here. Someone came and told me that Jake had gone missing.

So I went into the storeroom in case he was there, and there he was, dead as a doornail. Knife in the heart, by the look of it.'

'Who did it? Did anyone see?'

Feather looked around at the crowd, which suddenly seemed to have grown much thinner at the arrival of the police. The few men and women who were left shook their heads.

'We're looking for a rich-looking sort of bloke,' Feather announced to them. 'He'd stick out like a sore thumb around here. Did anyone see anyone like that? Long coat. Top hat. White scarf wrapped around his face.'

Again, everyone shook their heads, except for one man who asked: 'Is there a reward?'

'What's your name?' asked Feather.

'It depends if there's a reward,' said the man.

Feather turned to Cribbens. 'Sergeant, take this man and put him in the van.'

'What for?' protested the man loudly. 'I ain't done nothing!'

'This is a murder, the second here today, and I haven't got time to mess about,' snapped Feather. He turned to Mason. 'I'll need you, too.'

'Why?' demanded the potman. 'What have I done?'

'You found the body. You've got information that may help us find the person who killed your barman.'

'I ain't got any information!' said Mason.

'That's for me to find out,' said Feather crisply.

Mason gestured at the pub.

'But without me there's no one to look after it. Me and Jake was the only ones there.'

'Then lock it up.' Feather turned to the waiting Cribbens, who was holding the man he'd been ordered to put in the van firmly by the arm. 'Go on, Sergeant. And tell the driver to keep an eye on him while we get the body of the barman to the van.' He turned to Mason, who was looking agitated. 'You can give us a hand to carry him.'

'I can't,' said Mason. 'I've got a bad back.'

'You're a potman and washer-upperer, you do plenty of lifting. And you can rest your back when we get to Scotland Yard.'

When they got to Scotland Yard, Feather put the two men in different interview rooms. He left Cribbens to quiz the man who'd asked if there was a reward, while he questioned Eddie Mason, the potman.

'I don't know anything,' insisted Mason. 'I'm always out the back. Though today I had to look after the bar when Jake went out.'

'When was this?' asked Feather.

'It was soon after that other bloke came in,' said Mason.

'What bloke?'

'One of yours. Wilson, Jake said his name was.'

'Daniel Wilson?'

'I don't know. Jake said this bloke Wilson had been in asking questions and he had to go out. He was only telling me in case this Wilson came back.'

'And did he?'

Mason shook his head. 'Not while I was doing the bar. Then Jake came back.'

'Did he say where he'd been?'

'No.'

'How long was he gone for?'

'I don't know. About an hour, I think.'

'When did you last see Jake alive?'

'About an hour or so after he came back. I was feeling hungry, I hadn't eaten all day, so I told Jake I was going to get a bun from the baker's up the road. I went up there and got it, and stayed up there while I ate it. I knew if I came back, Jake would be on at me to do something and I wouldn't be able to eat the bun. Not enjoy it, anyway. They're really good buns. They got currants and things in 'em.'

'And when you got back?' prompted Feather.

'Jake wasn't in the bar, so I went into the storeroom to see if he was there, and he was. Only he was dead.'

'Were there any customers in the bar when you got back?'

'No, nor when I left. That's why I knew it was all right to go to the baker's, because there weren't any customers to look after.'

'And what did you do when you found Jake's body?'

'I went out in the street and told this little kid, Archie his name is, to go and fetch a copper.'

'Who's Archie?'

'He does errands for people.'

'Did he see who'd come in the pub?'

Again, Mason shook his head. 'No. He wasn't there when I went out to get my bun. I don't know where he was before. He just turned up as I came out of the pub.'

'Do you have an address for him?'

Mason looked at the inspector in disbelief. 'Address? You're joking. He's one of the street kids. They sleep on the roofs of buildings all over the place.'

Feather nodded, yes, he knew about these kids. Runaways or orphans, mostly. They gathered together in gangs for safety, and they slept on the roofs of buildings for the same reason, as well as being able to keep warm by being close to the chimney stacks.

Sergeant Cribbens was having even less success with Arnold Dibble, the man who'd asked if there was a reward.

'I never saw nothing,' he insisted. 'All I saw was this crowd outside the pub, so I went over to see what was going on, and that's when they told me a bloke had been killed in there. That's all I know.'

'So why did you ask if there was a reward for information?'

'A bloke's got to look after himself.'

'But you've just said you hadn't got any information.'

'And I haven't. But if someone tells me what they want, maybe I can find it. You know, ask around. All I need is a few coins to grease a few palms. A shilling or two.'

'You'll get any money that *might* be going *if* you come in with some good information that leads us to catch the bloke who killed the barman,' said Cribbens firmly.

'Well, that's no good,' protested Dibble. 'People want money up front, not promises of it later.'

Sergeant Cribbens fixed Dibble with a firm look. 'Listen, my old son,' he said. 'I've been in this game a good few years and I know when I'm being taken for a monkey. If your information's any good, I'll see what we can do about paying you. But we are not – and I repeat *not* – paying you on a promise. So nose around by all means. You'll find our blokes will be doing the same.' He leant forward to Dibble and told

276

him: 'We are not a charity, Arnold. Payment by results, that's the order of the day.'

After both men had been allowed to leave, Feather and his sergeant swapped notes.

'My one was a dead loss,' said Cribbens. 'He's a chancer. He saw nothing, but he says he'll find out, if we pay him up front.'

'I assume you put him straight?' groaned Feather.

'I did,' said Cribbens. 'How about yours?'

'Nothing. He was out buying a bun when the barman got killed. We'll have to flood the area with local bobbies asking questions, see what they come up with.' He sighed. 'Now to go and tell the chief superintendent about this latest killing. He's not going to be pleased.'

Feather was right, Armstrong wasn't pleased at all when the inspector told him about Jake Walker being stabbed to death.

'Another one!' he exploded in red-faced fury. 'We started off with two dead women. Then we had that bloke . . .' He struggled to remember the name.

'Edwin O'Tool,' said Feather.

'Then Joe Wallace has his throat cut. And now the barman at the same pub.'

'Jake Walker,' said Feather.

'Who gets stabbed to death. That's five people murdered, Inspector. Five!' He let out a groan. 'The commissioner's going to go mad when he hears about this. And the home secretary!'

'Do they have to be told, sir?' asked Feather.

'It'll be in the papers,' barked Armstrong. He got up. 'I'd better go and see the commissioner and tell him this latest before he reads about it in tomorrow's papers.' He looked at Feather, anguished. 'This could cost me my job, Inspector.'

'Surely not, sir.'

'Five dead and no suspects? They'll be looking for someone to blame. Unless we can lay our hands on this maniac before he kills anyone else.'

CHAPTER TWENTY-NINE

Daniel and Abigail were working together to prepare their evening meal when there was a knock at the door.

'Wonder who that can be?' wondered Daniel.

'The easiest way to find out is open the door,' said Abigail with a smile.

Daniel did, and returned to the kitchen with Inspector Feather.

'It's John,' he announced.

'You're just in time for food,' said Abigail. 'Lamb chops and mash? It's no problem to put another chop on.'

'Thanks, but Vera will have something ready for me. I've come to tell you about another murder.'

'Another?' said Abigail sharply.

'The barman from The Flower Pot in Seven Dials, Jake Walker. Stabbed through the heart.' He looked at Daniel. 'The potman at The Flower Pot said he nipped out shortly after you'd been.'

Daniel groaned. 'This is my fault,' he said. 'I threatened to go to the police and suggest they bring him in for questioning if he didn't tell me what he knew about the rich man. He must have immediately gone to see him and told him about the threat. I bet he asked for money to keep silent, the same as I expect Joe Wallace did. But they were both unlucky. It looks like this character made sure they stayed silent.' He sat down heavily on a chair. 'If I hadn't done that, he'd still be alive.'

'You don't know that for certain,' said Feather. 'Sooner or later he'd have tried to put the squeeze on this mystery man, and he'd have got it then. Are you any nearer to finding out who this rich man is? Have you got more on this Heppenstall character?'

'Only that we can count him out. He has a cast iron alibi for one of the murders, and as it appears both women were killed by the same person, that's him out of the frame.'

'But we've got another possible suspect,' said Abigail. 'Someone I knew when I was at Cambridge. Lord Powbry. His wife killed herself after she was rejected by Walter Sickert.'

'Rejected?' said Feather surprised.

'Yes, that was our reaction,' said Daniel. 'But it seems at the time Sickert was trying to prove to his wife he was the faithful husband.'

'That man's life seems to be a romantic disaster,' said Feather. 'What's your next move?'

'We meet Abberline at the National Gallery tomorrow morning at ten, introduce him to Stanford Beckett, and then we work out what we're going to do. Abigail's already volunteered to go and talk to Lord Powbry, see if there's anything suspicious there. This second murder at The Flower Pot makes me think that's where we might find some answers. Two men dead? That suggests whoever's doing it stays close to Seven Dials.'

'I'd be very careful if I were you,' warned Feather. 'As you said, two men dead. You don't want to be the third.'

After Feather had gone, Abigail looked at Daniel, concerned. 'He's got a good point. Walking around Seven Dials asking questions could be very dangerous.'

'As could asking difficult questions of Lord Powbry, if *he* turns out to our mystery man.'

'I'll be careful,' said Abigail.

'So will I,' said Daniel.

The next morning Daniel and Abigail were waiting for Abberline beside the main entrance to the National Gallery, and when he arrived – on the dot at 10 a.m. – they took him to meet Stanford Beckett, who shook his hand as warmly as if he was being introduced to royalty.

'Mr Abberline,' said Beckett. 'This is such an honour. I've read all about your exploits in the newspapers. I've followed your career with the greatest admiration. I feel both humbled and grateful to feel that you have agreed to join our investigation.'

After, Daniel and Abigail took Abberline to the gallery's cafeteria for coffee, where he asked, curious: 'Mr Beckett is a very effusive man. Does he greet everybody that way?'

'Not that we've noticed,' said Abigail. 'One can only assume he has a very high opinion of you.'

'Let's hope we don't let him down,' said Abberline. 'So, what's the plan?'

They told him the latest developments: the murder of Jake Walker at The Flower Pot; that Edmund Heppenstall was no longer a suspect because he had a cast iron alibi, and that Lord Powbry – formerly James Dowsett, a student with Abigail in Cambridge – had been added in as a possible suspect.

'It's all a bit tenuous,' said Abberline.

'That's true, but we haven't got a lot else to go on,' said Daniel. 'So Abigail's going to have a word with him, sound him out and see if he's got an alibi for the time of the murders; and I thought I'd go and make myself unpopular in Seven Dials by nosing around.'

'Setting a trap with yourself as bait?' asked Abberline.

'I hope not,' said Daniel. 'What thoughts have you had?'

'I was thinking about what you said, about the man who was with Wallace when he attacked you. You said that perhaps he was a pal of Wallace's, so I thought I'd go to Whitechapel and see if I can find any pals of Wallace's who might fit the bill. If so, we'll have our lead to this rich bloke.'

'It'll be like looking for a needle in a haystack.'

'True, but I know the place and the people. Remember, I spent years working there before the Ripper investigation.'

'They're suspicious of coppers in Whitechapel.'

'Not everyone. There were some good people there that I got to know when I was based there, before the Ripper murders. Some of them will still be around. One thing's for sure, when this sort of thing happens and there's the threat of a major influx of coppers in the area, the locals will be keen to help out. They don't like it when the place is flooded with coppers. You'll remember that from the Ripper investigation, Daniel. It interferes with regular criminal activity.'

Abberline stood and looked at the window display of Fenster's Funerals. All very tasteful. Black ribbons coming down from the top of the window and wrapped around bundles of white flowers. The flowers looked as if they were long past their bloom, wilted and shrivelled, but what was the point of spending good money on an expensive shop window display in Whitechapel, it would only get stolen at night.

He pushed open the door, causing the bell above the doorframe to give a gentle tinkling sound. A small, tubby, bald man appeared from the back of the shop and his face lit up in welcome as he saw who it was.

'Mr Abberline!' he said, and held out his hand.

'Mr Fenster,' smiled Abberline in return, and shook the funeral director's hand.

'It's been a few years since we've seen you round these parts,' said Fenster. 'We saw in the papers you'd retired.'

'It was the right time,' said Abberline. 'How have things been with you?'

Fenster shrugged. 'People die. It's the only thing that's guaranteed in life. What can I do for you?'

'Joe Wallace,' said Abberline.

'Ah yes,' nodded Fenster. He gestured at the back room. 'I've got him here. The police delivered him. Pauper's funeral, that one. The public purse.'

'I'm trying to find out who his friends were.'

'Friends?'

'Yes. We're trying to find out who killed him, and we're hoping we can find out who he went to Seven Dials to meet.'

Fenster shook his head. 'It's a long way to go to die. Lily said the police tried to say at first he'd killed himself, but he didn't.

Joe wasn't the type.' He looked thoughtful. 'Mostly, Joe just worked. He did stuff for Karl Ramsden and a butcher at Cable Street.'

'Yes, I've already been to see Karl,' said Abberline.

'Joe wasn't what you'd call the sociable type, so he didn't go to pubs much. Hardly ever. I think Lily kept an eye on their money.' He looked enquiringly at Abberline. 'Sergeant Whetstone's still at the local nick. He was looking into it after they brought Joe back. He might know something.'

Abberline sighed. 'I've already had a word with him. He's as wise as I am. It seems Joe kept his private business very much to himself.' He produced a small pasteboard business card, which he handed to Fenster. 'If you do hear anything, I'd be grateful if you'd get in touch.'

'You're not with the police, then?'

'Not officially, but we're working with them.'

'Ah, so you're working with your old sergeant, Daniel Wilson, and that Miss Fenton.'

'I am indeed.'

'How's that going?'

'Working with them, very good. This case? Banging my head against a brick wall.'

Abigail had to admit to butterflies in her stomach as she approached the address she'd been given for Lord Powbry. It was all of fifteen years since she'd last seen him in Cambridge at an event organised by the Egypt Society and there had been no contact between them since then. Surely he'd view her arrival with suspicion after all this time; and especially if he was the mystery 'rich man'. By all accounts the mystery 'rich man' had killed people who represented a danger to him, notably Joe Wallace and the barman at The Flower Pot. How would he react when Abigail started asking questions? James had always been a quiet sort, introverted, but astute. She had to be very careful how she raised the subject of his movements on the nights the two women were murdered. She'd just mention one of those nights so it wouldn't seem too obvious what she was after. At least, she hoped it wouldn't.

Her forthcoming trip to Egypt with Conan Doyle would be her lead in. Ask him if he was still involved with the Egypt Society, and if not, if he had any contacts there he could put her in touch with.

God, it's so feeble! she admitted to herself unhappily. She was supposed to be the internationally acknowledged Egyptologist, why would she be asking about some tiny university student organisation? It was so obviously a ploy. But what else could she use?

She walked up to the steps to the front door and pulled the bell pull. The door opened and a buxom woman of about fifty in a flowery apron looked out inquisitively at her.

'Good day,' smiled Abigail. 'My name's Abigail Fenton. I'm an old friend of Lord Powbry from his Cambridge days. Would it be possible to see him?'

Lily Wallace stood in the back room of Karl Ramsden's butcher's shop, her baby asleep in her arms, and watched as Mick Foley attacked a side of lamb on a wooden bench with a small hand axe.

'Are you listening to me, Mick?' demanded Lily.

Reluctantly, Mick put down the axe. 'Of course I am,' he said.

'But you're not answering me! Who was the rich toff

that Joe used to go off with?'

'I tell you I don't know!' answered Mick for the third time. 'I didn't even know there was a rich toff. All I know is that a couple of times Joe didn't turn up for work on the night shift, and later he said he'd had some private work.'

Lily sagged against the wall, feeling defeated. Mick was the fourth pal of Joe's she'd sought out to ask him about the mystery man in the carriage, and got the same response from him as she'd had from the previous three. No one knew what Joe had been up to, or who this rich bloke was, nor even where he came from.

As she left the butcher's she reflected that if only there had been another woman in Joe's life she'd have had more chance of finding out who the toff was. Men always talked to their women. Not necessarily to their wives. She and Joe didn't really talk, she was too busy with the kids, and Joe worked all the hours at different butchers. But *someone* knew.

Then she thought of where Joe had been killed. That pub in Seven Dials. What had he been doing there? Meeting the rich bloke, that was what. She was wasting her time asking questions here in Whitechapel. Seven Dials, that's where she should be. Talking to the people in that Flower Pot pub. Someone there would know who this rich bloke was. And she'd get them to tell her. There'd been that barman at The Flower Pot when she went there with the police, she'd seen him looking at her. He'd know, and if he didn't, he'd know who'd know. She could tell by the way he looked at her that he fancied her. Well, she'd get him to talk. Let him touch her up a bit first, then keep him waiting from going all the way until she'd got the name out of him. She smiled at the thought.

* * *

286

Daniel left The Flower Pot, heavy with feelings of disappointment and frustration. The potman, Mason, had insisted he hadn't even been at the pub when the barman, Jake Walker, had been killed. Nor had he seen anyone who could be described as rich in the pub, or near it, either before he'd gone off to the baker's to buy himself a bun, or when he'd returned to find Walker dead. The customers at the pub all told the same tale: none of them had been in the pub the previous day. Even if there was money to be made by talking, none of them had seen anything or knew anything.

Daniel didn't blame them: two men had been killed the day before because it was assumed they had been ready to talk. No one else wanted to die.

As Daniel made his way towards the actual Seven Dials clock, and thence home, a man watched him from the shadows of a tumbledown building.

Wilson again, he cursed silently and venomously. The man was like a damned terrier. Because of him, he'd been forced to kill two men. The last, the barman at The Flower Pot, had actually named Wilson as the reason he'd come looking for him. What did Wilson know? How close was he? There was only one answer; Wilson would have to die.

At her house, Jane Cobden picked up the invitation card that had been propped up on the mantelpiece and read: 'Mrs Walter Sickert and her guest are invited to the unveiling of two paintings from the collection of J. M. W. Turner, to be shown alongside two by Claude Lorrain at the National Gallery, London on the afternoon of Monday 22nd February 1897.'

'Are you going to this tomorrow?' she asked.

'No,' said Ellen firmly. 'I will not allow myself to be a figure of fun and humiliation, with those dreadful people sniggering about me behind my back.'

'They're not all dreadful,' said Jane. 'Two of Tom's authors are going to be there. Herbert Wells and the new one, Somerset Maugham.'

'One an unabashed lecher and the other a nonentity,' said Ellen.

'Tom has great hopes for Somerset Maugham.' She sighed. 'But I agree with you about Wells. No woman is safe with him. I wouldn't trust him in a convent. But then, the same could be said of Walter.'

'Which is exactly why I will not be going.'

CHAPTER THIRTY

The next morning, as they bathed and dressed ready for the event at the National Gallery that afternoon, Daniel and Abigail discussed what they'd learnt from their previous day's quizzing. The only fact that had surfaced was that the murderer couldn't have been Lord Powbry. Abigail had learnt from his housekeeper that Lord Powbry had been on his honeymoon in Germany for the past two weeks with his new bride and was not expected back for another two weeks.

'So, not that heartbroken by the death of his first wife,' commented Daniel.

Daniel had drawn a series of blanks, as had Abberline.

'We're no nearer,' sighed Abigail.

'Perhaps this afternoon will reveal a new suspect,' said Daniel. 'Mr Beckett did say we'd be meeting people who had reason to hate Sickert.'

'But hate him enough to kill five people?' asked Abigail.

'That may be what we're about to find out.'

'Mr Beckett should be pleased with the turnout,' commented Daniel as they walked into the main hall at the National Gallery. There was a large crowd gathered in front of four paintings hanging side by side. The majority were men, but there were quite a few women. Most had dressed up for the occasion, although some of the younger men had put on colourful jackets and hats to announce to those who didn't recognise them that they were serious artists.

'The usual smattering of celebrities,' Abigail murmured. 'The sort you get at all these occasions, keen to be noticed.'

'I don't recognise any of them,' said Daniel.

'That's because you don't move in artistic circles.'

They joined the crowd gathered before the main attraction, Abigail pushing her way through the throng to get a better view. The two paintings by Claude Lorrain, *Landscape with the Marriage of Isaac and Rebecca* and *Seaport with the Embarkation of the Queen of Sheba*, were now framed between two from Turner: *Calais Pier*, which dated from 1803, according to the plate beside the painting, and *Norham Castle, Sunrise* from 1845.

'Look at the Turners. Even though they were painted forty years apart, you can still see the same hand at work,' said Abigail admiringly.

'Really?' said Daniel. 'They look completely different to me. The *Norham Castle* one is vague, it could be anything, anywhere. But the other, the Calais one, is so detailed you can see the boats.'

'But look at the skies,' said Abigail. 'The light.'

'You sound like Sickert,' commented Daniel.

'Capturing the light in oils on canvas is what marks a great landscape artist out from an average painter. It brings the picture to life. You can *feel* it.'

'If you ever decide to give up being an archaeologist you could always become an art critic,' said Daniel. 'You have all the right phrases.'

They moved back from the four pictures to let others get closer. Suddenly Abigail groaned and whispered: 'Oh my God, Herbert Wells.'

'Who?'

Abigail nodded in the direction of a small, portly man with a moustache who seemed to be hovering on the fringes of those watching the paintings.

'The novelist. H. G. Wells,' she hissed. 'If he comes over to us, stay close by me.'

'Why?'

'He is a lecher and a pest.'

'Why don't you do what you've done before when men have acted inappropriately, punch him?'

'Because it wouldn't be the done thing on an occasion like this, Mr Beckett would be most upset.' She gave a smile of relief. 'It's all right, he's latched on to that blonde woman.'

'Who seems happy enough to encourage him, by the expression on her face.'

'Yes, well, different women have different attitudes to that sort of thing. Some actually encourage it.'

'We're supposed to be mingling and finding out the people who don't like Walter Sickert,' Daniel reminded her. 'I'm not sure how we're actually going to do that.'

'My suggestion is we go and stand in front of one of his paintings and wait until people stop by it and make disparaging comments about the work, and the painter.'

'Will they do that?'

'Oh yes, the art world is full of very bitchy people.'

'Where will we find his work? We know the portrait of Anne-Marie Dresser has been destroyed.'

'There's another in the British section,' said Abigail. 'Follow me.'

They left the main hall and Daniel found himself in a room with a variety of very colourful paintings, some large, some small, many of them depicting religious scenes or from Shakespearean plays.

'The Pre-Raphaelite Brotherhood,' said Abigail. 'What do you think?'

'Very serious,' said Daniel.

'Yes, well, they take themselves very seriously. They were set up as a loose group about forty years ago. The first founder members were John Everett Millais, Dante Gabriel Rossetti, William Holman Hunt and Ford Madox Brown.'

'Was it a requirement that everyone had to have three names?'

'I think they wanted to make themselves memorable. Their acknowledged artistic leader was John Ruskin, not himself primarily a painter but a critic.'

'The one whose wife ran off with Millais?' said Daniel, and he smiled as he added: 'See, I do take notice of what you tell me. So how did that work within the group?'

'Millais sort of drifted away from the others. He still painted,

292

but in a different style. More leaning towards the Impressionists. Although his most famous painting is the one that Pears soap used in their adverts.'

'The little boy in the velvet suit?'

'That's the one. "Bubbles". It earned him condemnation from some of his former Pre-Raphaelites who accused him of selling out to commercialism.'

'I assume those same artists also sold their paintings,' mused Daniel.

'Yes, but not to soap companies. They preferred to think of their art as pure.'

'Whereas, in fact, it was overromanticised tosh,' said a drawling voice behind them.

They turned and beheld a very thin young man in his early twenties, his hair parted in the middle hanging down in bangs below his ears.

'You don't approve of religious paintings?' asked Daniel.

'Oh, but I do,' said the young man. 'I've created quite a few myself, but—' Suddenly he stopped as a dreadful cough racked his narrow frame. He pulled a white handkerchief from his pocket and held it to his mouth as he coughed, the sound so painful that it sent a shudder through both Daniel and Abigail.

The young man looked briefly at the handkerchief before folding it and replacing it in his pocket, but not before both Abigail and Daniel had noted the blood on it.

'I really must use red handkerchiefs,' said the young man airily. 'Far less dramatic.'

With that, he walked off.

'Now there's a strange young man,' observed Daniel.

'Yes, in many people's eyes,' said Abigail. 'His name's

Aubrey Beardsley and he's one of the leading proponents of Art Nouveau.'

'Leading proponents?' asked Daniel, surprised. 'He's barely in his twenties.'

'Twenty-four, I believe.'

'Is any of his work here on exhibition?'

'No. Primarily, he's an illustrator working in ink, black ink on white paper seems to be his favourite. His main claim to fame are his erotic drawings, which have led to much muttering about him, and a view that he should be avoided as some kind of pervert.'

'Is he?'

'To be honest, I don't know, just what I read in the magazines. They attach him to the crowd that hung around with Oscar Wilde before he went to prison.'

'Homosexual?'

Abigail, looked thoughtful. 'Perhaps, although some people describe him as a-sexual. But when we get home, I'll show you some of his illustrations in my magazines.'

'Erotic images?' asked Daniel, startled.

'No,' said Abigail firmly. 'You won't find those sorts of works in the arts magazines I subscribe to. But his work is quite striking.'

'You like it?'

'I do.'

'Then I'm sure I will, too.'

Just then, an elderly man who'd been hovering near them approached them with an ingratiating smile aimed at Abigail.

'Excuse me, but it is Miss Abigail Fenton, isn't it?'

'Yes.'

'I'm sorry to be so bold as to interfere. My name's Algernon Farnsworth and I publish a quarterly magazine called *The Art of Egypt*.'

'Yes, I've seen it!' said Abigail in delight. 'It is most admirable! I was particularly impressed by the article you did on Flinders Petrie.'

'Who you worked with at Hawara.'

'I did indeed,' said Abigail. 'A most wonderful experience!'

'I wonder if you would consider writing an article about your experiences of that expedition for *The Art of Egypt*.'

Abigail looked doubtful.

'Surely the definitive piece about that has already been written by Petrie himself,' she said.

'Yes, but I know our readers would love to hear about it from the perspective of someone who was with Petrie and could give insights into the man and the mission.' He gave a hopeful smile as he added: 'And particularly by a woman. *The Art of Egypt* has been conspicuously light on articles by women.'

Abigail hesitated, and Daniel interceded: 'I really think this is something you need to think about positively, Abigail. It could be a very important step for you, and the world of archaeology.'

'Thank you for those words of encouragement, Mr Wilson,' said Farnsworth gratefully. 'It is Mr Daniel Wilson, I assume? I read that the National Gallery had commissioned the famous Museum Detectives, yourself and Miss Fenton, to look into the recent dreadful murders here.'

'Yes, I'm Daniel Wilson.' He smiled. 'But this evening is for art, and particularly for *The Art of Egypt*.' He turned to Abigail and said: 'I'll leave you to Mr Farnsworth to talk about this project for his magazine, while I enrich my own art education here.'

'Thank you, Mr Wilson. You are very considerate. I promise I shall return your companion to you shortly.'

Daniel bowed and walked away, leaving Abigail and Farnsworth to talk. He decided to head towards where the newly hung Turners were on display to eavesdrop and see if the name Sickert came up in any of the conversations, but as he moved in that direction, he found his path barred by a tall, well-dressed man in his sixties who looked at him coldly.

'Mr Daniel Wilson, I presume,' said the man, his tone curt.

'Indeed, sir.'

'I am Lord Yaxley.'

'Lord Yaxley,' said Daniel, and he held out his hand in greeting. To his surprise, Yaxley kept his own right hand resolutely at his side.

'I will not shake your hand, sir, because of the appalling situation you have brought my son to.'

'Your son?' asked Daniel, puzzled.

'Simon Anstis, the artist.'

Daniel frowned. 'I am sorry, Lord Yaxley, but with respect, any appalling situation your son finds himself in is totally of his own making.'

'You tricked him, sir, into being trapped here and assaulted with some nonsense about fingerprints, and then had him imprisoned in some dreadful police cell.'

'Your son destroyed a painting at this gallery, which he admitted to doing.'

'Under duress, sir, under duress. As a result, he has been banned from this establishment. Do you realise what that has done to him?'

'I would imagine he is unhappy about it, but he should have

thought of that before he set out to break into the gallery at night and destroy a painting.'

'He had reason, sir. The painting he inflicted some damage on was done by a so-called artist who has demeaned my son and his work for many years, which my son has borne with admirable sufferance, until finally he could take no more. Art is my son's reason for being alive. To paint, and to be part of that creative circle akin to himself, but thanks to you he has had that snatched away from him. He should be here today, but he has been publicly shunned and humiliated and banned because of you.'

'Again, sir, I would say that your son's banishment from this place, which I believe to be only temporary, is the result of his own actions. Hopefully he will have learnt from the error of his ways and will behave responsibly in the future.'

Yaxley glared at Daniel with an anger that caused his face to flush crimson.

'You have not heard the last of this, sir,' he said, then turned on his heel and stormed away from Daniel.

'What was all that about?' asked Abigail as she joined Daniel. 'Who was that extremely angry man?'

'Lord Yaxley, the father of Simon Anstis. He accused us – or, more exactly, me – of having ruined his son's life. In addition, he loathes Walter Sickert, so we've found at least one rich person who might be worth looking into.'

'I never realised that Simon Anstis came from a titled family.'

'Nor did I. That could explain how he is able to carry on his life as a painter, despite rarely selling any of his work.'

'The doting and wealthy father,' said Abigail.

'How did you get on with Mr Farnsworth?'

'Very well. He's got some old copies of *The Art of Egypt* outside in his carriage that he wants me to look at, to take on board the literary style that suits the magazine's readers.'

'I'll come with you and help you carry them,' said Daniel.

'I don't think there are that many,' said Abigail. 'Just one or two. His carriage is just over the road, by Trafalgar Square.'

'Nevertheless, I'll come with you just in case.'

'If you wait for me by the entrance, I'll get my coat from the cloakroom,' said Abigail. 'It'll be quite cold outside.'

She headed for the cloakroom, and Daniel made for the main entrance. He stepped outside and gave a little shiver. It was indeed cold. I should have got my overcoat at the same time, he thought. He started to turn when he became aware of someone very close behind him and he felt something hard jab into his back, and the next second there was the explosion of a gun going off and he felt a searing pain as a bullet tore into his flesh, ripping through his body, and he stumbled forward and felt himself falling . . .

CHAPTER THIRTY-ONE

Abigail sat beside the hospital bed where Daniel lay. His eyes were closed, his face deathly pale, and Abigail had to bend forward every now and then to reassure herself he was still breathing. It was one o'clock in the morning and Daniel had been brought to this private room in University College Hospital after a long operation, which had been carried out by Edmund Heppenstall. The bullet had torn deep into Daniel's right lung. Heppenstall had removed the bullet, along with a portion of Daniel's lung.

'He was lucky the bullet hit him on the right,' Heppenstall told Abigail afterwards. 'The same place on the left would have been into his heart and he'd have died immediately.'

'Will he recover?' Abigail asked.

Heppenstall had hesitated before answering: 'I hope so. He's a fit, healthy man, but he's lost a great deal of blood.'

As Abigail sat there, watching the unconscious Daniel, she made a silent prayer of thanks to Chief Superintendent Armstrong who'd instructed the hospital authorities that Miss Fenton was acting as an agent of the Metropolitan Police and as such must be allowed to stay with the patient at all times. She knew that hospital authorities did not approve of relatives being in the hospital outside usual visiting hours, and without the chief superintendent's intervention she would have had a struggle to be allowed to remain.

'Please, Daniel, don't die,' she whispered. 'Stay alive for me, for us. You'll still be able to function with part of one lung. Mr Heppenstall says so.'

We will be married, she thought. As soon as you are able to leave hospital. We will find a new house for us, just as we said. I will tell Mr Doyle I cannot go to Egypt. Not until you are fully recovered.

Suddenly she became aware that tears were rolling down her face.

He might not recover. He might die. The man who'd entered her life just three years ago and had become the most important part of her existence, even if now and then they disagreed, might die.

I cannot bear it, welled up in her.

She'd been walking towards the entrance of the National Gallery, now wearing her coat, when she'd heard the shot. Immediately there'd been confusion and panic.

'A man's been shot!' someone had yelled from out in the street.

She'd run out, and immediately recognised the body lying on the ground as Daniel. She threw herself down on her knees beside him and began to raise his head, before a uniformed attendant stopped her.

'Don't touch him, miss,' he warned her. 'I used to be a hospital orderly and moving someone who's been shot can sometimes make things worse for them.'

And so Abigail had sat herself down on the pavement beside Daniel's unconscious form, willing him to be alive. She heard the voices around her.

'What happened?' asked one.

'Someone shot this chap. Then he ran off. I saw him running towards Charing Cross Road.'

After that everything became a blur. Stanford Beckett appeared, horrified by what had happened. All the time Abigail refused to move, her eyes on Daniel the whole time, leaning forward as she did now to make sure he still breathed, only getting to her feet when the ambulance and the police arrived. The constable who appeared was none other than PC Wurzel, who recognised Abigail and Daniel, and immediately took charge, ordering the crowd to move back and sending another constable who'd appeared to find Inspector Feather. It was Wurzel who instructed the ambulance crew to allow Abigail to travel with them and ascertained that they would be going to University College Hospital.

The journey to the hospital had been a nightmare, the co-driver ringing a handbell loudly all the way to clear traffic from their route, and the vehicle rattling and jolting over the cobbles.

When they reached the hospital, Abigail had been directed to a waiting area while Daniel was rushed in on a trolley. Abigail had sat there for an hour in a state of terror at not knowing what Daniel's condition was. Inspector Feather appeared, joined shortly afterwards by Chief Superintendent Armstrong, and while Feather sat with Abigail, Armstrong proceeded to throw his weight around with the hospital authorities, almost threatening to impose martial law on the hospital.

When Armstrong joined them, he was able to tell Abigail that Daniel was being operated on, and by the best surgeon there was, a Mr Edmund Heppenstall.

'The same one?' asked Feather.

'It seems so,' said Armstrong. 'And I've told them that you, Miss Fenton, are here as an agent of the Metropolitan Police and my instructions are that you must stay with him at all times if he comes out of the operation.' As soon as he saw the look of anguish on Abigail's face he cursed silently under his breath, and corrected himself hastily: 'I meant, of course, *when* he comes out. They tell me that Heppenstall is the best surgeon there is. If anyone can save him, he can. He's in the best hands. I'm assured they'll look after both of you here, but if there are any problems, send for me.' He produced his pencil and notebook and wrote something down in it, then tore out the page and handed it to her. 'This is my home address if you need to get hold of me.'

'Thank you,' said Abigail, taking it.

After the chief superintendent had gone, Feather said to Abigail: 'He means well.'

'I know,' said Abigail. 'Do you know who did it?'

'No,' said Feather. 'We know that he disappeared up Charing Cross Road, but what happened to him then we have no idea. We have a description of him, but it could apply to so many. Average height, slim build, wearing a heavy topcoat. He had a scarf pulled up around his face so no one could make a guess as to how old he was.' He looked anxiously at Abigail. 'It must be connected to the mystery rich man we're looking for. It suggests Daniel and you are getting close. Have you got any possible suspects?'

She shook her head sadly.

'The men we looked into, none of them could have done it. Each of them had an alibi for at least one of the murders.'

'So we're no nearer to finding out our mystery killer,' said Feather resignedly.

'Oh, I'll find him,' said Abigail firmly. 'If it takes the rest of my life.'

Now, hours since that conversation with John Feather, she sat and looked at her unconscious lover, her partner, her husband in all but name, and her heart ached.

'I'll find him, Daniel,' she promised.

She went over in her mind everything that had happened since they'd first been contacted by Stanford Beckett. Somewhere in those memories was the answer, she was sure of it. They'd successfully tracked down Joe Wallace, why couldn't she use the same methods to find out who this mystery rich man was?

He had a carriage, and a driver. He'd cultivated the company of Kate Branson, picking her up at Charing Cross Station. Joe Wallace didn't have a butcher's van, or any sort of covered transport, so the bodies of both Anne-Marie Dresser and Kate Branson must have been delivered to the National Gallery in this rich man's carriage.

Joe Wallace had been killed in a privy of a tavern in

Seven Dials in Covent Garden.

Seven Dials, Charing Cross Station and the National Gallery were all within the same close distance to one another. The mystery killer was familiar with all three locations, shown by the fact that he'd known about The Flower Pot tavern in the tangle of narrow alleys and lanes that made up Seven Dials. He was also familiar with the underworld, both the fringe underworld of prostitutes and the hardcore violent world of Seven Dials. And he was familiar with the National Gallery. She reflected bitterly that all of this added up to someone like Walter Sickert, who inhabited all three worlds. Was that why these places had been chosen, because they all pointed to Sickert?

Who could hate Sickert so much they were prepared to murder, and had no concrete alibi for any of the murders?

Suddenly her bladder told her she needed to go to the toilet.

'I'll be back in a moment, my love,' she whispered, even though she knew he couldn't hear her.

The conveniences were on the next floor down. After using the toilet, she splashed cold water on her face in an effort to help her stay awake. If Daniel came round while she was sitting beside his bed, she didn't want him to see her fast asleep.

She climbed the stairs back to where his private room was, and as she approached it she became aware of a rustling noise coming from inside the room. A nurse, she assumed, but when she walked into the room, she saw the figure of a man standing over Daniel's bed holding a pillow and about to push it down onto his face.

'No!' she yelled, and hurled herself at the man. The man

dropped the pillow and swung a punch at her, which caught her on the side of the head and sent her crashing to the floor. She leapt to her feet and chased after the fleeing man, catching him as they reached the stairs. She grabbed at his coat and he swung his elbow back hard into her chest, then punched her again, this time in the face, smashing into her nose, filling her eyes with tears and sending her tumbling. When she pulled herself to her feet, she was aware she was clutching a torn fragment of a man's white scarf in her grip.

She ran down the stairs, looking over the banisters as she did so, but the man had gone and a door to the outside on the floor below was just swinging to a close. She continued hurrying down and pushed open the door and looked out. The street outside was empty and there were no sounds of running footsteps.

Desperate to make sure that Daniel hadn't suffered any harm, Abigail turned and ran up the stairs and back into his room. Daniel lay the same as before, on his back, his breathing shallow. The pillow the man had used to try to smother him lay on the floor.

'Is everything all right?' asked a nurse who had appeared in the doorway. 'I heard a shout of alarm and the sound of running feet.'

'Someone just tried to kill Mr Wilson,' burst out Abigail. 'I went to the toilet and when I came back a man was in this room trying to smother him with a pillow.'

The nurse gaped at her in bewilderment.

'Surely not!' she said.

'Yes,' said Abigail. 'I'm going to stay here in case he returns. But I need to send urgent messages to Chief Superintendent

Armstrong and Inspector Feather at their homes.'

'But it's the middle of the night,' the nurse pointed out.

'They told me to contact them if anything happened to Mr Wilson during the night,' Abigail told her firmly. 'An attempt to kill him fits that bill.'

CHAPTER THIRTY-TWO

Inspector Feather was the first to arrive after a hospital porter had been sent out with Abigail's urgent messages.

'My God, Abigail. The killer was here?'

'Trying to smother Daniel with a pillow,' said Abigail. 'I'd only left this room for a moment to go to the toilet. He must have been watching and waiting.'

'Did you catch a look at his face?'

'No. He had a scarf wrapped round the lower part of his face and a cap pulled down over his eyes.' She held out the scrap of cloth she'd managed to grab. 'I got this. It must have torn off his scarf.'

Feather took it, looked at it, then sniffed at it.

'It's got some sort of scent on it,' he said. 'What is it?'

'I have no idea,' said Abigail. 'It's not one I'm familiar with.' Then she stopped. 'Yes I am. I've smelt it before, but I can't remember where.'

There was the heavy tread of footsteps from outside, then the bulky figure of Chief Superintendent Armstrong thrust his way into the room. He looked down at Daniel and asked: 'How is he?'

'Still the same,' said Abigail. 'A doctor has checked on him since the attacker fled and says there's no change.'

'He tried to suffocate him, you said in your note.'

'Yes,' said Abigail. 'He'd have succeeded, too, if I'd been a moment longer.'

'And we have no idea who it was?' asked Armstrong.

'No, but I managed to tear off a piece of his scarf,' said Abigail.

Feather offered the piece of cloth to Armstrong, who put it to his nose, and then looked at it in distaste. 'My God!' he said. 'Detective Sergeant Rowbotham! He used to spray his clothes with this. We were glad when he left.'

'Lemon and bergamot!!' exclaimed Abigail suddenly.

'Yes, that's the stuff,' said Armstrong. He looked at Abigail, curious. 'How did you know?'

'Daniel mentioned a detective who used to wear this scent when we came across the smell before in Simon Anstis' studio.'

'Simon Anstis?' said Feather. 'The one who damaged Sickert's painting?'

'Yes,' said Abigail. 'He's our mystery rich man, the killer.'

'Artists aren't rich,' said Armstrong doubtfully.

'His father is,' said Abigail. 'Lord Yaxley.'

'Right,' said Armstrong determinedly. 'We'll find this Anstis and bring him in. But, in the meantime, just in case he tries anything again, we'll arrange a police guard outside this room. I'll fix that with the hospital authorities. And I'll also arrange for a cot bed to be brought in here. If you're going to be here all night, you'll need to get some sleep once the duty officer arrives to be on guard.' He turned to Feather. 'Wait here with Miss Fenton while I deal with that, Inspector. When I come back, I'll take over while you arrange for a rota of police officers to be on guard here until we catch this bloke.'

'Yes, sir,' said Feather.

He waited until the chief superintendent had gone, then he produced a long black wooden stick from his inner pocket and gave it to Abigail. 'A standard issue police truncheon, Abigail, just in case Anstis comes back. I promise you, this'll stop him in his tracks. I'll also come back in the morning to check on things.'

'Thank you, John.'

'With the cot coming, once the police guard is on duty, you can put your head down.'

'I doubt if I'll be able to sleep.'

'You'll be surprised. After the kind of shocks you've had, you will.'

It was three o'clock in the morning before the police constable reported for duty. He informed Abigail of his presence, then took up his position outside the door. Abigail checked on Daniel who was still unconscious, and then lay down on the temporary cot the hospital had provided. I'll just grab a half-hour, she promised herself; but it was half past six when the arrival of a nurse to check on Daniel woke her.

Abigail left the nurse to her duties while she went to the convenience to splash water on her face, and then went in search of a cup of tea.

She returned to the room, found the nurse was still at work, cleaning the wound in Daniel's back and checking his life signs, so she told the constable she would be going out to get something to eat and would return shortly.

There was a small cafe close to the hospital that served breakfast to mainly working people. She ordered and ate a fried breakfast ravenously, aware that she hadn't eaten anything since yesterday lunchtime before she and Daniel had left for the National Gallery. That done, she bought some newspapers from a street vendor and took them back to Daniel's room at the hospital. She'd hoped the nurse would still be there so that she could ask about his condition, and whether he was showing any signs of improving, but the nurse had gone. Determined to ask the next nurse who appeared, she ensconced herself in the chair beside Daniel's bed and began to read the papers. The banner headline on the front page of *The Telegraph* was 'Museum Detective Shot'.

Her eyes filled with tears and she thought: I can't cope with this at this moment, and she put the newspapers down and just sat, her eyes on the unconscious Daniel, which is where Fred Abberline found her when he arrived and knocked on the door of the room just after nine o'clock.

'I see you've got a police guard,' he said. He showed her the newspaper he was carrying with the banner headline. 'I came as soon as I saw it.'

'I was going to send you a note to tell you. I'm sorry.'

'That's all right, you've had other things on your mind.' He looked at the police truncheon lying on the bedside table. 'I see you've got a billy club, as we called them.'

'Inspector Feather gave it to me after Daniel was attacked here last night.'

'Attacked? Here, in the hospital?'

'Yes. I went to the toilet and while I was out of the room the killer came in and tried to smother Daniel with a pillow. I came in and caught him, but he got away. But at least we know who he is.'

'Who?'

'Simon Anstis. He's a would-be artist. The police are looking for him.'

'Well, if he comes back and you give him a swipe with that he'll know it. Lignum vitae. The hardest wood in the world. I've still got my old one. Did you know that when a copper retires from the beat he takes his truncheon with him? I bet Daniel's got his stashed away in a cupboard somewhere. It's a tradition because it's his own very personal weapon. Many coppers decorate their truncheons, paint it or put studs in it to mark it as theirs.' He looked at her, concerned. 'Did he hurt you badly? I can see the bruise on your cheek.'

'It was mainly my pride that was hurt because I let him get away. But, yes, he did punch me and it still hurts.'

'Have you read the papers?'

'I can't, not just yet.'

'I know how you feel,' said Abberline. He settled himself down on the temporary cot. 'I was the same when one of my colleagues got shot. We were chasing after some tearaway who suddenly pulled this gun out and bang! Bert went down and that was it. I couldn't look at a paper for two days after.' He looked at Daniel. 'Have they said how he's doing?'

She shook her head.

'The nurse came to check on him, so I left him to her and went out and had a bite of breakfast. By the time I came back, she was gone.'

'I can ask, if you'd like.'

'I don't know if they'd tell you. They're very close about saying anything, even to next of kin. I'm going to ask the next one who comes in to look at him.'

'Can I get you anything?'

'No, thanks for offering. Now there's a police guard on the room I feel all right about going out to get a bite of food or something.'

'What are the police doing to find this Anstis character?' asked Abberline.

'I don't know,' admitted Abigail. 'Whatever the usual procedures are, I suppose. Checking where he lives, people he knows.'

'I should be out there with them,' said Abberline. 'Armstrong doesn't like me, but in this case, I'd hope he'd let me be part of the search team. I'm still a good detective. I'm dogged. I'll keep going till I find Anstis.' Abberline took out his notebook and a pencil. 'So let me know everything you've got on him. Description. Addresses. Places he hangs out.'

Abigail gave him everything they knew about him along with the address of his studio. 'He murdered Joe Wallace in the privy of a pub called The Flower Pot in Seven Dials, so we assume he knows that area well. And his father is Lord Yaxley. I'm afraid I don't know where Lord Yaxley lives.'

'Don't worry, I'll find out,' said Abberline.

'Also, he's armed,' warned Abigail. 'He's got a gun.'

'So have I,' said Abberline, and he patted his inside pocket. 'And it's licensed.' He got up. 'I'll be back whether I've got news or not.'

'I'll be here,' said Abigail. 'I want to be here when Daniel wakes up.'

* * *

Abberline made his way to Scotland Yard, where he asked for Inspector Feather. The desk sergeant was new to Abberline, but one who obviously recognised the name when Abberline wrote it down for him on the visitor form.

'It's an honour to meet you, sir,' said the desk sergeant. 'Would you allow me to shake your hand?'

Abberline held out his hand and shook the desk sergeant's hand. 'Who do I have the pleasure of addressing?'

'John Richardson, sir.'

'Then it's my pleasure to make your acquaintance, Sergeant Richardson.'

The sergeant sent a message up to Feather's office, and shortly afterwards John Feather descended the stairs and walked across the marbled floor of reception, a welcoming smile on his face.

'Fred,' he greeted him, and the two men shook hands. 'Have you been to the hospital?'

'I have.'

'How's Daniel?'

'Still alive, thankfully. But still unconscious. Although that may be for the best for him at the moment, after what he went through.'

'And how's Abigail?'

'Bearing up. She's strong.' He looked towards the stairs inquisitively. 'Is the chief superintendent in?'

'No, he's gone to see the home secretary to make his report. I think he was glad of the opportunity to be able to give him some good news on this case for once: that we know who committed the murders and have a manhunt out for him.' His face looked sombre as he added: 'It's a pity it's at Daniel's expense. Do they think he'll pull through?'

'All they'll say is that the surgeon is the best man there is, and if anyone can save him, he can.'

'Mr Heppenstall,' nodded Feather.

'A former chief suspect,' said Abberline. 'I'm glad he never found out he was in the frame. So, what's happening at the moment? Any leads?'

'None that have paid off,' admitted Feather. 'We've tried all the places where Anstis is known to hang around, in addition to his studio, but so far nothing. He's gone to ground. The problem is he obviously has contacts in places like Seven Dials, and if he's hiding out somewhere like that it's going to be hard. Especially because he's obviously got money, so he'll be bribing people who can smuggle him out of London and maybe on board a boat.'

'Does he have money?' asked Abberline thoughtfully. 'Abigail told me about his studio, which doesn't sound very luxurious, and where it is I remember as being a bit rundown.'

'It still is,' agreed Feather.

'So where does this Simon Anstis keep his carriage?'

Feather stared at Abberline, stunned. 'Fred,' he said, 'you are a genius.'

'No, just a plodding old ex-copper. But it struck me that he has to keep this mysterious carriage of his somewhere. And then it struck me, maybe it's not his.'

'His father's,' said Feather. 'Lord Yaxley. Who's a very doting father by all accounts, who seems happy to provide everything his son wants to be an artist. Maybe he's also happy to let him borrow his carriage and drive it whenever he wants.'

'Have you called on Lord Yaxley?' asked Abberline.

'Yes, it was one of the first places we thought of. He told us

314

his son wasn't there.'

'How did he react to you asking for his son?'

'At first he was indignant, but then when we told him why we wanted to talk to him, he got defensive and looked unsettled.'

'So you didn't see him on your own?'

'No, the chief superintendent came with me. When it's someone that high in society, you need clout.'

'You told him you wanted to talk to him about the murders?'

'Yes.'

'And what did he say?'

'That was when he got most defensive.'

Even with the chief superintendent in attendance, their visit to Lord Yaxley's house had been short and their reception definitely nasty. It had begun with the butler opening the door a long time after they'd rung the bell. The butler had been dressed in a dressing gown thrown over his pyjamas, and his opening angry words had been: 'Do you know what time it is? It's the middle of the night! Why are you waking us at this hour? Who the devil are you?'

'Chief Superintendent Armstrong from Scotland Yard, and this is Inspector Feather. We wish to see Lord Yaxley.'

'At this hour? Out of the question! His Lordship is in bed.'

'This is a murder enquiry. Please rouse his Lordship.'

'I will do no such thing.'

'Then you will tell us whether Lord Yaxley's son, Simon Anstis, is here, or has been here tonight.'

'What's going on, Purkiss?' drawled an elegant voice, and a second man appeared, in his sixties, tall and thin, also wearing a dressing gown over pyjamas.

'Police, my Lord.'

'Police? At this hour?'

'Lord Yaxley, I presume,' said Armstrong, and he introduced himself and Inspector Feather again. 'We are in search of your son, Simon Anstis.'

'For what purpose?' demanded Yaxley coldly.

'We wish to talk to him regarding a series of murders.'

'Murders?' repeated Yaxley incredulously. 'Are you mad? This is my son we are talking about.'

'Is he in this house at this moment?'

'No, he is not. Now I will trouble you to leave. Purkiss, shut the door.'

'Yes, m'lord,' said the butler, and the front door slammed shut.

Feather looked at the chief superintendent. 'What do we do now, sir?'

'We leave,' grunted Armstrong. 'Without a warrant there's little else we can do.'

Now Feather was back at Lord Yaxley's house, this time with Fred Abberline in tow. The same butler, Purkiss, who'd opened the door to Feather and Armstrong during the night opened it again. This time he was dressed in a long frock coat over a striped waistcoat and dark trousers. He glared out at them.

'Remember me?' asked Feather. 'I was here before, along with Chief Superintendent Armstrong.'

'Who is it, Purkiss?'

As before, the tall elegant figure of Lord Yaxley hoved into view, and the butler opened the door wider so that Yaxley could see who was on his doorstep.

'The police again,' scowled Yaxley. 'What do you want? If you're still looking for my son, he's not here. And no, I don't know where he is. I would also suggest you are wasting your time looking for him in connection with any murders. My son is an eminently respected artist.'

'Yes, sir,' Feather. 'But actually, we're here to look at your carriage. I assume you have one?'

'My carriage?' repeated Yaxley in bewilderment. 'What on earth for?'

'Pursuant to the same case, sir.'

'These murders you keep on about and had the audacity to wake me up in the middle of the night over? This is an outrage.'

'Nevertheless, sir, this is a murder enquiry.'

'I don't care what sort of enquiry this is. Do you know who I am?'

'Yes, sir. Lord Yaxley.'

'A man with considerable influence in political circles, including many in the Cabinet.'

'Yes, sir,' said Feather, calmly but doggedly. 'May we look at your carriage?'

'No you may not!'

'May we talk to your carriage driver?'

'Again, no you may not. Now leave my property, and I must warn you that I shall be taking this unnecessary harassment up with the authorities, including my close acquaintance, the Commissioner of the Metropolitan Police.'

With that, he stepped back and the butler shut the door firmly.

Feather sighed. 'We won't get anywhere here without a warrant.'

'Did you notice the painting in the hallway?'

'Which one? There were loads of them.'

'The portrait of Lord Yaxley sitting in the driving seat of a four-wheeled carriage with four horses.'

Feather looked at him, worried.

'You're not suggesting . . . ?'

'Why not? If he can handle four horses, he can handle one. And he'd obviously do anything for his son.'

'Even this kind of murder and butchery?'

'Abigail said that Daniel told her Lord Yaxley hates Sickert. I think a search warrant might prove useful.'

Feather shook his head.

'We've got nothing to base it on. No evidence, none that will convince a magistrate. The fact that our suspect is Lord Yaxley's son means nothing, nor does a portrait of him driving a carriage, however much we think it helps our case. We need something concrete.' He gave a growl of frustration. 'We need to get hold of Simon Anstis.'

CHAPTER THIRTY-THREE

Simon Anstis entered the reception area of University College Hospital. In his hand he held a bouquet of flowers, encased in decorated paper. Inside the bouquet was a long, thin-bladed and very sharp knife.

Wilson and Fenton, he thought vengefully. They are the ones who've destroyed everything for me. Everything would have worked perfectly if they hadn't poked their noses in. Now, his life was in ruins. Well first he'd finish Wilson, and then he'd flee. Somewhere abroad. Change his name. Plenty of others had done it.

He walked up to the main reception and smiled at the woman behind the desk.

'Good morning,' he said. 'I wonder if it will be possible for me to visit Mr Daniel Wilson, who's a patient here. I'm an old friend of his.'

'I'm afraid Mr Wilson is not receiving visitors,' said the receptionist.

'I understand. Would it be possible for me to leave these flowers for him? I've been told there's a policeman on duty outside his room. I wondered if it would be all right for me to leave them with him.'

The receptionist looked doubtful. 'I'm not sure,' she said. 'I'd need to check.'

Antis smiled at her again. 'That's all right,' he said. 'I quite understand. I'll return another day.'

He walked away from the reception desk. Damn, he thought. This isn't going to be as easy as I'd hoped. Still, with just one policeman on duty outside his room, I can talk my way past him. A gentleman with upper-class manners and educated voice can go anywhere.

He went back to the double doors leading to the street, and – as he'd done before on his failed attempt to smother Wilson – he made for the stairs to the first floor where Wilson's private room was situated. A solitary policeman was on duty outside the room.

'Good morning, Officer,' smiled Anstis. 'The receptionist said I could come up here and leave these flowers for Mr Wilson on the chair beside his bed. I'm an old friend of his.'

The constable looked uncertain. 'I need to get permission from the matron first,' he said.

'Of course,' nodded Anstis genially. 'I'll wait here while you go and see her.' As the constable looked like he was about to insist Anstis left and returned later, Anstis added: 'That way, if anyone comes and wonders where you are, I can tell them. We don't want you getting in trouble for deserting your post.'

The constable hesitated, then nodded. 'I won't be a moment,' he said.

Anstis smiled and waited until the constable had disappeared round the corner. Then he took the knife from the bouquet, abandoned the flowers on the chair beside the door, pushed open the door and walked in.

Daniel Wilson lay in the bed, still unconscious, pale, barely breathing.

So, still alive, but not for much longer, thought Anstis vengefully.

He approached the bed, the knife held to one side ready to plunge it into Wilson's heart. He pulled back his hand, and then heard a swishing sound behind him, and the next second pain of a level he'd never experienced before flooded through him as something crashed down on his wrist and he heard and felt the bones in his wrist break.

He screamed and spun round and saw the enraged features of Abigail Fenton, and then she swung the heavy police truncheon at him and his face exploded in blood and pain and everything went black.

Fred Abberline sat next to a wall at one side of the interview room in the basement of Scotland Yard. In the centre of the room Chief Superintendent Armstrong and Inspector Feather sat looking at the forlorn figure of Simon Anstis, whose damaged face was heavily bandaged and whose broken right arm was encased in plaster and in a sling.

Abigail was still at University College Hospital, watching over Daniel. Armstrong had generously invited Abberline to sit in and observe the questioning of Anstis. 'That way, you can tell her what happened,' Armstrong had grunted. 'Save me doing it.'

Anstis didn't need persuading to talk. Armstrong's opening question 'Why did you do it?' had been like releasing a dam. All the hatred and anger and misery poured out from him.

'It was about Sickert. I hated him. No – more than hated him. There isn't a word to describe the depth of my feelings of anger and hatred towards him. It began when he mocked my work. He called me an "amateur dauber", and a "would-be Sunday painter". And he said it to others, abusing me to them behind my back so that people laughed at me and disparaged my work. Meanwhile, the critics heaped praise on Sickert's work. The top people flocked to have their portraits painted by him. Some people bought my work, but very few, and then only to find favour with my father.

'And then Sickert brought Anne-Marie back from France with him and installed her in a room. I fell in love with her as soon as I saw her. More than love, it was a passion like I'd never experienced before. She agreed to model for me, naked. The same as she did for Sickert. But whereas she allowed Sickert to have her completely, she kept me at arm's length. She deliberately played with my feelings. I think she may have used my interest in her to titillate Sickert.

'With that, and his mockery of me as an artist, I knew I had to get rid of him if I was ever going to find some kind of inner peace. But if I just killed him, or got someone else to do it for me, I knew it would just elevate his position as an artist. He would be seen as the great British artist who died too young. And Anne-Marie would mourn him instead of coming to me for comfort after his death. I had to do more than just have him killed, I had to discredit him. Disgrace him, so that the critics and the people would shun his work and Anne-Marie would recoil from him in disgust. But how?

'And then I remembered that there had been rumours at the time of Jack the Ripper of Sickert having been part of a conspiracy that carried out the murders. As luck would have it, I was having a jacket made for me by a tailor's in Bethnal Green, Barrowman's. I went there because they'd made clothes for my father, and he said I could put it on his account there. While I was there, being measured, I got talking to the tailor's apprentice and when he asked me what I did, I told him I was an artist. At that he became very sullen. I asked him what was the matter with artists, and he told me that his mother had had an encounter with one and she died as a result. I asked him where he came from, and when he told me Whitechapel, I realised that it was possible he was one of the children of a Ripper victim. So I brought up the name Sickert, and he went into a rage, saying that he was the man who'd killed his mother in conspiracy with the Queen's doctor and her grandson, and how they'd got away with it because of who they were.'

'This was Henry Nichols?' asked Armstrong, checking the name on the notes he'd been given.

Anstis nodded. 'He told me he wasn't the only one who felt this way. He said there was a childhood friend of his whose mother had also died at the hands of this trio, but who's death hadn't even been attributed to the Ripper, so there was no chance of him trying to claim compensation. Not that any of them ever got compensation, but there were rumours that they might be able to. He said this friend of his, a butcher, was even angrier than him about the injustice of what had been done, and that no one had been tried. Not that there was much they could do about it: the Queen's doctor was dead, and so was her grandson. The only one of the three still alive was Sickert, and he was untouchable because of all the famous and influential people he knew.

'That's when I had my idea: how I could discredit Sickert in the eyes of everyone, and have him executed as a filthy, loathsome murder. I got Nichols to introduce me to his butcher friend.'

'Joe Wallace?'

Again, Antis gave a nod. 'I met Wallace and told him I shared his anger at Sickert, and that it was unjust that he was still walking about free, while his mother and the other victims had no chance of justice. But then I told him there was a way to get retribution for what had happened to his mother and the others and have Sickert pay with his life, for him to be executed and everyone would know that he was the Ripper. I told him that there was a young woman who was a prostitute who also modelled for Sickert. I told him she was sick and on the point of death. I said that when she died, if I brought her body to him, he could inflict on her the same kind of wounds that had been inflicted on the Ripper's victims. Then we'd leave her body at the National Gallery, where she'd be recognised as one of Sickert's models, and I'd send an anonymous letter to Scotland Yard naming Sickert as the person who'd killed and butchered her.'

'You were already planning to kill Anne-Marie?'

'No!' Anstis' face became a mask of pain and anguish. 'I loved Anne-Marie. I'd never hurt her.'

'Then who?'

'Kate Branson. I found out that she'd modelled for Sickert, and where her pitch was at Charing Cross Station. I went there to make her acquaintance. Get her to trust me.'

'Which she did.'

'Yes. She was a nice girl, but a necessary casualty to make sure that Sickert was arrested and tried. I made contact with her over a few weeks and was building up to the point where I would kill her, when everything changed.

'Anne-Marie had come to my studio for another sitting, and this time she became . . . scornful of me. She'd always been scornful before, teased me, but this time she was worse. She taunted me, repeated the words that Sickert had used about me: an amateur dauber and a would-be Sunday painter. She also then thrust her naked body at me and began to describe what she and Sickert would do together. It was too much, and for the first time ever I hit her, and she fell, and struck her head on the fender. At first, I thought she was just unconscious, but then I realised she was dead. I'd killed her! I hadn't meant to, it was the taunting and everything else that overcame me and I lashed out, and now she was dead.

'What could I do? Go to the police? Tell them it had been an accident? They wouldn't believe me. And then I thought of my plan for using Kate Branson. It would be the same, except it would now be Anne-Marie.

'I put her in my father's carriage and drove to Whitechapel. I collected Joe Wallace. We took the body to a shed where he did the work, cutting her up. I guess for him her body was just another piece of meat, but for me it was misery. I couldn't stay in the shed and watch. When he'd finished, he brought her body out and we put it in the carriage and took it to the

National Gallery, where we left it. I drove Joe home, then left a note at Scotland Yard naming Sickert. As I'd hoped, Sickert was arrested. But then I heard he was being released. It was so unjust!

'On Wednesday I contacted Joe and told him the disaster that had happened, and that Sickert was going to get away with it. Luckily, I told him, another woman who had been his model had also just died. We'd do the same to this woman as we had to Anne-Marie and leave her body at the National Gallery. This would clinch it that Sickert was the one responsible.'

'Wasn't Wallace suspicious about these women turning up dead so soon after one another?'

'I'm afraid that women who lead that kind of lifestyle often die young, and in tragic circumstances. Growing up in Whitechapel, Wallace knew that.'

'So you picked Kate Branson up that night, killed her and took her to Wallace at Whitechapel.'

Anstis nodded. 'The second time was easier. The first time, I was on edge in case we were caught leaving her body by the gallery.'

'But then, Sickert was allowed to leave the country.'

'I was furious. And desperate. I'd been keeping watch on Sickert and I knew he had some drunk staying at his studio, so I persuaded Joe to go there with me and kill him. I was sure that would put the final nail in Sickert's coffin.'

'But it didn't,' said Armstrong. 'And then we got on to Joe.'

'He came to see me, begging for money. He wanted me to get him out of the country. I told him I would, that I knew someone at Seven Dials who could arrange it. He believed me because everyone knows that everything can be bought in Seven

Dials. I thought that once I'd killed Joe and left the razor there, that would be the end of it. I'd have to find another way to discredit Sickert, but at least I was safe. But then the barman at The Flower Pot contacted me. He said he knew who I was and what I'd done, and he wanted money to keep quiet. I couldn't let that happen. If he knew, then just like Joe Wallace, he could talk.'

'So you killed him.'

'He told me that Daniel Wilson was looking for some rich man they believed was the person behind Joe Wallace and the killings.'

'So you shot Daniel Wilson.'

'It was the only way. I was sure the police would have been happy to think the case ended with Joe committing suicide, but Wilson and that Fenton woman were like terriers.' He looked down at his broken wrist. 'That woman did this. She should be charged.'

Feather looked down at the piece of paper Abberline had passed to him before the interview started, and said quietly: 'The carriage you used has been identified as belonging to your father.'

'No!' shouted Anstis, alarmed. 'No one could identify it! That's rubbish!'

'Let me put it another way,' said Feather calmly. 'The driver has been identified as your father.'

'Impossible!' said Anstis, staring wildly around. 'He was masked!' And then, as he realised what he'd said, he collapsed, falling face forward onto the table, his body heaving with sobs.

Armstrong looked towards Abberline and nodded, then at Inspector Feather.

'Good work,' he said. He looked at the constables and ordered. 'Take him away to the custody cells.'

As Anstis was lifted from his chair and led out of the room, Armstrong turned to Feather. 'Time to bring in Lord Yaxley. And I'm coming with you, Inspector.'

CHAPTER THIRTY-FOUR

Chief Superintendent Armstrong led the way up the gleaming white marble front steps to the imposing black hardwood front door of Lord Yaxley's residence. He was followed by Inspector Feather, Sergeant Cribbens, Dr Snow, a uniformed sergeant and the two constables. At the kerb stood their two vehicles, a police van and a carriage.

Dr Snow had been added to the team at the tentative suggestion of Inspector Feather.

'Why?' Armstrong had demanded aggressively when Feather made the suggestion.

'If you remember, sir, he was able to identify the speck of sawdust Wilson and Miss Fenton found in the boot print in Sickert's studio, which tied Joe Wallace to O'Tool's murder. If we locate the carriage at Lord Yaxley's, he might find traces of evidence inside it that will link the carriage to the murders of the two women.' Then he added quietly: 'And Dr Snow is the home secretary's nephew.'

Armstrong's face broke into a slow grin. 'Point taken, Inspector.'

Armstrong pulled on the bell pull and they heard the ringing sound from inside the house. There was a few minutes' wait, then the door opened and the butler looked out at them.

'Chief Superintendent Armstrong from Scotland Yard,' announced Armstrong imperiously.

'The tradesmen's entrance is at the side,' said the butler curtly, and began to close the door; but Armstrong planted his boot in it to stop it.

'I have a warrant to search this house,' he snapped. 'You will direct me to Lord Yaxley.'

'What's going on, Purkiss?' called a voice, and then the elegant figure of Lord Yaxley appeared.

'Police, your Lordship,' said the butler in a tone of great disapproval.

'Again!' raged Yaxley. 'This the third time I've been bothered in this way.'

'But the first time with warrants,' said Armstrong. 'One for your arrest, Lord Yaxley, as an accomplice to murder. The other a warrant to search these premises.' He looked coldly at Yaxley. 'We have your son in custody, and he's made a full confession.'

Yaxley stared at the chief superintendent, and then he began to retreat into the house.

'Get him!' Armstrong shouted at the uniformed sergeant and one of the constables, and the two rushed in and grabbed hold of Yaxley and hauled him back to the doorway. Purkiss, the butler, stared at the police, and at his master, in bewilderment.

'Put him in the van,' ordered Armstrong. 'And the butler, too. I'm not taking any chances on him messing with evidence before we've had a chance to look at everything.'

'No!' howled Purkiss, and he backed away.

'Sergeant Cribbens!' snapped Armstrong.

Cribbens stepped forward, grabbed the butler by an arm and twisted it up behind his back, making the butler cry out in pain.

'Come on, you,' snapped Cribbens.

'Put them in two separate holding cells,' said Armstrong. 'We'll be with you once we've gone over this place.'

'You can't do this!' raged Yaxley. 'I'll have you sacked!'

Struggling and resisting, Yaxley was forced to the police van and pushed inside, and locked into the van's cell. Purkiss, all the fight gone out of him, trudged unhappily up the wooden steps and into the back of the van, where he was also locked in.

'Right, Inspector, Dr Snow, let's get to work,' said the chief superintendent grimly.

Abberline returned to the hospital and found Abigail still beside Daniel's bed.

'Any news?' he asked.

'He's still breathing,' said Abigail. 'I'm waiting for Mr Heppenstall to arrive. The sister said he'd be along. How did it go with Simon Anstis?'

'A full confession,' said Abberline. 'It also looks like it was Lord Yaxley who drove the carriage on the nights of the murders.'

'Anstis' father?'

'Yes. The chief superintendent and the others have gone to

bring him in.' He smiled. 'A bit of a coup, I think.'

Suddenly both stopped and turned their attention to Daniel, caught by a sudden rasping sound.

'He coughed,' said Abigail, and she bent down to listen to him. Daniel was still prone, but his eyelids flickered, and then opened.

'Where am I?' he asked hoarsely.

Abberline patted Abigail on the shoulder.

'I'll find a nurse,' he told her. 'And then I'll leave you two together. I'll be back later.'

The short, round woman wearing an apron and with the worried expression looked at the chief superintendent.

'Where are you taking the master?' she asked.

'To Scotland Yard,' replied Armstrong. 'He's helping us with our enquiries.'

'I heard you say "murders",' said the woman anxiously.

'That's right,' said Armstrong. 'Who am I addressing?'

'Mrs Phillips, the housekeeper.' She looked bewildered. 'You took Mr Purkiss as well?'

'We did. Now, can you direct us to where Lord Yaxley keeps his carriage?'

'In the stables,' she said. 'In the courtyard.'

'And where do we find the driver?'

'Bert Stoke. He doesn't live in, he lodges with his sister.'

'Do you have his address?'

'Yes, I've got it in my book.'

As Mrs Phillips left to get Stoke's address, Armstrong turned to Feather.

'Right, once we've got his address, you go and see him,

Inspector. Find out about the carriage's movements, and when he drove it and when he didn't. I'll stay here with Dr Snow.' He then turned to Snow and said: 'You use whatever instruments you've brought with you to go over that carriage, inside and out, but especially inside. If they used it to transport the bodies, there might still be traces we can use as evidence.'

'Yes, sir,' said Snow delightedly. He patted the large bag he'd brought with him. 'I've brought a magnifying glass and bags with me, and a scalpel and tweezers to take samples that I can examine properly back at the laboratory.'

'Excellent,' said Armstrong. He gave a grim smile. 'If you can nail him with what you find, Doctor, I'll make sure this laboratory of yours becomes permanent.'

Abigail stood to one side and watched as Edmund Heppenstall carried out his examination. Daniel had been helped to sit up by two nurses and now he rested against a heap of pillows. He'd been turned on his side, then on his back, for Heppenstall to examine the gunshot wound, which had now been cleaned and re-dressed.

'You're coming on well, Mr Wilson,' said Heppenstall. 'Even though you may not feel it.'

'Who shot me?' asked Daniel, his voice still hoarse.

'I'll let Miss Fenton answer those kinds of questions,' said Heppenstall. 'I handle medical matters only. The main thing for you now is rest. You're going to be here at least another week before we can consider letting you go home. And after that I'll arrange for a district nurse to call in on you to check the wound.' He turned to Abigail and said: 'I would ask that you don't tire him, Miss Fenton. A few minutes more now, but then he needs rest. Proper rest. I suggest you go home. The staff here will take good care of him.'

'May I return later?'

'No. Leave it until tomorrow. And late morning, no earlier. I'll leave you now so you can say goodbye, but I shall return in ten minutes and will insist you leave if you're still here.'

After Heppenstall and the nurses had left, Abigail took her seat beside Daniel's bed and took hold of his hand.

'He's a good man,' she said. 'He saved your life. I'm glad he wasn't our killer.'

'So am I,' said Daniel. He frowned. 'But we still don't know what happened to his wife.'

'Sssh,' said Abigail with an apprehensive glance towards the door. 'This is not the place to talk about things like that, not if you want the staff to treat you kindly. Mr Heppenstall is viewed as some sort of saint here.'

'It's still an unanswered question,' said Daniel. 'Who shot me?'

'Simon Anstis. He's been arrested and he's made a full confession.'

'So, we got the killer.'

'We did.' She squeezed his hand. 'We'll talk more when I come tomorrow. I don't want Mr Heppenstall throwing me out when he returns, he might bar me.' She leant forward and kissed him gently on the mouth. 'I love you, Daniel. Mr Heppenstall bought you back from the dead, so now you have to do as he says and rest. I'll never forgive you if you try and do things and end up dying. Promise me?'

'I promise,' said Daniel. He forced a smile. 'I'll make sure I won't die because I have no intention of leaving you, Abigail. I'll see you tomorrow.'

Bert Stoke was a small man in his fifties and he looked at John Feather in surprise when the inspector introduced himself.

'Scotland Yard? Why are Scotland Yard coming to me and asking questions?'

'You are the carriage driver for Lord Yaxley?'

'Yes, but not just his driver. I also do general handyman stuff for him. Small repairs to the house, that sort of thing.'

'May I come in?' asked Feather.

Stoke nodded and took the inspector into the small parlour.

'Are you the only one who drives the carriage?' Feather asked as he took a seat.

'Mostly, but sometimes his Lordship likes to drive himself.'

'Did you drive the carriage on the nights of 14th and 17th February?'

'No, his Lordship gave me the night off both nights. Said he didn't need me. Funnily enough, when I got to work next morning on the Monday, the 15th, the first thing I did was check on the horse as I always do, and I was sure he'd been out. I always make sure he's wiped down before I stable him for the night, but it looked to me as if there was mud around his hooves. I asked his Lordship, but he said I must have missed the mud the last time I took him out. In fact, he got quite short with me about it, but I know I didn't miss the mud. I'm very particular.'

'What about the night of the 17th?'

'Well, that was another funny thing. I had an arrangement to play in a dominoes match. I'm part of a team and we play on

Wednesday nights at the Rose and Crown, so I make that my night off. But I always check with his Lordship in case he's got a change of plans and might need me. But that night he said again I wasn't needed.'

'Does that happen often, him not needing you?'

'Not really. He likes me to be available and if he needs me in an evening and he hasn't told me beforehand, he sends someone to fetch me. So I was quite pleased to know I wasn't going to be called for. It meant I could enjoy my dominoes with an easy mind.'

'And when you got to work on the morning of Thursday 17th February, did you notice anything about the horse that might indicate it had been out?'

'Not the horse, no. But there was a smell of cleaning fluid inside the carriage.'

'Did you ask Lord Yaxley about it?'

Stoke shook his head. 'No, not after the way he'd had a go at me when I mentioned the mud on the horse's hoof the day before. I didn't fancy getting another earful. His Lordship can get quite nasty when he's in a bad mood.'

CHAPTER THIRTY-FIVE

Abigail fell onto the armchair in their living room, sinking into its soft cushions, and closed her eyes. She'd had barely three hours' sleep since she and Daniel had woken on Sunday morning, and everything that had happened, the two attacks by Simon Anstis, and the agony of waiting to find out if Daniel would ever wake, had taken its toll of her. She could just feel herself slipping away, when a knocking at the door pulled her back to reality.

She forced herself up and along the passageway to the door, which she opened to find John Feather and Fred Abberline standing side by side.

'My God, you look like thinner versions of Tweedledum, and Tweedledee,' she said.

She led them through to the kitchen, where she filled the kettle and put it on the range. Then she realised the range had gone out.

'Sorry,' she apologised, 'force of habit. Usually Daniel keeps the embers ready to kick into life.'

'That's all right,' said Feather. 'You sit down, I'll do the range.'

Gratefully, Abigail sat down, Abberline joining her while Feather set to work to clean out the ashes in the grate and lay the fire.

'We turned up at the hospital at the same time to see how Daniel was, and were told you'd gone home and that Daniel was recovering, but not allowed visitors,' said Abberline. 'So we decided to join forces to fill you in on everything.'

'The hospital wouldn't tell us how he was,' said Feather. 'How is he?'

'Recovering, thank God,' said Abigail. 'He needs rest, which is why they sent me packing and have stopped all other visitors. What happened with Lord Yaxley?'

'He's under lock and key,' said Feather. 'We got all the evidence we need from the carriage to prove the bodies were transported in it. Dr Snow was in his element. He took samples of everything. He found tiny grains of sawdust in the carpet, proving that Joe Wallace had been in it. He also found minute traces of bodily fluids, as well as fibres from the clothes both women wore. They may have thought they'd cleaned the inside, but not well enough to hide things from someone like Dr Snow with all his paraphernalia and his microscopes.' He lifted the ashcan. 'Where do these go?' he asked.

'Outside,' said Abigail. 'You'll see the ash pit. Paper, wood and coal are in the scullery.'

Feather left to dispose of the ashes.

'By the way, Catherine Heppenstall has turned up,' Abberline told her.

'What?' said Abigail, surprised. 'Dead?'

'Very much alive. Emma heard that she turned up at her parents' house the day before yesterday. I intended to tell you when I saw you before, but what with one thing and another, and Daniel waking up.'

'Where had she been?'

'Appearing up north in a travelling show. Liverpool, Manchester, Carlisle, Newcastle. She's also changed her name. She's now known as Lola Lamprey.'

'Why did she come all this way south to see her parents?'

'I don't think it was just to see her parents. From what Emma's heard she came to London to ask Edmund Heppenstall for a divorce. Apparently, she wants to get married to one of her fellow performers. I think she's hoping for a divorce settlement. So, it's lucky we didn't pursue the idea that Heppenstall murdered her.'

'Daniel was still kicking himself over that,' sighed Abigail.

'But he was right about the butcher. And the rich toff behind him. That was great detective work.'

Feather reappeared, carrying a bucket of coal, along with old newspapers and kindling.

'I'll soon have this going for you,' he said, kneeling down beside the grate. 'I bet you're desperate for a cup of tea.'

'I'm more desperate for some sleep,' yawned Abigail.

Abberline and Feather exchanged looks.

'Then up you go, lass, and put your head down,' said Abberline. 'Me and John will get this range going and make ourselves a cuppa, and then we'll head off. We'll lock the front door and pop the key through the letter box.'

'No, you've come all this way, I should be a proper hostess.'

'You are, but first and foremost you're a friend. Go on, up you go. We've got the main news. We'll catch up with everything else later.'

Abigail looked at them, gratefully. 'Thank you,' she said. 'I don't know what we'd do without you.'

Despite feeling that she'd sleep right through to the next morning, Abigail woke in the middle of the night as the memories of the shooting of Daniel and Anstis' attacks on him flooded through her mind. Automatically, she reached out across the bed for Daniel, but found only the empty sheet, and suddenly she remembered that he was still at the hospital. But he was alive. Or was he? Fear struck her at the thought that he may have had a relapse, and she had to fight the urge to get out of bed, dress, and hurry to the hospital. No, she told herself. It's irrational. If anything bad had happened they'd send a message to her.

But would they?

From that moment on, try as she might, she couldn't sleep. She went downstairs and made herself a cup of tea, silently thanking John Feather for getting the range going. It was another two hours before she felt sleep overtaking her and she headed back to bed, uttering silent prayers that Daniel was still alive.

The first thing she did when she arrived at University College Hospital at half past ten the next morning was to stride up to reception and ask how Mr Daniel Wilson was. There was a heart-stopping moment's hesitation while the receptionist turned the pages of notes in front of her, then she smiled at

Abigail and said: 'He had a good night. He's awake. He's had breakfast.'

Abigail wanted to grab her and kiss her at this news, but instead she restrained herself to a smile of thanks, before heading up the stairs.

Daniel was sitting up in bed, a newspaper open in front of him, and he smiled broadly as Abigail came into the room.

'Good morning!' he said. 'Thank you for saving my life. They told me what you did to Simon Anstis.'

She kissed him, then sat down beside the bed.

'You'd have done the same for me.' She noticed a very large bouquet of flowers in a bowl on a side table. 'Where did the flowers come from?'

'Ellen Sickert.'

'She came to see you?'

'She came, but they wouldn't let her in. Mr Heppenstall has decreed that I'm only allowed one visitor, you. Any more would hamper my recovery. So she left the flowers with a note. She also, according to the sister, is paying the bills here for my hospitalisation and treatment.'

'Is that what she says in her note?'

'No, no mention of it. But the sister told me that she went to see the almoner and made arrangements for all bills regarding my treatment to be sent to her. She feels guilty because of what happened to me, that I was shot because of the case.'

'Well, she's right.'

'Yes, but she doesn't have to feel guilty over it.'

'I didn't bring you any flowers,' admitted Abigail. 'In fact, I didn't bring you anything. I wasn't sure if they'd allow you to have sweets or fruit.'

'I don't need anything except you,' said Daniel.

'By the way, Fred Abberline turned up at home yesterday with John Feather. They've got all the proof they need that Lord Yaxley drove the carriage on the nights of the murders. Oh, and Catherine Heppenstall has turned up. Only now she's calling herself Lola Lamprey.'

'Lola Lamprey? My God. Why?'

'It's her new stage name. She's been with some travelling show in the north of England.'

'How did you find this out?'

'Through Fred Abberline. Emma learnt that Catherine came south and visited her parents in Clapham as part of her journey to ask Mr Heppenstall for a divorce.'

'So I got that wrong,' said Daniel ruefully.

'But you got everything else right. Joe Wallace. The mystery rich man, who turned out to be Simon Anstis. Daniel Wilson, detective extraordinaire.'

'We did it together,' said Daniel. He looked down at himself ruefully. 'How long do I have to stay here?'

'Mr Heppenstall said at least a week, depending on how you heal. Remember, he said that yesterday?'

Daniel shook his head.

'I don't remember much about yesterday. Except you being here.'

'The bullet did a lot of damage. Mr Heppenstall says the main thing you have to do is rest and let your body heal.' She looked at him carefully as she said: 'I was wondering if a hospital is the same as a ship.'

'In what way?'

'With regard to getting married. The captain of a ship can

marry people, I wondered if a matron or someone senior was allowed to do the same.'

'Get married?' asked Daniel. 'Here?'

'Why not? Things are always getting in the way of us whenever we start thinking about it. You're not going anywhere any time soon.'

'I'm not sure if it would be legal.'

'It is,' said Abigail. 'I went to see Sir Bramley Petton about it this morning, and he told me that under the Marriage Act of 1836 it is legal for people to get married in a place other than a recognised place of worship providing a local registration officer is present. There's a chaplain at the hospital who can conduct the ceremony and, if you're in agreement, I can ask him if he'd marry us.'

'Is this a proposal?' asked Daniel. 'I mean, a *serious* proposal?'

'Yes.'

Daniel looked around the room. 'We won't get many people in here.'

'All we need is us, the chaplain and the registrar, John Feather as best man, and a witness for me.'

'Your sister, Bella?'

Abigail looked doubtful. 'I'm not sure she'd approve of the setting.'

'But she'd be very upset if you didn't ask her.'

'So you agree? Us getting married, here?'

'If the hospital agrees.'

'I'm sure they would. It would be wonderful publicity for them. The Museum Detectives marry at UCH.'

'I don't think they'd care for that. They'd have everyone else wanting to do the same.'

'Yes, you're right. So, no publicity.'

He smiled. 'And, when I get out, we'll find our new house. Somewhere with indoor plumbing.'

'Yes,' she said. She took his hands in hers. 'This feels like a whole new life starting for us. And I love it.'

ACKNOWLEDGEMENTS

This book is fiction but, like the others in the Museum Mysteries, includes real people and real events from the time in which it is set. Walter Sickert features heavily as a suspect in the murders, and as a suspect in the original Jack the Ripper murders. In fact, the idea of Sickert as a suspect is a relatively recent concept: in 1976 a book by Stephen Knight (*Jack the Ripper; The Final Solution*) suggested that the Ripper murders were a conspiracy involving the Duke of Clarence, Sir William Gull, along with Walter Sickert. This idea was later developed into a TV serial. This was not the first to suggest Sickert as the Ripper: Donald McCormick's *The Identity of Jack the Ripper* (published in 1959) also named Sickert as a suspect. Then, in 2002, the famous American crime writer, Patricia Cornwell, published a non-fiction book (*Portrait of a Killer: Jack the Ripper – Case Closed*) naming Sickert as Jack the Ripper and citing evidence she'd gathered in support of her claim. These made me think: if the evidence that is being cited in support of these theories was known in 1888 (the time of the Ripper killings) then surely Inspector Abberline, a very astute, clever and experienced policeman, would have been aware of them, and would at least have had Sickert in for questioning; but there is no record of that happening.

I have long been interested in Sickert. I was born and brought up in Camden Town, London, which was the inspiration for much of Sickert's work, and where he had his studio. He was one of the founders of the Camden Town group of painters. Many of his paintings were set inside the Bedford Music Hall, Camden Town. As a child in the 1950s I was often taken to see shows and pantomimes at this famous theatre. The Old Bedford was closed in 1959 and demolished in the 1969. As I grew up, I developed a great liking for Sickert's art and wanted to know more about him, and discovered that Sickert seemed to have known and mixed with almost everyone of importance in Britain. He worked as an assistant to the artist James McNeill Whistler; he was an actor in the 1870s and 1880s, including appearing with Henry Irving's Lyceum Theatre company. In 1927 he was introduced to Winston Churchill by Churchill's wife, Clementine. Sickert was a friend of Clementine and her family. It was Sickert who taught Churchill about painting using photographs, and I was stunned when I visited Chartwell in Kent, Churchill's home, to see a large painting entitled *Tea at Chartwell*, painted by Churchill, which showed a group of people enjoying tea in the dining room with Churchill and his wife; the group including Walter Sickert and his wife.

Please forgive this rather long discourse, but I hope you'll see why writing this book gave me the opportunity – in the light of recent retrospective claims about Sickert with regard to Jack the Ripper – to bring in events that plausibly *might* have happened at this time to bring Sickert and Abberline together. After all, Elizabeth I and Mary Queen of Scots are often shown in films and novels as meeting – yet the two never actually met. So, bearing that in mind, I hope you'll forgive this artistic licence with regard to Sickert and Abberline.

JIM ELDRIDGE was born in central London in November 1944, on the same day as one of the deadliest V2 attacks on the city. He left school at sixteen and worked at a variety of jobs, including stoker at a blast furnace, before becoming a teacher. From 1975 to 1985 he taught in mostly disadvantaged areas of Luton. At the same time, he was writing comedy scripts for radio, and then television. As a scriptwriter he has had countless broadcast on television in the UK and internationally, as well as on the radio. Jim has also written over 100 children's books, before concentrating on historical crime fiction for adults.

jimeldridge.com

If you enjoyed *Murder at the National Gallery*, look out
for more books by Jim Eldridge . . .

To discover more great fiction and to place an order
visit our website
www.allisonandbusby.com
or call us on
020 3950 7834